"You'd be w
lightly where Julie Cameron
is concerned."

"How's that, Unc?" Tough L.A. cop talk, for sure.

"Lots of reasons. First of all, she comes from one of the most prominent ranching families in this part of Colorado."

"Good for her. What else?"

"She's got an older brother with a real bad temper."

That scares me, Max thought contemptuously. "What else?"

Gene scowled at his nephew. "People like Julie. *I* like her. She's a little flighty and she can be stubborn—boy, can she be stubborn!—but beneath that brash exterior lurks a heart of pure marshmallow."

All Max had noticed was that *around* that heart lurked a body he wouldn't mind getting to know a whole lot better.

"Yeah, sure," he said to placate his uncle. "Whatever you say. So let's talk about this big bad gang of horse rustlers I'm supposed to bring to justice."

Dear Reader,

I'm in love with the American West and the entire Western myth. I could never resist a story about strong, handsome cowboys and beautiful, feisty cowgirls. When I began writing stories of my own, I became even more caught up in the Western mystique.

The natural result was a miniseries for Harlequin in 1993 about the Taggarts of Texas. Since several of my formative years were spent in the Lone Star State, I relished the opportunity to write the kind of books I love to read.

When I moved to the Centennial State a while back, it quickly became apparent that Texas and Colorado are "the same, only different." Both have lots of cows, cowboys and cowgirls, and some of the finest and friendliest people on earth. Other than weather, the biggest difference I noticed was that the only Coloradans who say "y'all" are transplanted Texans.

Naturally, I found another Western miniseries evolving from new surroundings and experiences: a May Day snowstorm, a trip over Independence Pass with my heart in my mouth, a swim in the world's largest hot-springs pool at Glenwood Springs…and the exploits of an old gray mare renowned as an escape artist.

All these adventures and discoveries—and many more—ended up in the three Camerons of Colorado books about a ranching family chock-full of rugged individuals. I hope you'll enjoy the stories of Ben, Maggie and Julie, and then…who knows where my love of the West will lead?

Maybe… Hey, maybe Thom T. Taggart of Texas and Etta May Cameron of Colorado ought to get together! Or what about—

Sincerely,

Ruth Jean Dale

Ruth Jean Dale
THE CUPID CHRONICLES

Harlequin Books

TORONTO • NEW YORK • LONDON
AMSTERDAM • PARIS • SYDNEY • HAMBURG
STOCKHOLM • ATHENS • TOKYO • MILAN
MADRID • WARSAW • BUDAPEST • AUCKLAND

ISBN 0-373-70687-1

THE CUPID CHRONICLES

Printed in U.S.A.

THE CUPID
CHRONICLES

PROLOGUE

July, Los Angeles, California

MAX MACKENZIE hustled the gorgeous blond actress-sometime-girlfriend out of his apartment, down the stairs and into her sports car, trying not to choke on that brown stuff they called air in Los Angeles. A coughing spell wouldn't do his fractured ribs a helluva lot of good. And after all he'd been through today, he was in no mood to cope with a possessive female, regardless of her attributes.

He was giving her the bum's rush and she knew it. She braced one of those long sleek legs inside the car and the other outside. "But, Maxie, baby," she complained, caressing his jaw with manicured fingertips, "you're hurt. Why don't you let me stay and make it *all* better?"

"Yeah, right—if you don't kill me before you cure me." Max tried to maneuver his left arm, with its fresh plaster cast, beyond her reach.

"You'd go with a smile on your face," she promised, rubbing her hands over his chest seductively. "Why don't you just let me—"

"Another time. I got some stuff to take care of."

She pouted prettily. "Promise?"

"Anything." Anything to get rid of her.

Limping back into his apartment, Max closed the door and sagged against it, allowing himself the luxury of a groan. It made him feel better. Moving slowly and carefully, he navigated the clutter of old newspapers and beer cans and dirty socks until he reached the battered metal desk that served as his command headquarters. He had to knock a forty-pound telephone book and an empty cereal box off the chair before he could lower himself painfully onto the cracked-plastic-covered padding.

He hurt all over, but at least he wasn't missing any vital body parts. Hell, the bullet hadn't even hit anything important, had just torn the muscles in his left arm and tweaked a bone. No big deal.

His reluctant gaze finally settled on the telephone answering machine, blinking like a movie marquee run amok. After staring at it for several minutes, he punched *play* and leaned back gingerly in the chair to listen to his messages. God, he felt rotten.

"Max, darling, you said you'd call—" Max tapped the *skip* button.

"Hey, buddy, you all right? I called the station and they said—" *Skip.*

"This is Mitchell from the *Times*. I hear you're the hero who sprung a bunch of hostages over at the Burger Bonanza on Primero Avenue, shot the stuffing out of some poor homeless kid in the process. I got some questions for you, man—" *Skip.* Damned reporters.

"Remember me? Jimmy introduced us last week and I gave you my telephone number—" *Skip.* Remember her? Hell, he didn't even remember Jimmy.

"C'mon, Max, this is your old pal Kevin. I admit Mitchell's an obnoxious idiot, but you gotta talk to someone sooner or later. Deadline's fast approaching, my man—" *Skip.* Editors should be above that kind of whining.

"...of TV channel 14... Channel 11... 560 Radio..." *Skip, skip, skip.*

"Maxwell Cosmo Mackenzie, keep your hand off that *skip* button! Listen up! This is your mother talking." He could just imagine Liz Mackenzie gritting her teeth and searching for words with which to castigate her thirty-three-year-old son, as if he were an errant teenager.

But she got her way; hers was one message he didn't skip.

"This is your last chance, buster," she went on relentlessly. "The big family reunion is tomorrow in Simi Valley and you'd better be there *or else.* No excuses, and I mean none, Maxwell. You've been acting downright weird lately, but that's no excuse. Unless you want your butt tossed out of this family—" *Click.*

She hung up on him. That was a switch.

Max got up and poured a couple of inches of scotch into a dirty glass. He'd learned to drink whiskey at his father's knee long before he'd reached legal drinking age. Now he drank it rarely, but every once in a while he just needed . . . false courage?

Staring out the window of the third-floor apartment in his seedy neighborhood, Max, a Los Angeles Police Department veteran, admitted that his mother had a point. He *was* getting weird.

What the hell was happening to him? In the eighteen months since his divorce, he'd lived increasingly close to the edge. He'd been accused of acting like a trigger-happy wild man; he'd been called a macho jerk; and it'd been suggested he was a hot dog more interested in fame and glory than in the greater good. A couple of weeks ago the department shrink had finally murmured the dreaded b-word: burnout.

Well, he was certainly fed up with everything, not just the job. Phony town, phony people. In L.A., every cabdriver was working on a script, every lifeguard on every crowded beach had an agent. Max had busted a drug dealer the other day, an accessory to murder who was ticked off because he'd have to miss an open call for street punks at one of the film studios. "It's one'a the majors, man. Why don'tcha gimme a break? I'll turn myself in the minute it's over, honest, man."

Yeah, once Max would have argued about that "weird" tag bestowed on him by his own mother, but now he wasn't so sure; he'd found himself sympathizing with the guy. When you started feeling sorry for the bad guys . . .

He stared out the window, frowning at the neon sign across the street, the one flashing *vacant* over and over and over. That was how he felt: mentally vacant. Out to lunch. A doughnut shy of a dozen.

He splashed more scotch into his glass, wondering what the hell burnout felt like.

His father probably could have told him, if he hadn't died in a hail of gunfire when Max was seventeen. Maxwell Cosmo Mackenzie, Sr., had been a good cop, a lousy husband and an absentee father. Maxwell Cosmo Mackenzie, Jr., was following so closely in his father's footsteps it was scary. Fortunately Junior's wife was smart enough to become his ex-wife before they got around to having a kid, but the rest was right on.

A few hours earlier, Max had survived his own hail of bullets, emerging from a hostage screwup with nothing worse than a slug in his left arm, plus assorted abrasions and contusions and cracked ribs. He'd also shot a man—a boy really—with his own gun. Now there'd be an investigation, with all the hassle and publicity that went with it. God, how he hated seeing his personal business splashed all over by the media. Over the years, he'd been called a hero and he'd been called a rogue cop, and neither rap was worth sh—

The telephone rang, and Max stood there in the dark listening to his mother's voice, coaxing now: "...all be there, even your Uncle Gene from Colorado and your cousins from Philadelphia. I'm sorry I was cross, Max, but sometimes you can be so...obstinate. Please, as a personal favor to your mother who loves you—"

Max picked up. "Yeah, Ma, I'll be there. And before you hear it on the eleven o'clock news and go bonkers, I think I oughtta tell you..."

CHAPTER ONE

August, Cupid, Colorado

JULIE CAMERON was *not* a happy camper.

Hands on her hips, she stood in the middle of the newsroom of the *Cupid Chronicles* and glared at the door behind which her boss, Gene Varner, was hiding his cowardly self.

Gene was editor, publisher and owner of the only newspaper in town, but this newsroom, humble though it might have been, was Julie's turf. She'd worked for the *Chronicles* off and on since high school. She'd done it all: sports, life-styles, photography. She'd even spent a miserable week in classified, a horrible experience she had no intention of ever repeating. She'd delivered papers, dummied pages, written headlines and editorials.

But today at the mature age of twenty-six, she was the star news reporter and had been for three glorious years, ever since her predecessor had run off with the milkman—actually a former dairy farmer from Garden City, Kansas.

Julie hadn't wished anyone bad luck, but once the city beat was hers, she was fiercely protective of it.

Thus she could hardly be expected to take kindly to Gene's bombshell.

Gene Varner was bringing in a nephew from California to learn the newspaper business. The mere thought of it made Julie's blood boil. She'd be damned if some hotshot from California was going to horn in on her turf, even if blood *was* thicker than water.

Avis Vaughn, the newspaper's bookkeeper, had kept her wary eye on Julie both before and after Gene's rambling proclamation. Finally the pretty black woman spoke up. "It won't be so bad, Julie. At the very least, he'll be able to type. You keep saying you're working too hard and need help."

"Help, yes, but how much help do you think I'm going to get from the boss's nephew?"

Avis shrugged. "He's probably a perfectly nice man," she said reasonably. "Gene is."

"Nice?" Julie invested the word with all the scorn she was feeling. "Nice! He's got to be an idiot—the nephew, I mean, although Gene's not looking any too good at the moment, either. Who in their right mind would leave California for this wide spot in a mountain road?"

Avis smiled. "Your sister-in-law did."

"Oh, well, Betsy." Julie shrugged the notion away. "That's different."

"How is it different?"

"It just is." Julie stalked to a beat-up old oak desk and threw herself into the chair, wobbly casters trembling. "Did you hear Gene say this guy had any experience?"

"No."

"Neither did I. Did Gene say how old he is?"

"No."

"I didn't think so. Did you hear Gene say when he's coming?"

"No."

"Me, neither." Julie banged clenched hands down on her desk blotter. "I've got a bad feeling about this, Avis. Gene's not leveling with us. This guy must be the pits."

"Relax, girl. You're the star here. Gene's not about to mess with you."

Julie liked the sound of that. Better for a reporter to be feared and respected than loved and ignored, she always said. "You really think so? Because if he did, I'd be out of here—" it took her three tries to snap her fingers "—like that."

"He knows." Avis turned back to her computer. "You've been threatening to move on to the big time for ages. Heck, Julie, you're the franchise! He's not going to take any chances on losing you."

"I hope not," Julie grumbled, but Avis's remarks had mollified her considerably. Of course Gene wouldn't stab her in the back after all she'd done for the *CC*. Why, she'd never even taken a sick day, not in all the years she'd worked here. Let some old Johnny-come-lately nephew match that.

Avis was right, Julie comforted herself. She *was* the newspaper. Everybody came to her with their stories. She got scoops all the time. Of course, it was considerably easier to get scoops when you worked for the only newspaper in town, but that wasn't her fault.

She turned back to the story she was writing about street improvements over on Lovers' Lane. Typing a couple of words, she let her fingers grow still over the keyboard. Her gaze wandered pensively around the newsroom, while melancholy thoughts swept over her. She'd spent many an hour in this newsroom, most of them happy. Some of them incredibly exciting. Only a few of them filled with dull drudgery. That was the stuff Gene's nephew was welcome to take over, she decided.

The *Chronicles* office, ideally located on Main Street smack-dab in the middle of town, was practically a second home to her. A hardware store was located on one side, and Second Street on the other. In back was a parking lot, shared by the newspaper and the marshal's office and jail. Cupid City Hall, an old brick building erected more than seventy years before, took up the rest of the block. Across Second Street to the northeast was a ball field and Cupid Elementary School. The rest of the town radiated out from that center core.

All nice and handy for an ambitious reporter like Julie Laverne Cameron.

The newspaper office itself was basically two big rooms, one for the production of the news and the other for the printing of same on an antiquated offset press. A counter ran the entire width in front, providing a not-very-effective barrier to customers, news sources, friends and strangers who might drop by. Once through the door, visitors had a view of the entire news and business operation with its motley array of second-hand furniture and computers.

Gene's office was located off to one side of the newsroom, and his door was rarely closed. Today was an exception.

Coward.

The bell over the front door jingled, and Julie looked up automatically. It was her brother Ben's wife, Betsy. Co-owner of a popular local café called the Rusty Spur, she came in carrying a paper bag and wearing a big smile.

"I brought you some lunch," she announced. "Things must be hopping around here if you don't even have time to keep a lunch date." She looked around the placid nearly deserted office.

Julie groaned and smacked her hand to her forehead. The last thing she'd said over the breakfast table at the ranch before heading to work this morning was that she'd meet her sister-in-law at the Spur for lunch at twelve-thirty. "Betsy! I'm sorry, I flat forgot." Which was no wonder, after Gene's bombshell.

"That's okay." Betsy lifted the hinged section of counter and walked through. "Standing up a relative is not exactly a crime. I forgive you. In fact, I've brought you a meat-loaf sandwich on that buttermilk bread you like so much.''

She plunked the bag down on Julie's neat desktop and plunked herself down on what Julie called the witness chair. It was where she grilled her sources— mercilessly, she liked to think.

"Sounds great." Julie opened the bag, caught a whiff of Betsy's homemade bread and groaned in anticipation. Back in California, Betsy had trained to be a chef; pastry and baked goods were her specialty. Once she'd started baking for the café in which she'd inherited a half interest, business had boomed.

"So what's going on?" Betsy asked, looking around curiously. "Hi, Avis. Nice to see you. How's Bobby?"

"He's fine. It's nice to see you, too—and nothing's going on." Avis rose. "Julie just likes to holler before she's hurt. Once she gets her dander up, there's no reasoning with her." With a smile, she headed for the files at the back of the room.

"It's nepotism, plain and simple." Julie took a big bite of her sandwich, which was scrumptious. When she could talk again, she added, "Gene's bringing in his nephew to learn the newspaper biz."

When Betsy didn't react, Julie gave her a verbal nudge. "You know what this means, don't you?"

"Apparently not."

"It means," Julie said with feigned patience, "that he's going to get in my way, sure as shootin'. Fine," she added wrathfully, "that's just fine. But he's not going to stick his nose into the *good* stuff. He can do the church rummage sales and the giant vegetables and the service clubs and the obituaries and the millions of rewrites, but he's not getting close to City Hall or the cop shop. Period." She glared at Betsy. "I mean it."

Betsy blinked. "I believe you. I'm sure Gene will, too. I've always thought he was a reasonable man."

"You don't know him as well as I do," Julie said darkly. "When he gets a bee in his bonnet..." She shook her head and pursed her lips. "One thing's for sure, this new guy isn't getting *close* to the biggest story in Cupid history. It's *mine.*"

Betsy nodded sagely. "The gang of rustlers," she whispered, as if one of their number might be lurking nearby.

"The gang of rustlers," Julie agreed grimly. "When they started operating in *my* territory, it became *my* story. I'll follow it to the bitter end. Why, it could win me a Pulitzer."

Betsy's eyebrows soared skeptically. "Really?"

"Why not?" Julie shrugged. "Whatever, it's my story and it will by God remain my story, or I'll know the reason why."

And she attacked her meat-loaf sandwich as if it offered a threat to that resolve.

"TODAY'S THE DAY," Julie announced the following Tuesday at breakfast.

Almost the entire Cameron clan was at the table, including Grandma, brother Ben, Betsy and their three kids. Joey was nine, Lisa Marie was eight, and Catherine, usually called Cat, was three.

Ben reached for another of Betsy's feather-light biscuits. "What day?"

"The day Gene's nephew starts work."

"What's his name?" Grandma asked.

Julie grimaced. "Cosmo Mackenzie. Do you believe it?"

"I knew a Cosmo once," Grandma said. "Didn't like him much, though."

"I knew a Mackenzie once," Betsy said, frowning in thought, "but I don't remember where. Maybe," she suggested hopefully, "this new guy will be cute."

"Maybe," Julie retorted, "he won't."

Ben nodded wisely. "You know what that means, Betsy. Once my baby sister makes up her mind, you can't change it with dynamite. This poor clown could look like John Wayne—"

"Mel Gibson," Betsy inserted.

"—and it wouldn't make any difference to her. He's toast."

Betsy nudged her husband with an elbow. "Now, Ben, Julie isn't *that* close-minded. She'll give him a fair chance."

"Yeah." Ben snorted derisively. "Give him a fair trial and then hang the guilty bastard, right, Jewel?"

"Don't call me Jewel!"

"Hear that?" Ben winked at Betsy. "Fairness isn't the issue here."

"Leave your sister alone, Ben Cameron." Grandma called for peace, but she was stifling a smile. "You run the ranch and let her run the newspaper."

"I don't run the newspaper." Julie tossed her napkin beside her plate. "I only work there."

"But—" Lisa Marie looked around in confusion "—*I* thought you run it, Aunt Julie. Didn't you, Joey?"

Joey shrugged. "Nah, I thought some guy did, but I didn't know he was new." He pushed back his chair. "You done, Lisa? Let's go see if those calves got outta the corral again last night."

Depressed, Julie watched the kids scamper away. Out of the mouths of babes: "Some guy" ran everything—except Julie Laverne Cameron. No guy would *ever* do that.

JULIE WAS LOADED for bear before Gene ever produced his nephew, who by then had taken on an awful significance in her mind. Even so, she was hardly prepared for the sight of him in the flesh.

It was nearly eleven when Gene came out of his office, someone trailing along in his shadow. Which, of course, wasn't that unusual, since Gene was a beefy six-footer who tended to dominate through sheer size. Julie knew that beneath his intimidating exterior lurked the heart of a pussycat.

"Can I have your attention, everybody?"

He sounded nervous, Julie thought. *Good.* She waited, resisting the desire to slide her chair back from her desk for a better view of the skulker behind her editor and publisher.

Everybody in the room responded obediently: photographer, sports editor, advertising salesman, bookkeeper. Expectation hung over them all like a dark cloud—at least, it seemed dark to Julie.

Gene cleared his throat. Since the death of his wife, Grace, almost a year ago, he'd begun to look his age, which was somewhere in the late fifties. *My gosh, is he about to introduce the next publisher of the newspaper?* Julie wondered in sudden panic.

Gene pressed on doggedly. "I'd like you to meet my nephew," he said, stepping aside. "This is Cosmo Mackenzie, my favorite sister's only child. I know you'll all make him welcome."

Julie grabbed at her desktop for support, inadvertently knocking off a single paper clip—and of course, everybody in the room must have heard it drop. *The man's left arm was in a cast.* He wouldn't even be able to type, and typing ability was the bare minimum. This guy wouldn't be any kind of help at all in a newsroom.

But then she looked at the rest of Cosmo Mackenzie, and suddenly an arm cast seemed like the least of his disabilities.

Gene's nephew, a man who appeared to be in his early thirties, was a genuine, deluxe, twenty-karat nerd. His hair, a nondescript brown, was slicked straight back with something that made it shine like patent leather. With his right hand, he pushed nervously at the nosepiece of round frameless eyeglasses and smiled uncertainly.

The man was hopeless, but his clothes were possibly even worse; Julie stifled a groan. His droopy short-sleeved shirt, with its busy brown-and-rusty-orange pattern, was buttoned right up to the neck. His shirttail had come untucked, and the sides billowed over his hips, making him look almost as beefy as his uncle.

And as if all that wasn't enough, he moved with the grace of the terminally clumsy.

"Oh, dear," Avis whispered to Julie. "He looks like Michael Douglas in that movie where he played a nerd engineer who went bananas on some freeway in California and started shooting everything that moved."

"Aaaa-men," Julie agreed, speaking out of the side of her mouth. "Does the word 'doomed' mean anything to you?"

That muttered aside earned Julie an alarmed glance from Avis. "You or him?" she asked sharply.

With a slump-shouldered stance and apologetic smile, Gene's nephew looked around the room. "Gosh, Uncle Gene," he said into the deafening silence, "I've never been in a newspaper office before. This is swell." He nodded to everyone in general, a silly-looking smile on his square-jawed face.

"Yes, uh . . . Cosmo, let me introduce the team." Gene took his nephew's elbow and steered him forward, as if the guy couldn't be trusted to follow. "Say hello to Avis Vaughn, who keeps our books. Avis, my nephew, Cosmo Mackenzie."

Avis stood up, smiling; Julie had to give her credit, the woman was *cool*.

"Pleased to meet you." Avis offered her hand. "Cos—" she cleared her throat "—Cosmo, is it?"

"That's right." Cosmo spoke with a curious self-effacement. He seemed almost pathetically eager to please. "It's a family name."

"Uh . . . right. And your friends call you . . . ?"

He frowned. "Cosmo." He pumped her hand vigorously. "Glad to meet you, Avis. We're going to be great friends."

"I'm sure," Avis agreed weakly, and sat back down as if suddenly too weak to stand.

Gene dragged Cosmo on. The publisher didn't seem able to meet Julie's disbelieving stare. "This is Julie Cameron, my number-one reporter."

An eager smile lit Cosmo Mackenzie's face. He grabbed Julie's right hand and pumped it enthusiastically. "Wow, oh, wow, a real reporter. I can't believe this is happening. It's great to meet you, Julie, just great. We're going to make a great team."

He had the grip of a rodeo bulldogger. Julie tried to wiggle her numb fingers free. Then what he'd said sunk in. "Team! We're not going to be a team. No way."

He looked crestfallen. "We're not?" Frowning, he glanced at his uncle. "I thought this was one big happy family."

"It is," Julie said quickly, "but—"

"No problem, then. I'll catch on quick. Wait and see." He spoke with all the confidence of the totally lame. "Do you believe in fate?"

The sudden change of direction threw Julie even farther off-balance. "Fate?"

He nodded. "This was meant to be."

"What was?" He had her so far out of kilter that for a moment she almost wondered which of them was temporarily disconnected. Surely he wasn't implying that they—she and he— A shudder ran down her spine.

He smiled; his teeth, at least, were good, strong and straight and white. "Me, in a newsroom. I think I've got printer's blood in my veins."

"Uh, I think the expression's ink—printer's ink."

He nodded and squeezed her fingers just a little bit tighter. "That's right. See, in my other life I was an insurance salesman."

Julie let out her breath in a soft moan. "I almost could've guessed."

"Thanks." He looked flattered, not offended. "Insurance is okay. I liked it and all. But then I tripped and fell down some stairs and broke the old wing." He lifted his cast and waved it around.

Julie ducked. "Careful, don't hurt yourself." *Or me, please.*

"Gosh, I'm sorry." He lowered the cast with an apologetic hunch of his shoulders. "Anyway, when that happened, I took it as a—" he rolled his eyes toward the ceiling "—kind of sign from heaven that it was time for me to pursue my dreams."

"We should all pursue our dreams," Julie agreed faintly. She'd stopped tugging at her fingers, which had lost all feeling, and just stood there with her hand hanging limply from his.

Cosmo nodded. "Which reminded me of Uncle Gene." He glanced fondly at the publisher, who stood there with his mouth hanging open. "I've always envied the exciting and glamorous life of a journalist. Maybe I'll start as an investigative reporter and see how it goes."

"Investigative reporter!" Julie finally managed to wrench her hand free. Unconsciously she set about rubbing a little feeling back into her fingers. "You can't even *type!* How do you expect to—"

"Uh-uh-uh, one big happy family," Cosmo reminded her. "I'd help *you* if you had a temporary infirmity." His gaze met hers and held. He smiled. "Gosh, Julie, we're going to get along like gangbusters. You can teach me the ropes, introduce me around town. You can be...well, like my sponsor."

Gene tugged at Cosmo's arm. "That's fine, just fine. Now come meet the rest of the staff."

He dragged his nephew away, but not before Julie made a startling discovery: Cosmo Mackenzie had green eyes behind those awful glasses, the greenest eyes she'd ever seen on a real live person.

She'd always hated green eyes; green indicated jealousy, didn't it? *Cosmo's jealous of my privileged position at the newspaper. Investigative reporter, indeed!* This was even worse than she'd imagined.

It only took Gene and Cosmo a few more minutes to make the rounds for individual introductions to all the *CC* employees. Steaming, Julie watched their progress.

Jeez. Wait'll the cowboys at the Hideout saloon got a load of this guy. She shuddered. Introduce Cosmo Mackenzie around town? Sponsor him?

She'd sooner write obituaries.

Up to and including her own.

HIS OFFICE DOOR closed and the portly publisher sank into his chair. Pulling a handkerchief from his hip pocket, he mopped his forehead and spoke to his nephew. "Thank heaven that's over. For a minute there..." He shuddered. "So what do you think of my staff, Max? Are they on to us?"

"Call me Cosmo," Max warned.

"Of course. Cosmo. I wouldn't want to slip up in front of anyone," Gene agreed. "But about my staff...?"

"Your staff doesn't have a clue." Max longed to unbutton the collar scratching his neck, but like his uncle, he had to be careful about slipping out of character. When you went undercover, the least thing could do you in. "Leave your staff to me," he added. "I can handle her—them, with pleasure."

Gene looked anxious. "You'd be well advised to tread lightly where Julie Cameron is concerned."

"How's that, Unc?" Tough L.A. cop talk, for sure.

"Lots of reasons. First of all, she comes from one of the most prominent ranching families in this part of Colorado. The Camerons are pioneer cattle folks and held in high regard."

"Good for them. What else?"

"She's got an older brother with a real bad temper."

That scares me, Max thought contemptuously. "What else?"

"I guess you could say her personal popularity around here is high. She's sort of Cupid's answer to Scarlett O'Hara, if you catch my drift." At Max's blank look, Gene added, "You know, Margaret Mitchell's book?"

"If Joe Wambaugh didn't write it, I haven't read it. Spell it out."

Gene scowled darkly. "People *like* Julie. She was even named Miss Cupid a few years back—on a write-in vote, no less."

"Go on," Max invited, unmoved thus far.

Gene sighed. "*I* like her. She's a little flighty and she can be stubborn—boy, can she be stubborn!—but she's got the right instincts. She talks a much tougher game than she plays. Beneath that brash exterior lurks a heart of pure marshmallow."

All Max had noticed was that around that heart, whatever it was made of, lurked a body he wouldn't mind getting to know a whole lot better. Julie Cameron looked like too hot a little number to be stashed away in the middle of nowhere.

Knowledge which elicited a sigh. In his present situation, it was highly unlikely he'd be able to make any time with her; duty before pleasure. But you never could tell...

"Yeah, sure," he said to placate his uncle. "Whatever you say. So let's talk about this big bad gang of Western outlaws I'm supposed to bring to justice."

MAXWELL C. MACKENZIE, Jr., had let himself be lured to Cupid, Colorado, to round up the bad guys and teach the hayseeds how it was done. Funny, how life hinged on unrelated incidents all leading to a time and a place never consciously chosen.

If Max hadn't been shot rescuing hostages from a deranged gunman, he'd never have gone to the family reunion in Simi Valley, no matter how mad his mother got. But he *had* been shot, and the only way to convince her he was all right was to let her see for herself. And if he was going to do that, it might as well be at the family reunion she'd spent the past twelve months putting together, so all the aunts could ooh and ahh over him, and all the uncles and cousins could pound on his good shoulder and talk macho.

They had, except for Gene, who'd watched all the attention Max was getting with a thoughtful expression. When Gene got the chance, he sidled up to his nephew for a few private words. "I suppose this means you'll be put on admin leave until the powers that be decide whether you're a hero or a deranged psycho yourself," he suggested.

"Bingo," Max said. "You been talking to my lieutenant?"

Gene laughed. "Being in the newspaper business, I'm familiar with law enforcement." He studied his nephew. "So you're a free man, at least for a while. How long you think it'll take them to reinstate you?"

Max shrugged. "Who knows?" *Who cares?* "There's medical leave involved here, too." He hoisted the cast. The way he felt at that moment, he wasn't sure he *wanted* reinstatement.

"So what do you plan to do with all that free time?" Gene asked. "Because if you don't have any plans, I might have something that'll interest you...."

And it had. Max wasn't sure why, but he was rather fond of his uncle Gene and wouldn't mind doing him a favor, especially now that Aunt Grace was dead and their two daughters grown and moved back East.

Gene was living all alone now in a big old house on the edge of some hick town in Colorado. His only company was Grace's two cats and her horse; Gene's horse had been stolen, and he was obviously pretty unhappy about that, unhappy enough to try to coax his nephew into tracking down the gang of horse thieves who did it.

Horse thieves. It'd be a piece of cake. Not cars, not drugs, not jewels or even money, but *horses,* four-legged animals that went *neigh.* Why the hell would anyone heist a horse these days?

The very thought made Max laugh, and it felt good. Damned good. Why not? It wasn't as if he had anything better to do with his time.

Besides, he had something to prove to himself: that he could do the job without violence. No shootings, no fireworks of any kind, he promised himself. He'd go undercover as—he broke into a delighted grunt of laughter—a reporter. He'd go to work for Uncle Gene so he could snoop around to his heart's content, messing with people's minds and their lives and never being called on it.

There was only one problem, and Gene quickly put his finger on it.

"Max, you wouldn't happen to know a dingbat from a column rule, would you?" the newspaperman had asked hopefully.

"A what from a who?"

Gene sighed. "I was afraid of that. I guess we'll have to cook up a story to cover your ignorance."

Thus had been born Cosmo Mackenzie, insurance nerd and wanna-be investigative reporter.

So what if he'd never been east of Las Vegas except in an airplane? He was ripe for a change. There had to be something better than L.A. with its concrete canyons and pea-soup skies, its hustlers and opportunists. Hell, at this point he was ready for *any* change, even for the worse.

Not that he thought there was a chance of the worse happening. Max was supremely confident he'd be up to the challenge.

Rustlers, he thought. *Give me a break!*

ON THE OTHER SIDE of Gene Varner's door, Julie Cameron was in a stew. This was even worse than she'd expected, which hardly seemed possible.

Cosmo Mackenzie was not only a dweeb with delusions of grandeur, he was a handicapped dweeb with one arm in a cast. Even if he knew anything about newspaper work, which he didn't, he wouldn't be able to do it until the cast came off.

Her only consolation was the knowledge that once he found out how hard the work was, he wouldn't last a month. Californians, she thought scornfully; everybody knew how flaky they were.

Still, that didn't keep her from wanting to try her hand at a newspaper job in the Golden State—the big time. Someday her opportunity would come, and when it did, she'd grab it.

In the meantime, if anyone was going to be stuck doing Cosmo's work, it wasn't going to be her. *He's your problem, Gene, and welcome to it.*

Investigative reporter. *Give me a break!*

CHAPTER TWO

GRANDMA CAMERON eyed Julie over the chicken-fried steak that night. "Whatcha waitin' for, hon?" she prodded. "Tell us all about him. Does he really have two heads and breathe fire?"

"Ha, ha, very funny." Julie spooned more gravy onto her steak.

Joey propped both elbows on the table, his gray eyes bright. "Are we talkin' dragons here?" he wanted to know hopefully. "Because if we are—"

"Please remove your elbows from the table."

"Ah, Mama—"

"Do as your mother says, son."

Joey did, and Betsy gave him an approving pat on the shoulder. "When are you bringing him to the Spur so I can get a look at him, Julie?"

"Never, if there's a God. This guy is..." Julie darted a cautious glance at the three children. Joey and Lisa Marie, as usual, were totally tuned in to the adult conversation. Only Cat remained happily unaware as she struggled to convey bits of potato to her mouth with an uncooperative spoon.

"He's what, Jewel?" Ben teased.

"Don't call me that!"

"He's what, Julie?"

"He's…not my type. My first impression is that he's not anybody's type, if you catch my drift."

Lisa Marie nodded sagely. "He's a nerd," she confided to Joey. "Too bad. Aunt Julie's been between boyfriends for a long time now—maybe a month."

In fact, Julie had been between boyfriends longer than that. Six months, to be exact. It'd been that long since the termination of her most recent engagement. Before that, however, she'd never been without dedicated male admiration and attention.

She sighed. Sometimes she thought she'd met and rejected every even remotely eligible man in this part of Colorado. The pickings were getting slim indeed, and the arrival of Cosmo Mackenzie did nothing to improve the situation. The day would never come when she'd be *that* hard up.

Maybe she should just write men off as more trouble than they were worth.

JULIE DIDN'T FIGURE her opinion of Cosmo Mackenzie could get much lower, but he proved her wrong the first time he sat down at a computer terminal—hers, naturally. The *Chronicles* had none to spare for "the new guy." He'd managed to put off that fateful moment for days. Finally caught, he looked at her with a blank expression.

"Now what?" he asked.

She showed him: how to start a story, how to file a story, how to recall a story, how to log in a story so the editor would know it was there.

Then she showed him again. And again. He tried earnestly to pick out the appropriate keys with his one good hand, his determined gaze glued to the keyboard and his movements slow and inaccurate.

Finally she had to ask the dreaded question. "You *do* know how to type, don't you?"

He looked up with that ingenuous expression she was beginning to recognize, the one that indicated some simpleminded interpretation of a complicated subject.

"Oh, sure," he said brightly. "As long as the letters are on the keys, I've got it licked. And yours are."

Julie wanted to scream. Instead, she reached past him to retrieve a packet of unopened mail, her arm brushing his shoulder. She yanked away from even that brief contact, not wanting him to get the wrong idea. Apparently he already had, for he gave her a glance she could only interpret as hopeful.

Leafing rapidly through the envelopes, she extracted one. "Let's see how you do with a basic rewrite. This is a good one to start with—the monthly meeting of the Ladies' Literary Tea Society."

His astonishing green eyes grew wide behind the dweeb glasses. "You haven't even opened the envelope yet. How do you know what's in it?"

"I know," she said, taking out a single sheet of paper and attaching it to the copyholder, "because the same release comes in every month. Every month I rewrite it and put it in the paper." She straightened, hands on hips. "Do your stuff, Cosmo."

"Sure, Julie." He turned to the terminal with clear resolve.

For ninety seconds or so, she waited. Nothing happened. "Well?" she prompted. "You can start any time now. I haven't got all day here."

"Oh, sure." Another of those uncomprehending smiles. "What is it you want me to do again?"

"Rewrite the story!"

"Oh. The story. Sure." Turning his attention to the flickering screen, he studied that for a few moments, then gave the same attention to the handwritten piece of onionskin fluttering from the copyholder.

Julie resisted the urge to grab his good right hand and slam it down on the keyboard. Finally he voluntarily raised that hand, allowed it to drift experimentally in the appropriate direction, drop lower...hesitate.

"Will you get a move on?" Julie burst out. "Do something, even if you do it wrong! I don't expect perfection, but you've got to start somewhere. You should already be finished with that one and on to the next."

"Really?" He sighed. "Maybe I could start on something a little...bigger. I don't know anything about a ladies' club. How can I write about something I don't know anything about?"

"Why," she asked sweetly, "should you be any different from any other reporter? If we only wrote stories about what we know, there would be great gaping holes in the newspaper. Our readers wouldn't like that. The paper would go out of business. That would throw us all out of work."

"Gosh," Cosmo said. "And all because I don't know anything about a ladies' club." He scratched his left thumb where it emerged from the cast. "It's just that I don't think I'm suited for society reporting. Why don't you do all the women's stuff and I'll do the manly stuff? Couldn't I write about a murder? Or a bank robbery—that would be nice."

"A murder or a bank robbery would *not* be nice. Besides, the last murder we had around here was in 1967, and we haven't had a bank robbery since...since before that." Technically true; being the home of a bank robber who worked out of town was different.

"Come on!" He gave her a dubious glance. "Crime is rampant across the land—I watch television. What does your sheriff do with his time? You do have a sheriff, don't you?"

"We have a marshal, and most of the time he's handing out parking tickets and driving drunks home."

"That's all?" Cosmo frowned. "I thought as a journalist I'd be rubbing elbows with the criminal element on a daily basis. Now you tell me Cupid doesn't even *have* a criminal element."

He looked so disappointed she gave an exasperated sigh. "I didn't say that, exactly. Once in a while somebody gets thrown in the pokey for fighting. We've had a bit of cattle and horse rustling over the years." She hesitated, knowing she should stop while she was ahead but still incensed by his attitude. "We did have one famous desperado. Maybe you've heard of him—old Ethan Turner, the Outlaw Grandpa."

Cosmo's mouth dropped open, revealing those strong white teeth. "You had a grandpa who was an outlaw? What's this world coming to?"

"Exactly." There! She felt justified.

"I'll interview him." Cosmo started from the chair. "Just tell me where—"

Julie stopped him with a hand on his shoulder; it was like grabbing hold of a block of concrete. Still, he responded to even that light pressure and sat down obediently.

"He's serving time in the big house for bank robbery. He's got some no-account kin living on a ranch north of here, so maybe you'll get lucky and one of them will try something. In the meantime—" she tapped the news release with one finger "—get busy. We all had to start at the bottom."

He sighed and his big shoulders drooped beneath the yellow-and-maroon rayon shirt. "Maybe if you went away and came back later?" he suggested. "I know you're only trying to help, and you've been the soul of patience and courtesy, but you kind of—" he licked his lips and darted her an anxious glance "—make me nervous?"

"Oh, Cosmo." Here he was, being downright ingratiating, while making her aware she'd been neither patient nor courteous. She threw up her hands in defeat. "Have it your way. I'll be back in an hour or two."

"Take your time."

And he turned around to face the task at hand with such determination she actually dared to hope.

Those hopes were dashed upon her return when she found a message on her screen:

uncle genr isss takn me t lunch, he siad you cn wruite thos fastr than me. love c.mackenzie p.s unk sez we got spilchek whichh willm clen upp m copy. 2what is copy???

Swearing a blue streak, albeit under her breath, Julie sat down and within fifteen minutes, had batted out the ladies' club brief and another half dozen of its ilk.

And all the while she was also promising herself that she would not—repeat, *not*—continue doing this guy's work for him, nephew or no. In fact, she wouldn't have anything more to do with him, period, the wretched undeserving—

Cosmo and Gene returned, bringing with them an air of excitement. Julie looked up, stone-faced, from her computer terminal.

"Finish all those rewrites?" Gene asked cheerfully.

"Yes!" The keyboard shuddered with the force of her blows. "Did you have a good *lunch?*" She banged harder.

"As a matter of fact—" Gene and Cosmo exchanged conspiratorial glances "—we ran into Dwight and—"

"Dwight!" Julie bolted from her chair. Dwight Deakins was the marshal of Cupid. She knew he'd been to Denver to talk to the big crime boys about local problems with rustlers but hadn't realized he'd returned. "What— Gene, you get back here this minute!"

But Gene was heading for his office. "Cosmo can fill you in," he called just before closing the door.

Gritting her teeth, Julie turned to the big lug standing there grinning like a Cheshire cat. With one finger, he pushed his eyeglasses back into place on the bridge of his nose.

"Gosh, yes, Julie, I'll be glad to tell you everything," he declared. "And then maybe you can help me write the story? Gene says it'll be page one."

"I'll—" Julie bit off her words; she'd been about to say, *I'll page-one you, Buster!* But what was the point? Cosmo, it seemed, had a skin like a rhinoceros, and nothing she might say would pierce it. She couldn't intimidate him, which left her only one recourse.

Wherever Cosmo Mackenzie went from now on, she'd be right there, keeping an eye on him. He'd just stolen a story from her; it was the first time and the last time.

Fortunately what he'd stolen wasn't much, just the news that Colorado horse thefts might be linked with similar thefts in Kansas and Oklahoma.

"Marshal Deakins says that horse rustling has become a modern crime," Cosmo reported. "Some stolen horses go to good homes and people who have no idea their new horse was stolen. But some of the horses are sold for meat."

"That's gruesome!" Julie, a horse lover herself, shuddered.

"He says about sixty percent of stolen horses end up in slaughterhouses. Some of the more valuable are stolen-to-order, and the rest are just unloaded as fast as possible. He says—"

"I don't want to hear any more about what he says!" Julie turned away. She knew a lot more about the probable fate of stolen horses than she was willing to share with this upstart, and she wasn't pleased that he'd managed to worm so much information out of the marshal.

As far as she was concerned, Cosmo had completely worn out his welcome, chilly as it had been.

WITH COSMO on board, Julie's workload seemed to double, instead of decrease. Not only was she doing all the work she did before, she was endeavoring to teach him to do something—anything! He seemed to be trying his best, but nothing good ever resulted from his efforts. Good? Not even usable!

Since he was living with his uncle in the big old house over on Lovers' Lane, she didn't worry too much about his after-hours activities, at least at first. Gene Varner had become a real homebody since his wife's death. If it wasn't for his pets and horses, she didn't know what he'd have done. Then those rotten horse thieves had taken his pinto, leaving just Grace's old gray mare. No wonder Gene was rabid on the subject of rustlers.

Cosmo might be—might be?—*was* worthless at the office, but Julie could see he was offering Gene valuable companionship. It made her feel a bit more forgiving toward the newest and most incompetent member of the *Chronicles* team—but only a bit.

Unfortunately Gene hadn't hired Cosmo as a companion but as a journalist. That knowledge rubbed Julie raw.

She didn't even want to *think* about what Gene was paying his nephew. If it was more than she was getting, it would make her crazy; and it *had* to be more, since her own paycheck was so pitifully small.

How much were nephews worth on the open market?

Glaring across the newsroom at the broad back of her nemesis as he chatted with Bob Mays, the sports editor, she reminded herself it was time to get off the dime and look for a better job. Just because she'd taken a shot at the big time in Denver a few years ago and hadn't liked it didn't mean she was doomed to a life of small time. She had quit the Denver job, they hadn't fired her, and Gene had welcomed her back with open arms.

Besides, she didn't want Denver and never had. She wanted California. And that dumb cluck over there had given up the Golden State for *this*.

Cosmo wandered into Gene's office, and Bob headed for the door, his path leading him past Julie's desk.

"Nice guy," he said, jerking his head toward the publisher's door. "Knows his sports, lemme tell ya."

Julie stared after the diminutive form of the middle-aged sports junky, wondering if she'd heard right. *Consider the source,* she rationalized. Bob would be crazy about Jack the Ripper if he could quote baseball statistics.

Just the kind of thing Cosmo would be good at. Passive, undemanding... nerdy. She turned back to a feature on civic beautification.

"Oh, Julie! Could you come in here a minute?"

Gene beckoned from his open doorway. With a sigh, she rose to answer the summons.

Cosmo sat in Gene's chair, legs crossed and feet on the desk. Julie stared. He wore plain brown lace-up shoes with thick soles, and navy blue socks with a pattern of ivy crawling up his ankles. He looked very pleased with himself.

Frowning, she addressed Gene. "You rang?"

"I'd like to talk to you about something." He glanced at his nephew. "Cosmo, would you mind waiting outside?"

"Sure, Unc." Cosmo didn't as much swing his feet off the desktop as drag them off; they landed on the carpeted floor with a loud thunk. Looking rather smug, he departed.

Now Julie was really puzzled. "What's up?"

"Several things." Gene resumed his own chair, and Julie perched on the corner of the desk. "First of all, I want to thank you for looking out for Cosmo during his first week."

"Has it been a week already?" Julie said, unable to scotch the sarcasm.

Gene nodded. "Time flies. So how's he doing, Julie? Really."

"Really?"

"Really."

For a moment, she considered her options. She'd be perfectly justified if she screamed and hollered, but what good would it do? She was sure Cosmo would have a job at the *CC* as long as he wanted one, regardless of any objections she might raise.

On the other hand, Gene was obviously so happy to have his nephew here that she'd feel guilty raining on his parade—too much, anyway.

So she shrugged and said cautiously, "He's . . . catching on."

Gene let out his breath in a gusty sigh. "That's great, just great. You've been swell about this, Julie."

"It was . . . nothing." The lie hurt her conscience.

"I know better. I'm much obliged."

She was feeling more and more uncomfortable. "No need. If that's all—"

"Not quite," he said quickly. "I've got another favor to ask you. Cosmo's spending all his time either at work or entertaining me at home. That's no kind of life for a young man. I wonder if I could prevail on you to, I don't know, invite him out?"

Julie fell off the corner of the desk, luckily landing on her feet. "You don't mean on a *date!*" She'd sooner die.

"Oh, no, nothing like that." Gene's ruddy cheeks turned an even brighter shade. "I mean, like, for a cup of coffee."

Oh, God, not at the Rusty Spur. That was where Betsy worked and the rest of the Camerons hung out. They'd never let her live this guy down.

"Or," Gene went on, "for a drink, even. Hey, why don't you take him to the Hideout, Julie? You know, introduce him around. I'd consider it a great favor."

"Gene, you know I don't want to disappoint you, but I don't even like to think about the reception he'd get at the Hideout." She shuddered. "Some of those old boys can get pretty rowdy. Cosmo might . . . get hassled."

"Don't worry about that," Gene said blithely. "I'm not asking you to baby-sit, just to help him get to know a few people." He put on his most forlorn expression. "Is that too much to ask, Julie? Tell you what I'm gonna do. I'm gonna give you the rest of the week off."

"Gene, it's Friday already and—" she glanced at her watch "—five-fifteen."

"Mere coincidence. You two young people—"

His door opened and Cosmo reentered, his expression eager. "Are we all set?"

Set up was more like it, Julie thought crossly. Still, she knew when she was licked. "C'mon, Cosmo," she said with more resignation than invitation. "I'll buy you a drink."

She walked past him and through the door. Behind her, she heard him say an enthusiastic, "Thanks, Uncle Gene. I won't forget this!"

Neither would she. Gene Varner owed her big time.

IN CUPID you knew you were an adult when you could get a drink at the Hideout without showing any ID. Located on the southwestern edge of town, the Hideout was a true cowboy honky-tonk, a place for "singin', dancin', drinkin' and fightin'."

In other words, completely alien to the likes of Cosmo Mackenzie. Nevertheless, Julie led him doggedly through the door, turned left at the stuffed buffalo and headed toward the antique bar along the wall. To the right were booths, and in the middle, behind the wall that screened the entry, was the biggest dance floor in this part of the state.

Cosmo stopped and stared. "Is that a buffalo?" he asked.

"That would be my guess." Julie gestured impatiently. "You coming or not?"

"Sure. What's the rush?" He looked hurt. "Gosh, Julie, you sure are acting uptight. Are you ashamed of me or something?"

His question made her uncomfortable. "Whatever gave you that idea?" She led the way to the bar and propped one foot on the rail.

"I dunno." He emulated her, but his foot slipped off the shiny brass; on the second try, it stuck.

A not-so-smooth move much appreciated by Charlie Gilroy, the bartender. He walked up, grinning. "Long time no see, Julie. What can I do you for?"

"Hi, Charlie. I'll have a glass of white wine, I guess. Uh...do you know C-Cosmo?" She didn't think she'd ever get used to saying that name.

Charlie's heavy eyebrows soared. A chunky man in his late thirties, he prided himself on having seen them all—but Julie could tell that the barkeep considered Cosmo in a class by himself.

Cosmo lifted his arm above the bar to offer his hand for a shake. "Pleased to meet you, Charlie."

Charlie ignored the hand. "You ain't from around here, I take it."

Julie laughed. "You sound like a B movie, Charlie. You gonna give him till sundown to get out of town?"

"Won't have to," Charlie said. "I'll leave it to them boys over in the corner."

Julie glanced in the direction he indicated and groaned. There in the back corner, just in front of the partition blocking off the rest rooms, sat as motley a looking crew as you were apt to find in Cupid, Colorado.

Johnny King was her own age: twenty-six. She and her twin, Jason, had gone to school with Johnny, but they'd never been friends. Johnny was a smart aleck and a troublemaker. Jason had tangled with him more than once.

As she watched the wiry Johnny, he reached across the table to cuff his companion alongside the head. Beau Turner grinned his goofy grin and said something, then rubbed his ear. At six foot two, Beau was at least four inches taller than his companion, not to mention two years older, but Johnny was the one in charge. Beau was no smarter than the law allowed. As a Turner, he had a lot to live down right off the bat. Like a grandpa in prison for bank robbery and a father who drank copious amounts of cheap wine out of brown paper bags.

The third member of the little group was the shocker, though: Scott Hale, he of the shiny blond hair and shiny red Corvette. Scott Hale, the first man Julie Cameron had ever loved.

Or thought she'd loved. Looking back on that time five years ago, she now realized her feelings for him had had more to do with her starry-eyed notions of big-city glitz and sophistication, which Scott had seemed to represent, than true feelings of affection and respect.

She turned back to the bar, knowing she should never have let Gene get her into this. There were a few others in the room, as well, but if there was any real trouble, it would come from that dark table in back.

Charlie rapped his knuckles on the bar to get Cosmo's attention. "You want anything, fella?"

Cosmo screwed up his face in concentration. "I believe I'll have . . . a sloe-gin fizz."

Charlie's jaw dropped. "You'll have a *what?*"

Cosmo smiled pleasantly. "A—"

"Beer!" Julie jammed one elbow toward his ribs, hitting the cast, instead. It was like banging into a wall. "He'll have a beer."

"But—"

"Shut up, Cosmo." She gave Charlie her most winning smile. "He's putting you on, honest. Bring him a Coors. I'll have a white wine."

The bartender looked bemused. "Yeah, sure." He moved away.

Julie rubbed her throbbing elbow and glared at her companion. "What are you trying to do, make yourself a laughingstock?"

"But . . ." He shook his head, which did nothing to dislodge his plastered-down hair.

"Real men may eat quiche, but they don't drink sloe-gin fizzes in the Hideout."

Before he could respond, a glass of wine and a beer slid across the bar. "Catch me later," Charlie said, moving off.

Cosmo fumbled in his trouser pocket. "Here, let me."

Julie picked up the two drinks. "He said to pay him later. Let's get a table." *As far away from that terrible trio as we can.*

"You mean he trusts us?" Cosmo slid out a chair for her.

She sat down, surprised but pleased by that small courtesy. "Not us. He trusts *me*. He's known my family all his life, and me, all my life. If I tried to stiff him for a couple of drinks, he'd know where to find me." She offered the beer. "You, he doesn't know from Adam."

Cosmo sat down in the chair opposite hers. "Oh." He sounded disappointed. "Still, it must be nice to live where everybody knows your name."

She thought she heard a genuine touch of longing in his voice, as if he hadn't realized such places existed. To her surprise, she found herself responding seriously, without a trace of sarcasm or scorn.

"This is real small-town America," she said. "There are still a lot of people in this town who don't lock their cars or their houses at night. If you need something, all you have to do is ask—you don't have to steal it."

She twirled the stem of the wineglass between her fingers. "Of course, they're not saints. They'll do you the favor but probably hold it over your head for the rest of your life."

"That sounds like a fair trade to me," he said. "Back in California—"

"Why, if it ain't little Julie Cameron . . ."

A couple of booted and blue-jeaned locals leaned over the table grinning—but not at her. They were getting an eyeful of Cosmo, no doubt about it.

"Hi, guys," she said, remembering why she was here. "This is Gene's nephew, Cosmo Mackenzie. Cosmo, this is—"

The two burst into raucous laughter. Without waiting to be introduced, they ambled away shaking their heads. One by one and two by two, other customers drifted by to get a better look at the yahoo sitting across from Julie Cameron. With his unfashionable glasses and slicked-back hair, high-buttoned and baggy short-sleeved shirt, he was an oddity, all right. Even the women giggled behind their hands.

Cosmo seemed delighted with the attention. Julie wasn't; she'd be razzed about this for the rest of her life. She wished everybody would just leave them alone—but that would defeat the purpose. She was facing this public humiliation to introduce Cosmo Mackenzie around. As soon as she'd done her duty, she'd be out of there.

At a lull between gawkers, Cosmo leaned forward with his elbows on the table to speak in a confidential tone. "There's three fellows back there in that dark corner who keep looking over here and laughing. Why don't they just come on by like all these other friendly people?"

"You don't want to meet them, Cosmo, trust me."

"Oh, but I do," he said. He sipped his beer much the same way she sipped her wine. Daintily. "Who are they, anyway?"

"The big one is Beau Turner. Beau's . . . well, you might say he's rowing with only one oar in the water."

"Turner." A light bulb went on in Cosmo's eyes. "Is he related to the Outlaw Grandpa?"

"Yes, but don't ever say anything about that in front of him. He doesn't take kindly to that title."

Cosmo nodded wisely. "How about the other two?"

She was reluctant to go into it but couldn't think of a graceful way to change the subject. "The little one is Johnny King. He's kinda wild, always in trouble but nothing really serious." She glanced toward the bar and added quickly, "I've finished my wine, so I think I'll just be running along—"

"How about the third guy?"

That firm voice hardly sounded like Cosmo's. She looked at him with surprise. "Why, that's . . . Scott Hale."

"Should I recognize the name?"

If Cosmo wasn't wearing his usual guileless expression, she'd have sworn he was putting her on. "Of course not. I'm just a little surprised to see him here. He moved away a few years ago, and I haven't seen him to talk to in—"

"Get ready," Cosmo interrupted pleasantly. "He's on his way over."

IT WAS ALL Max could do to keep that phony-baloney grin on his face while Julie made the introductions. Obviously this Scott Hale made her very nervous.

Not King and Turner, though, who traded insults with her like old friends—well, maybe just old acquaintances. King was a scrapper, a brawler, a bully when he thought he could get away with it; Max zeroed in on the type without effort. Turner seemed genuinely friendly, sticking out a big paw and, when King knocked it aside, looking genuinely confused.

As for Hale, he had a certain oily smoothness Max immediately disliked. That and the shiny blond hair and the speculation in those blue eyes when he turned them on Julie.

King took the initiative, his lip curling. "This your new boyfriend, Julie?"

"No, this is not!" Temper made her brown eyes sparkle with golden highlights. She took a deep breath. "Cosmo is a co-worker. We're just having a friendly little drink, that's all." She stood up abruptly. "And now we're finished." Her wineglass was still half-full. "Let's go, Cosmo."

Not quite yet, he thought, trying not to meet the gaze of any of the three men who crowded around the table. This was no time to issue challenges. "Aw, one more, Julie." He tried to sound pleading, when snapping orders came so much more naturally. "Okay?"

"Not okay. I'm going to the Spur. If you stay here, you're on your own, if you get my drift. Do you?"

He nodded, enjoying her efforts to force those full ripe lips into a forbidding line. "Aw, come on, Julie..."

"Aw, come on, Julie," Johnny King mocked. "Why don't you set back down and have a friendly drink with *us*."

She ignored Johnny. "I won't be responsible," she reminded Max. She took a step. "I'm going."

Max sighed. "Then I guess I'll see you Monday in the office," he said regretfully. "Have a nice weekend."

"Yeah, Julie," King called after her retreating form. "Have a nice weekend and don't worry about your *boyfriend*. We'll see he gets home safe, won't we, boys?"

And he guffawed and straddled one of the empty chairs.

CHAPTER THREE

"JULIE, YOU DIDN'T!"

Betsy, horrified, looked across the counter at her sister-in-law.

Julie slumped on her stool at the Rusty Spur Café. "What was I supposed to do? I didn't even know Scott was back in town. I didn't have much interest in a friendly drink with him."

"I'm sure you didn't." Betsy finished wiping the counter and stood there holding the rag in her hand. She only worked one evening a week, and this week, that happened to be Friday. "That's a bad bunch," she said after a moment. "From what you've told me, Cosmo Mackenzie is a babe in the woods."

"I guess you could call him that." Julie glared down at the gold-veined pattern of the countertop, adding defensively, "But I gave him every chance to come with me. And I made it perfectly clear I wouldn't be responsible for anything that might happen if he didn't. He's a grown man." She bit her lip. "What else could I do?"

Betsy didn't look impressed. "That certainly gets you off the hook, doesn't it."

Meeting her pretty sister-in-law's reproachful gaze, Julie had a sinking feeling she wasn't off the hook at all. Blast that Cosmo Mackenzie! She could only try to appease her conscience with the knowledge that if he didn't know how to handle himself by now, he wouldn't learn any younger.

But regardless of that, he was *not* Julie's responsibility.

WITHIN THE FIRST fifteen minutes, Max had confirmed his initial impressions of Johnny King and Beau Turner and found out something brand-new about Scott Hale.

The slick son of a bitch had once been engaged to Julie Cameron. Johnny King took great delight in pointing out that Scott and Julie had been together, as he put it, for months.

Max sipped his beer. "Maybe she'll take you back," he suggested to Hale.

"Nah, it was years ago," Hale responded. "You're welcome to her."

"Hey," King objected, "if she's up for grabs, don't forget me."

Turner guffawed. "Old Jason'd beat the shit out of you for even lookin' at his sister," the big man opined. His little brown eyes narrowed on Max. "You, too, I bet."

"Hell," King scoffed, "Jason's out gettin' his brains scrambled at some rodeo. I've had my eye on Miss

High and Mighty for years. This might just be a good time to take me a little run at—"

Cosmo stood up suddenly, the thick heel of one nerd shoe jamming down hard on King's booted toes. This apparently accidental mishap elicited a yelp of pain, which Max pretended not to hear. "Any of you boys want another drink?" he invited. "My treat."

Hale stood up. "Not me. I've got to get back to Denver tonight."

Beau Turner looked pleased. "I'll have me another brewsky."

King shot Max a venomous glance; he was trying to massage his toe through boot leather. "Make it a pitcher, dude. And watch whose feet you're steppin' on, or I'll arrange a cast for your other arm."

"Sure thing." Max fought his smile. The dynamic duo still sitting at the table had obviously been drinking for some time, and they weren't thinking quite straight—if they ever had.

This might turn out to be fun, after all.

For the next thirty minutes, Max mostly listened, neatly cataloging everything he heard and coming to a few conclusions.

He learned that Johnny had just been fired from his job on a highway crew repairing roads around Cupid, through no fault of his own, naturally—the bastards were out to get him for no reason. Every word Johnny uttered revealed him as a mean little drunk, although he apparently came from a decent family.

Whereas Beau might be a decent man from a dysfunctional family. Beau's father was a drunk, and his mother had run away years earlier with "the gas-meter man." His grandfather—Beau looked around carefully to make sure no one who might contradict him was listening—was "out of town." With all that being the case, Beau worked on the family ranch—when he worked. That left him plenty of time to spend with his good buddy Johnny.

It was quickly obvious that although Beau was a follower, Johnny was no leader. Probing carefully, listening to the bits and pieces as they came out, Max found himself sympathetic to the big guy. Beau, with his broad goofy grin, was strangely likable.

Kind of like a bigger dumber Cosmo Mackenzie.

"How 'bout you?" Johnny slurred the words and poked a finger into Max's chest. "Julie Cameron's kinda high-class for a nosy nobody like you, even if you do have money." He took another swallow from the beer Max had brought.

"I but worship Julie from afar," Max said gravely, "and I've only got enough money to buy drinks for my friends occasionally. I'm just in town to learn the newspaper business from my uncle Gene. To tell you the truth, I've never been west of Las Vegas before, and I want to learn as much as I can about everything. Besides, I never knew any cowboys before."

Johnny gave Beau an exaggerated wink. "You wouldn't know a cowboy if one spit in your face. Me'n Beau can teach you plenty, though. Let's go outside and have the first lesson. Tenderfoot like you oughta be grateful for a chance like this."

Beau looked unhappy. "Aw, Johnny, he's already one arm short of a pair."

"So?"

"So...I ain't finished my beer."

"Bring it." Johnny staggered to his feet.

Max rose with alacrity. "I appreciate you taking the trouble."

"No trouble." Johnny drained his beer and burped. "Is it, bud."

Beau frowned. "I dunno, Johnny. There's a lotta beer left in that pitcher."

"Stay here'n drink it, then," Johnny snapped. "Who the hell needs you anyhow?"

"No, no, I'm comin'."

Johnny herded Max toward the back of the room. Someone else occupied the table in the corner where he and the boys had been sitting earlier, and Johnny managed to kick the man's chair leg as they passed.

The man, a long drink of water in standard cowboy costume, surged to his feet, his female companion giving a little shriek of alarm. "Watch what the hell you're doin', King," he snarled.

Johnny whirled drunkenly, his squinty eyes and two-fisted pose belligerent. "Whatcha gonna do if I don't, Tom Purdy?"

"I'm gonna kick your butt from here to Denver, that's what I'm gonna do." Tom Purdy hitched up his jeans, getting ready to do just that.

The woman, a thirtyish looker with big hair, jumped up and grabbed the man's arm. "Oh, Tom, please don't get in a fight."

He tried to shake her off. "Set down, Lorrie. This is no concern of yours."

"It is so. You promised..." Her worried gaze appealed to the other three men before settling on Max.

Who politely dipped his head in her direction. "I'm sure Mr. King didn't intend offense—"

Johnny whirled around. "Don't you go apologizin' for me!"

"Or," Max said, smoothly changing course, "maybe he did. But your friend, Mr. Purdy, is right. It's nothing to worry your pretty little head about." *Take care, Max,* he warned himself. *Don't start having so much fun you give yourself away.*

The woman laughed. "You're new around here." She batted her eyelashes at Max, the emergency apparently forgotten.

"I am."

Tom Purdy gave Max a shove. "Hey, you quit makin' time with my girl."

Max blinked, pretending great surprise. "Is that what I'm doing? I beg your pard—"

Johnny gave Purdy a shove. "Butt out. If anybody's gonna work this dude over, it'll be me'n ol' Beau here."

"Yeah." Beau had been watching with rapt attention. Now that his chain had been yanked, he roused himself. "Want me to hold 'im while you punch 'im out, Johnny?'' He grabbed Max's elbows and hauled them back.

Lorrie let out another little shriek. ''What're you guys doing? You can't just gang up on a one-armed stranger that way. Tom, help him!''

Tom's lip curled. ''What the hell for? I don't like him any better'n they do.''

''But it was Johnny King who kicked your chair, not Mr. Mackenzie. Mr. Mackenzie is a gentleman!''

Johnny ignored the brouhaha building between Tom and Lorrie. Cocking his right fist, he sighted down his arm. ''Quit weavin' around—dammit, hold him still, Beau,'' he directed, letting fly.

Beau was strong, but he had no reason to suspect Max was, too. Therefore the big guy was completely unprepared for his captive to wait until the last possible second, then duck to the side just enough to allow Johnny's fist to sail past his ear.

But not harmlessly. It clipped Beau square on the chin.

Beau released Max and reared back, rubbing his jaw. ''Why'd you go and do that?'' he bellowed, glaring at his friend.

''The son of a bitch moved!'' Johnny stumbled into Tom, knocking the man ass over teakettle. When Tom went down, he took his chair with him.

Lorrie screamed, but not for her erstwhile escort. She grabbed Max's arm. ''Quick, run! Tom'll be killin' mad once he gets himself untangled.''

"But I didn't do any—" Max stepped back and Beau hurtled between them and into the table, which splintered and collapsed beneath his weight "—thing. This is all a big misunderstanding."

"Aargh!" Johnny launched himself into the air, body spread like a net with arms high and fingers curved into talons, reaching for revenge. An almost negligent straight arm from Max changed Johnny's direction in midflight. He landed on Tom Purdy, who'd finally managed to struggle as far as his knees.

"Oh, my goodness!" Lorrie covered her mouth with both hands. Her horrified gaze flew between Max and the pile of bodies on the floor.

The bartender came rushing up, followed by several curious patrons. "What in the holy hell!" He stopped short. Nobody was standing except Max and Lorrie. Max could see the man's thoughts on his face: *This don't make no sense.*

Max tsk-tsked and shook his head disapprovingly. "I believe they've consumed a little too much beer," he confided. "I'd like to buy this lady a drink, and then I'll settle up and be on my way."

"Sure thing." The barkeep frowned, obviously still having trouble figuring out what had happened. Somebody at the bottom of the pile groaned, and onlookers started dragging off bodies.

Lorrie cocked her head and regarded Max with a slight smile that was a little confused, a little not. "Do you really have to go?"

Max smoothed back his waxed hair with both hands, although it was unmussed by the evening's events. "I'm afraid so."

She pouted. "Maybe we'll see each other again?"

"If the fates be kind."

She gave him an uncertain smile. "You're weird, Cosmo Mackenzie, but I like you. I'm not real clear what just happened here, but maybe it's better that way."

"Maybe it is," he agreed.

"Don't worry about them three. They'll be too embarrassed to even ask what hit 'em."

"That, too, may be for the better." With a jaunty salute, Max tossed a few bills onto the bar and departed the Hideout in pursuit of Julie Cameron. He was feeling *good*. With any luck, she'd still be at the Rusty Spur.

SHE WASN'T, but Max didn't realize that until he'd already taken a seat. Then the pretty blond waitress approached, and he damn near fell off his chair.

Maxwell Cosmo Mackenzie never forgot a face, and he'd seen that face before: Elizabeth Ross. Several years ago in Los Angeles, she'd thought she and her daughter might be the targets of a stalker. Her movie-star husband had just died, and she wasn't in the best shape herself. Max had been called in to handle the case, and because it was potentially high profile, he'd been warned to treat the woman with kid gloves—all right, threatened with dire reprisals if he didn't.

There'd been a female fan following her around, as it turned out, but with nothing more sinister in mind than to get close to the wife and child of her dead idol. Max had tried to ease Mrs. Ross's fears, but hadn't been sure he'd succeeded.

He hadn't seen or thought about her since. Was he hallucinating now? Maybe he was mistaken. Maybe—

She placed a glass of water on the table and smiled. "Hi," she said brightly. "Our special tonight is chicken and dumplings with—" She broke off in the middle of her practiced spiel and stared at Max in wide-eyed confusion.

Damn, this woman did look like Elizabeth Ross, but why would the widow of a movie star be slinging hash in a roadside diner in Cupid, Colorado?

"Hey, Betsy!" A man at the counter waved his mug in the air. "Can I get a little more coffee here?"

"Wait your turn, Cleve." She turned back to Max, still looking completely off-balance. "You're new in town." She slipped her pencil and order pad into an apron pocket and thrust out her hand. "I'm Betsy Cameron."

Another Cameron; could he handle more than one? "I'm Cosmo Mackenzie. I think I work with your sister-in-law at the *Chronicles?*"

Her lips curved in an easy smile, but she still looked vaguely uncertain. "Julie's mentioned you."

"I'll bet she has." Max laughed. Which might have been a mistake.

Betsy blinked and seemed on the verge of saying something he was sure he wouldn't want to hear. "Yes, well . . . I'm glad to see you made it out of the Hideout in one piece. I scolded Julie for leaving you there with that awful Johnny King."

"Me and Johnny and Beau are good buddies," Max protested. It was all right; she hadn't recognized him.

Her eyebrows arched. "You think so, do you? I wouldn't count on that, if I were you. But back to business—what can I bring you, Cosmo? Are you here for dinner or just a cup of coffee?"

"Coffee, I guess." He looked around. "I thought Julie would be here."

"You just missed her. She's on the way back to the ranch." Betsy turned away. "Care for a piece of pie with that coffee?"

Ah, yes—Julie had said her sister-in-law was quite the baker. "What kind do you have?"

"Lemon-meringue and chocolate-cream . . ." She peered back behind the counter, twisting to get a better view of the pie cabinet. "Looks like a couple pieces of apple and maybe one of peach."

Max's mouth watered. "Peach."

"Can I put a slab of ice cream on that for you?"

"Yes, ma'am." He busied himself with silverware rolled in a paper napkin, wishing she wouldn't linger.

"You know," she said slowly, "I have the funniest feeling we've met before." She sighed. "Oh, well. It'll come to me."

He sure as hell hoped not. Disbelieving, he watched her walk away. Big L.A. cop about to have his cover blown, week two. Or maybe not... What were the chances she'd remember a brief meeting at such a traumatic time in her life?

Slim and none.

THE PIE WAS GREAT. Max ate quickly, determined to get out of the Rusty Spur before Betsy Cameron could figure out where she'd seen him before. She was busy fortunately, and he didn't think she'd have time to dwell on it.

He thought wrong. When he walked to the cash register at the far end of the counter and she reached out to take his money, he saw sudden knowledge lighten her clear blue eyes.

"My God, I know you! You're—"

"Hey, don't give me away." Max looked around anxiously. Although there were several customers in the café, no one seemed to be paying them the least bit of attention.

"But you're—"

"Mrs. Ross, please don't say any more. We need to talk."

"I'm not Mrs. Ross now. I'm Mrs. Cameron—call me Betsy. What in the world are you doing here, Detective Mackenzie? I knew the minute I heard your last name that it was familiar, but I don't recall your first name being Cosmo." She cocked her head and looked at him with a smile. "Or maybe you made that up."

"I didn't make up a damned thing." Reaching around the big glass jug of pennies on the counter, he grabbed her wrist and dragged her down to the end, where they could talk without any chance of being overheard. "Look, will you let me explain before you blow my cover?"

Her eyes went round as buttons. "Are you working undercover in Cupid? How exciting!"

She led the way to the table in the back, the one farthest away from the other diners. He followed, his mind racing over his options.

Which boiled down to exactly one. He'd have to level with her and hope she'd keep his secret. He didn't much care to do that but saw no other way.

She sat down and leaned forward eagerly, her forearms on the tabletop. "Tell me everything," she urged in a stage whisper. "Who are you after, a murderer?" She recoiled. "Not L.A. gang members in little old Cupid! I read in the papers that Denver's getting a lot of those hoodlums, but surely not here."

"Nah, nothing like that." Max rested his cast on the table and sighed. "I'm not here for the LAPD. As a matter of fact, I'm on administrative leave. I was involved in a hostage situation out there a few weeks back and got my—"

"That's right. I read about it in the Denver papers, but I didn't make the connection. You're a hero!" She sat up straighter. "You managed to slip inside that fast-food store and mix with the hostages. Then when you

got a chance, you jumped the gunman. Oh!'' Those
wide astonished eyes again. "You got shot!"

"It was nothing," he said modestly.

"Nothing!" She looked at his cast. "Is that why
you're wearing that?"

"Well, yeah, the bullet clipped a bone." He
shrugged. "No big deal. But the first thing that happens after a shooting is a complete departmental re-
view. Since I was going to be on administrative leave
and sick leave, anyway, I let Gene talk me into coming
to Cupid to do a little job for him."

"Then Gene Varner really is your uncle?"

Max nodded.

"What's the job?"

"Horse thieves. Gene is really ticked off about that
gang that's been stealing horses—especially *his* horse."

She nodded sympathetically. "I know he is. He and
Julie write editorials about it all the time. But why
would a big-city policeman like you be willing to take
on something this...this inconsequential? I mean,
you're used to dealing with murderers and psy-
chos..." Her voice trailed off and her expression became pensive. "You were right about my stalker. She
was harmless."

He smiled. "I know. Some people do foolish
things..." *And I hope my leveling with you isn't one
them.* "You seem happy now. I'm glad."

"Thank you. I'm very happy. I married a wonderful man, and I've put all those California years behind

me." She laughed lightly. "But we must seem like real hicks to you, Mr. Mackenzie."

"Call me Cosmo. And before you ask, that really is my name. I'm Maxwell Cosmo Mackenzie."

"I remember now! One of the other officers called you Max."

He nodded. "But I'd appreciate it if you'd forget that until I've finished with the job I came here to do. Gene and I just thought it'd be easier for me to get to the bottom of the rustling if everybody thought I was an inept but well-meaning reporter who'd be no threat to anyone. It's been my experience that strangers don't tend to open up much to out-of-town policemen, especially those with no jurisdiction."

She nodded. "Who else knows?"

"Only Gene, and now you." Time to ask the sixty-four-dollar question. "Can I count on you to keep my secret, Betsy?"

"From everybody?" She looked startled, perhaps a little worried. "Even my husband?"

"Especially your husband. I hear he's got quite a temper."

She laughed a bit ruefully. "That's true. How about Julie?"

"Especially Julie, too. She could blow my cover sky-high if she knew." He frowned. "She's not suspicious, is she?"

"No. She thinks you're a total nerd." Betsy giggled. "I must admit, you've got a pretty good disguise. Fortunately for the success of your mission, Julie already had it in for you before you ever arrived. Once she makes up her mind, it takes an act of God to change it."

Max wasn't sure he liked the sound of that. If he'd met Ms. Julie Cameron in his "super cop" role, he'd have shown her a few moves unknown to nerds anywhere. He shoved aside wounded vanity. "I met a guy at the Hideout tonight who says he was engaged to Julie once."

"Scott Hale, right? I heard he was back in town."

"Right."

Betsy nodded. "That was several years ago, when I first came to Cupid. He never was right for her. She's been engaged a few times since then, too, but she never could bring herself to marry any of them."

"Sounds a little peculiar to me," Max grumbled, thinking about how incensed he'd been by Hale. Nor was he happy to find out there'd been others. What was she, a one-woman welcome committee?

Obviously not; Cosmo was a strikeout, wasn't he? She had her standards.

"Not if you know Julie." Betsy's face softened when she talked about her sister-in-law. "She's all heart. She falls in and out of love like other women fall on and off diets. Nothing is ever trivial to her."

"A butterfly, huh?"

"Not at all." Betsy looked offended. "Julie is one of a kind. She has so much to give that it's hard to find a guy worthy of her—*my* opinion, not hers. If she ever found the right guy..." Betsy blinked and looked past him. "Oh, dear, I've got to get back to work. The cook is glaring at me." She jumped up.

"Hey, wait a minute. Is my secret safe with you, or should I just pack it in and go on back to the Big Orange?"

"Don't do that." She smiled. "I won't breathe a word—unless I have to."

Unless she had to? What did that mean? Whatever; he supposed he'd have to be satisfied. What the hell. He'd just dodged a bullet.

The first one, anyway. How many more awaited him in this one-horse town?

"By the way," he called after her, "the pie was great."

She tossed him a grin over one shoulder while reaching for plates loaded with hamburgers and fries. "I know. I made it."

She winked, which earned Max a curious glance from the middle-aged couple seated near the door.

CHAPTER FOUR

JULIE KICKED OPEN the back door of the Straight Arrow ranch house and walked into the laundry room, holding her gloved hands out carefully to keep from touching anything. She'd been out in the barn helping Ben doctor a sick cow, and she was covered with mud and blood and crud and who knew what. If she entered the kitchen before cleaning up, Granny would have her hide.

But they'd saved the cow, to her great relief. Bossy was part of Julie's own small herd, started when her father gave her a couple of calves on her tenth birthday. She even had her own brand: the Arrow J. When she wasn't at the *Chronicles* office, she could often be found out on the range with Ben or working in the barns and corrals.

Betsy came in from the kitchen. "I thought I heard you in here," she said, then stopped abruptly and made a face. "Ugh! Is that what I think it is all over you?"

"Probably." Julie sprinkled on powdered soap, added more water and scrubbed her hands and arms until they were red. "I saw you drive in a while ago. Good night at the Spur?"

Betsy shrugged. "An okay night." She raised one eyebrow. "A friend of yours was in."

Julie groaned. "Not Scott."

Betsy shook her head. "Mr. Mackenzie. C-Cosmo."

"Hard to say, isn't it." Julie spoke wryly. "What kind of name is Cosmo?"

"Maybe a family name," Betsy suggested.

Julie reached for a towel. "Was he in one piece?"

"Looked like it."

"That's a relief. I really did feel a little bit guilty about leaving him there alone with those guys, but..." She shrugged. "Did you introduce yourself?"

"Yes. I must say, he speaks more highly of you than you do of him."

"That's supposed to make me happy?" Julie tossed the towel on top of the washing machine. "Did he, uh, look like he'd been involved in any kind of altercation?"

"He looked cool as a cucumber, not a hair out of place."

"Considering the stuff he puts on it—" Julie pointed to her own tousled hair "—that's no wonder." She hesitated, reluctant to ask the question on her mind but incapable of abstaining. "So what do you think of him?"

Betsy cocked her head, her eyes bright with speculation. "I think he's quite nice," she said firmly, "and not a nerd at all."

"Wait a minute, are we talking about the same guy?"

Laughing, they walked into the kitchen.

A LOT OF STRANGE RUMORS were floating around town the next week concerning events at the Hideout Friday night. Avis had heard about a big fight, but nothing to indicate Cosmo was involved; the life-styles editor, Mary Louise Davis, said her husband had heard the new guy at the *Chronicles* got drunk and fell over Tom Purdy's foot—accidentally or on purpose.

The sports editor, Bob Mays, said he'd gone into the Hideout just as Cosmo was leaving and had found a big to-do with some drunks in the back: Tom Purdy might have been one of them, Bob couldn't be sure. Beau Turner was there, and Johnny King, bellowing like a cut bull. Johnny apparently blamed Cosmo for the whole thing, but Bob didn't see how Cosmo could've been involved when he didn't have a scratch on him, and the others, in a word, did.

When Cosmo walked into the newsroom whistling, everybody shut up. But they couldn't help casting curious glances in his direction.

Julie assured herself that she honestly didn't give a hoot what had happened after her departure that night. Nevertheless, when he came out of Gene's office and stood grinning in front of her desk, she heard herself saying, "So what was all this excitement at the Hideout the other night?"

"Excitement?" He pushed his glasses higher onto his nose, looking puzzled. "What excitement?"

For a moment she just looked at him. Then she gave an exasperated sigh. "Never mind. I'm sure it was exaggerated. Let's get to work."

She didn't give it another thought until midafternoon when she ran into Lorrie Anderson, working behind the counter at Rocky Pizza across the street. Lorrie offered a diet soda and a grin.

"So how's Cosmo today?"

Julie stared at the woman. "Where did you meet Cosmo?"

"Friday night at the Hideout."

Aha! "Maybe you can tell me what happened, then. I've heard all kinds of wild stories."

"Nothin'." Lorrie looked absolutely owllike, her lips clamping shut around the single word.

"Come on, Lorrie," Julie cajoled, "something must have happened. Everybody in town's talking about it."

"Let 'em talk," Lorrie said airily. "All I know is, Cosmo's kind of . . . cute."

"Cute!" Had all that peroxide affected Lorrie's brain? "Are we talking about the same Cosmo who works—and I use the word laughingly—at the *Cupid Chronicles?*"

Lorrie shrugged. "You know another Cosmo?" She turned away. "Tell him I said hi, okay?"

Julie nodded, stunned. When she relayed the message, Cosmo grinned.

"Nice girl, that Lorrie," he said. "Now, about this rewrite you gave me . . ."

And that was that.

MAX WAS A STITCH in the side Julie couldn't get rid off, no matter how many deep breaths she drew. They spent hours working together in the office every day, and when Cosmo ventured forth, she tried to keep right on his heels, since she didn't trust him as far as she could throw him.

But as time passed, she didn't find handling this interloper getting much easier. At work he was the next thing to useless. In town he was an embarrassment, asking stupid questions and generally revealing his ignorance on virtually every subject—even insurance, according to the town's only insurance agent.

Julie spent a lot of time rolling her eyes and groaning. But she also found herself watching for him to come in each morning and waiting for him to go home each night. As a certain well-known professor complained, she was growing accustomed to his face.

Not, she assured herself, that she liked him any better with the passage of time. But she also had to admit she found no spite or malice in him. Cosmo Mackenzie was the closest thing to a pacifist she'd ever spent time with. He always seemed willing to give the benefit of the doubt, which made her crazy sometimes but was gratifying when applied to herself.

If only he could learn to type and follow orders.

Dream on, she thought crabbily, staring down at one of his so-called crime stories: "A woman suffered a black eye when accosted by Main Street the other day."

She had to wonder what weapon Main Street had used in the attack.

MAX WAS GETTING the lay of the land and figuring out who the players were. With Julie dogging his heels, he began with a tour of Main Street, meeting the businessmen—business*persons*, Julie corrected—and clerks and customers alike.

Cupid, he was not surprised to discover, was a whole lot different from Los Angeles. Here he was greeted with smiles, not middle fingers; service was not grudging nor attention stinted; and everybody knew who he was before he opened his mouth.

"Gene's nephew . . . Hey, me'n Gene go way back. Welcome to Cupid. Cosmo, is it?"

His name usually elicited a snicker, occasionally a guffaw. "Family name," he'd say, shrugging helplessly. "My mother thought he'd leave me his money. He left it to Disneyland for all the happy hours he'd spent there—like they need it."

That never failed to gain him sympathy. From everyone except Julie.

Julie was an experience all by herself. She didn't trust him as far as she could throw him, yet there wasn't a thing she could pin on him. Baiting her quickly became one of Max's favorite pastimes.

"Tell me again about the five *W*'s?" he'd ask, and strive for the proper submissive expression while she berated him for forgetting yet again.

"Who, what, where, when, why!" she'd shout.

And he'd ask, "Where did you say the h-word fits in there?"

"And sometimes *how!*" she'd yell.

He wanted to tell her she was cute when she was angry. Her brown eyes would turn dark and turbulent, and her full lips would quiver with indignation. A becoming shade of rose would tint her high cheekbones and—a big plus—she always sucked in a deep breath to calm herself.

Julie had a hell of a bod by any standard of measurement. Her breasts were high and full, just the way he liked them, and her hips curvy, which made her waist look tiny. She didn't exactly seem unaware of her physical attributes, more...indifferent. He knew she didn't do aerobics or run or pump iron to keep her figure.

But whatever she was doing sure as hell worked for Max. Maybe he could—

No, dammit! He wasn't going to blow this project just so he could cozy up to the luscious Julie Cameron. She'd still be around when the job was over.

Of course, she probably wouldn't be talking to him then. She barely was now.

Life, he consoled himself, was full of tough choices.

But then the rustlers struck again and choice was no longer a consideration.

MAX SPRAWLED in a chair in front of Gene's desk, his feet propped on a stack of papers. "Julie's out there having a fit," he said. "You'd think they were her horses that were stolen."

"You just don't get it, do you." Gene shook his grizzled head. "When somebody steals your horse, it's not like he took your bicycle. A horse is part of the family. A man who'd steal a horse is the lowest form of human life in the West."

"Lower than murderers?"

Gene frowned. "We don't have murders in Cupid. Last one was long about—"

"Julie told me—1967, domestic violence. I looked it up. Now about this horse theft..."

Max laid out the details gathered through a few judicious phone calls and lots of "professional courtesy": a ranch near Greeley, five horses, one a kid's pet. Best of the bunch was a roper worth thousands, the rest nondescript and probably already sold to a slaughterhouse in Texas.

Gene shuddered. "Dog food."

"More likely people food. Horse meat is a popular dish in a lot of countries."

"It'd be like eating...eating a dog."

Max shrugged. "Dog meat is a popular dish in—"

"Stop." Gene looked green. "When I think of someone eating Gwendolyn, it's enough to make my blood boil."

Max could understand that. Gwendolyn was really a member of Gene's family. The old mare would stand at the fence and beg for treats, nuzzling the unwary with her head just like...

A dog.

Max cleared his throat, surprised at himself. He wasn't one to get sentimental about...about much of anything. "Whatever. It looks like the job was pulled by the same bunch, according to the authorities. Used a trailer, actually made a couple of trips before anyone knew what was happening. Not much to go on unfortunately.''

''Damn!'' Coming from the gentle Gene, that was something. ''Dwight have anything to say? For that matter, what do you think of our marshal?''

Idly Max tried to scratch an itch just beyond his pencil's reach between his skin and the plaster cast. He considered his uncle's question. ''Dwight Deakins,'' he said at last. ''What do I think of him . . . Hell of a nice guy but decades behind in law-enforcement techniques. If all the small-town lawmen in this state are like Dwight, it's a wonder nothing more important's been stolen than a few horses and cows. Are there any crown jewels locked up in Denver? If so, this state's in trouble.''

''Very funny.'' Gene didn't look as if he meant it. ''Dwight likes to work on gut instinct.''

''That and a buck-fifty will get him a cup of coffee in L.A.'' Max sighed. ''I have to admit I'm not getting very far myself.''

The damned pencil was too short. Max reached for Gene's dull-edged letter opener. ''I'd sure as hell like to see them pull something here in Cupid again. If they follow the pattern set so far, we should be next up.''

Gene looked surprised. ''You mean they're hitting Cupid every other time?'' His normally pleasant expression turned savage. ''Hanging's too good for a horse thief. I hope they *do* hit here so you can bust their butts. I say throw 'em in jail for the rest of their miserable lives.''

Max laughed. "I know you have strong feelings, but that sounds a tad extreme."

Gene scrunched up his face. "Sorry, but when they took my pinto, they went too far. That was the best horse I ever had. Thank God they didn't get Gwendolyn, too." He picked up his coffee cup, saw it was empty and put it down again. He spoke in a more ordinary tone. "So how are you getting along with Julie?"

Max smiled. "Not as well as I'd like to."

"Now, Max—"

"Cosmo."

"Okay, Cosmo, I told you to leave her alone. I don't want any broken hearts left behind in Colorado when you go back to California."

And he would be going back, Max realized with a start. Funny, he hadn't given California much thought since arriving in Colorado.

Time sure flew when you were having fun.

"And one more thing..."

"Yeah?" Max regarded his uncle with raised eyebrows.

"Will you go have Doc Kunkle look at that cast? You're driving me crazy, always digging at it. When's it supposed to come off, anyway?"

"Sometime this week, maybe next." Max hadn't realized he was getting on anyone's nerves.

"Well, go see if you can get it cut off now, why don't you. At least then you'll be able to type. That should appease Julie a little."

"I don't need a doctor for that," Max said. "You must have a saw at home somewhere. We can cut it off tonight."

Gene looked appalled. "Are you kidding? I'm no doctor—"

From the doorway behind Max, Julie's voice shocked him: "You've *got* to be kidding, Cosmo."

Max slid his feet from the desk, banging them awkwardly on the floor. He was glad Julie was behind him, for it took him a couple of seconds to crawl back into his nerd persona. He found himself stuttering: "B-but it w-won't be—"

"Absolutely not." Julie marched into the room and stopped, her fists on her hips and indignation on her face. "Honestly, Cosmo, I haven't got the first idea how your mind works. If that cast comes off too soon or too late, you could spend the rest of your life with . . . with a crooked arm or something."

Max tried for brave. "But I want to pack my own weight around here, Julie. Even with a crooked arm, I'd type better than I do now."

She rolled her eyes. "I have a strong suspicion that your typing skills will be minimal even with two good arms."

"Now, children." Gene reached for his telephone. "There'll be no further argument on the subject. I'll even call Doc and set up the appointment. How's that?''

That could mean trouble, Max realized, his back to the wall. There was a bullet hole under the cast, along with a broken bone. The bone would be mended, but he'd have the scar from the bullet for life. What if the good doctor asked a lot of embarrassing questions?

Maybe he wouldn't. How much could you expect from an old sawbones this far out in the boonies? Maybe he'd just cut the cast off and send Max on his way.

Julie's smile had an edge to it. "To make sure you do what you're supposed to, I'll drive you over there," she announced.

Trouble with a capital *T.*

JULIE PARKED in the small medical office/infirmary on Lovers' Lane and climbed out to wait for Max. He'd tried every way he could think of to get her to let him come alone, but she wouldn't be swayed. Now she followed him into the office and seated herself in the waiting room as if for the duration.

Rose Kunkle, who was not only the doctor's wife but his nurse and receptionist, stood up with a professional smile. "Doctor's expecting you, Cosmo."

Max took a deep breath. "Here goes nothing," he said to Julie.

At least, he *hoped* it would be nothing.

"Hmm," Doc Kunkle said for about the thirtieth time. "Hmm." He looked up, his shrewd blue eyes amused. "So who shot you?"

Max almost fell off the examining table. "What are you talking about?" he blustered, yanking up his shirt and pulling it over his stiff left arm without even pausing long enough to brush away the bits of plaster clinging to his skin. "Do I look like the kind of guy people shoot at?"

"Yep." Doc Kunkle slid up the billowing sleeve of Max's shirt and lifted the recently liberated left arm, turning it slightly to reveal a hell of a lot more than Max wanted revealed. "You were lucky." He released the arm and turned to wash his hands. "What are you, a cop?"

Max buttoned his shirt, using two hands to do the job for the first time in ages. "Who the hell are you, Sherlock Holmes?"

"Dr. Kunkle, you may presume." Doc looked positively delighted. "It wasn't so tough. I assessed your overall physical condition, which is great—you're hard as a rock." Doc thumped his disgruntled patient's shoulder. "Then I noted all your scars—hardly typical for an insurance agent, at least an honest one. Naturally I'd assume any nephew of Gene Varner's to be honest as the day is long."

Max glowered at the doctor, completely pissed off. "So your advice to me is to keep my clothes on," he suggested sarcastically.

"For starters. I was suspicious before I even started on the cast. Come on, Cosmo, did you really think I wouldn't know a bullet scar when I saw one? Or two, counting that other one just below the third rib in back?"

"They told me you were an old half-blind guy who couldn't see a bread truck if he was starving to death."

Kunkle laughed heartily and slapped his knee. "That's a hot one. I may wear glasses—I need 'em to see, unlike you—but I'm still playing with a full deck, m'boy."

So the old goat had even checked out the glasses. Great. Max slipped the offending eyewear back in place. "What'll it cost me to keep you quiet?"

"The truth." Doc sat down at the small desk in the corner and leaned his chin on a fist, his face alight with curiosity. "There's nothing I like more than a good secret, and this better be—good, that is. Of course, I'll have to tell my wife, but other than that—"

"What?" Max yelped. "For the love of... Why? Soon everybody in town's gonna know."

"Who else you taken into your confidence?" Doc demanded. "Besides your uncle of course. He *is* your uncle, isn't he?"

"Yes, he's my uncle, and who else knows is none of your business. About your wife—"

"Oh, she won't tell anyone if I ask her not to," the doctor said confidently. "But I'll have to let her in on it because she came in during the examination—remember when she brought in that folder and left it on the desk?"

Max frowned. "Sure, but what—?"

"She saw you, boy." Doc grinned. "And that woman is nobody's fool. The condition you're in doesn't match the condition you're supposed to be in, you know? I wouldn't exactly call you Arnold what's-his-face, but you're no ninety-eight-pound weakling, either."

"Well, no, but—"

"Never mind that. Start talking. If you convince me you're a good guy, I'll convince Rose. If you fail..." He made a sibilant sound, drawing his forefinger across his throat.

Max started talking.

JULIE WAS GETTING tired of sitting in the doctor's waiting room like the patient little wife or something. She was merely bored, however, not lonesome, for Rose Kunkle kept up a running commentary.

Among all that pleasant if inane chatter, Rose said one thing Julie couldn't figure out. It was upon her return from taking a file in to the doctor.

She'd come out with her eyes wide. "Hit *me* like a ton of bricks," she'd announced. "Your young man is a real stud muffin! Hubba-hubba!"

Julie, in the vernacular, had all but dropped her teeth. Cosmo Mackenzie, a stud muffin? Rose Kunkle needed new glasses!

Julie was still pondering the imponderable when the inner door opened. Doc Kunkle and Cosmo walked out together, Doc's hand on the younger man's shoulder. The lower edge of a gauze bandage extended below Max's left sleeve, but the cast was gone.

Julie stood up. "Is he all right, Doc?"

"Right as rain." Doc Kunkle positively beamed. "Now, *Cosmo,* you remember what I told you."

Cosmo shifted from foot to foot, looking distinctly uncomfortable. "Sure, Doc, I will."

"And if there's anything you need, *anything at all,* you just call on me. Got it?"

"Uh . . . I got it." Cosmo fumbled beneath the hem of his voluminous wine-and-green-patterned shirt for the wallet in his hip pocket. "What do I owe you?"

Doc shrugged him away. "I'll send you a bill," he said. "I know where you live." He laughed uproariously as if he'd made a terrific joke.

Even Rose was looking at Doc as if he'd lost it. "Merciful heavens, Amos, what are you finding so hilarious? I've got the bill right here—"

"Later." Doc waved her off. "Now you take care," he said to Cosmo. "Don't want you fallin' down any more stairs. Next time, more than an arm might get . . . busted."

And he winked.

Cosmo said plaintively to Julie, "Get me out of here."

She did, but with many a puzzled glance.

SO HE'D DODGED another bullet, Max was still trying
to convince himself as they pulled into the parking
space behind the newspaper office. Doc wouldn't give
the game away—if he could just control his glee at being in the know.

Julie threw open her door and jumped out, Max
following more slowly. This was getting complicated.
Now three people knew, in addition to Gene. How
much longer would they be able to keep their mouths—

"Yo, Julie! Over here!"

Max turned toward the jail at one edge of the parking lot. Marshal Deakins stood in the doorway, beck-
oning furiously.

He met them halfway.

"What?" Julie demanded.

Max heard the excitement in her voice, but made no
comment. Both she and Deakins were ignoring him,
and that suited him just fine.

The marshal gave a great honking laugh. "They
turned Ethan Turner loose yesterday!"

Julie gasped and took a step back, which inadvertently brought her up short against Max's chest. Automatically he leaned toward her, touching her
shoulders lightly with his hands.

Damn, she felt good! Two-handed men had it all
over the other kind.

She gave him a quick astonished glance and jerked
away. To Dwight she said, "You've got to be kidding!
He's got *years* more to serve."

"I know it," Dwight agreed, "but I guess some smart lawyer got him off early. Anyway—" he grinned broadly "—here's the best part. He's comin' home to Cupid. The old bandit is moving back to the family ranch, where he'll have ol' Beau to corrupt, like the kid needs it."

He beamed at the two of them as if he'd given them a wonderful present. "So whaddaya think of that?"

CHAPTER FIVE

WHAT DID JULIE CAMERON think about the return of eighty-six-year-old Ethan Turner, the Outlaw Grandpa?

Judging by her response, not very damned much, Max realized.

"He's behind this rustling!" she cried. "Why didn't I see it? He's got to be the brains of the gang, and now he's getting out of prison and can run things himself."

Dwight grimaced, casting a glance at Max that sought his support, man to man. "Now, Julie, don't go off half-cocked. I wasn't suggesting any such thing. Ethan's paid his debt to society—"

"Ha! They're letting him out early, you said."

"Well, yes, but—"

"He's got a criminal record. Once a criminal, always a criminal."

Max couldn't let her get any more worked up without at least trying to set her straight. "Didn't you say the old guy robbed banks?"

Julie shot him a hostile glance. "Yeah. So?"

"So—" he chose his words carefully "—would a guy who robs banks necessarily be interested in heisting horses?"

She shrugged impatiently. "Stealing's stealing."

Dwight hooked his thumbs on his gun belt and shook his head. "No, it ain't, Julie. We got nothin' on Ethan. I just told you because it's news."

"It will be when I get through with the story," she agreed grimly. She turned toward the back entrance to the *Chronicles* building. "Thanks, Dwight. I'll take it from here."

Max watched her go, his mouth turning down in disapproval. Sight unseen, Ethan Turner had his sympathy. Bank robbers, in his experience, had a fondness for cash. If old Ethan had wanted to do it the hard way, he'd have gone in for horses or cattle in the first place.

What the hell was Julie's problem? It was almost as if... as if she had something personal against the old guy.

Slowly Max became aware that Dwight was studying him thoughtfully. The lawman cleared his throat.

"See you got the cast off."

Max nodded. "Doc Kunkle removed it." He flexed the newly liberated arm.

"Doc, huh. That's good." Dwight turned away, then hesitated. "You were pretty quick to pick up on the hole in Julie's crime theory."

"What crime theory?" *Be careful, Mackenzie.*

"That old Ethan's the brains behind the rustler gang. I don't think he is, either."

"Uh, do you have any other suspects?"

"Yeah, I got me some suspects, but I ain't talkin' till I got some hard facts. In the meantime, I hope Julie doesn't rouse a lynch mob to meet the Outlaw Grandpa. She's the one can do it.''

With that, Max had to agree. Later when he repeated the conversation to Gene, he asked the question uppermost in his mind: "So why *is* Julie so rabid on the subject of this old outlaw?''

Gene looked uncomfortable, hemmed and hawed, then finally sighed and said defensively, ''You can't entirely blame her. When Ethan got busted for those bank robberies a few years back, Julie was the first one to rush to his defense. He swore he was innocent, and she, being pretty much a rookie reporter at the time, believed him. She even talked me into going way out on a limb to support him, editorially and in every other way.''

A light dawned. ''And then it turned out he was guilty...''

''As sin,'' Gene confirmed. ''Julie was devastated. She went to visit him in jail, hoping there'd be some explanation, and he wouldn't even see her—but he talked to the big boys in Denver. She'll never forgive him for that.'' Gene shook his head. ''And I'm not real sure I will, either. In Cupid, we look out for our own—until they stab us in the back. Then it's Katy-bar-the-door.''

ETHAN TURNER arrived in Cupid in Beau's beat-up old pickup the following Friday, the day after publication of an inflammatory editorial in the *Chronicles*. Trailing the Turners into town were a couple of television crews from Denver and several out-of-town reporters, intent on interviewing the Outlaw Grandpa—and no doubt grilling him about insinuations in his hometown paper that bank robbing and horse stealing were not that far apart in the lexicon of reprehensible crimes.

Julie, who'd written the editorial and badgered Gene into publishing it, was disgusted to see what it had wrought. "Look at that media circus," she groused, peering out the front window of the office. "I think they got him cornered down there at the Rusty Spur."

Max looked through the dirty window glass and down the block. Sure enough, he could see TV trucks and a mess of traffic around the café at the far end of Main Street. "Reporters," he said with distaste. "They'd step on their own mothers to get a story."

Julie recoiled. "Watch it! I'm a reporter, too. So are you, sort of."

Max tried to cover up. "I meant, present company excluded, of course." But he'd meant exactly what he said; he'd had more experience than he'd ever wanted with the media, all of it bad. A few weeks on the other side of the fence had done nothing to change his basic opinion about the kind of scavengers they were.

"I suppose I should go on down just in case there's anything new," she said after a moment. "You can work on those rewrites until I get back."

"I'll go with you."

"Now, Max, there's no need for both of us to go." She put her hands on her hips and regarded him belligerently.

"Then I'll go and you stay," he suggested. "I've never even seen the Outlaw Grandpa. I'm curious."

"You're curious." She raked him with a scornful glance, which had absolutely no effect. "Okay, come along if you've got to, but stay out of the way."

He'd stay out of the way, all right. Count on it.

IN THE CAFÉ Ethan Turner apologized for his lurid past and then shut up, which of course wasn't good enough for the piranhas of the press. As an interested but theoretically uninvolved observer, Max felt a stab of sympathy for the old man with the erect carriage and uneasy expression.

At eighty-six, Ethan Turner was whipcord lean in well-worn cowboy garb, but he had an air of fragility about him that pierced Max's studied uninvolvement. With a full head of white hair and a luxurious mustache, the old man was the epitome of the weather-beaten cowboy. Blue eyes looked out of his leathery face with a kind of helpless melancholy, as if they'd seen things other people hadn't.

"Boys," he said, holding up gnarled hands, "I paid my debt to society. I'd be much obliged if you'd just let me be."

But, of course, they wouldn't. Even Beau was pushed aside in the feeding frenzy to obtain any tiny newsworthy morsel. Julie was right in the thick of it, although not actively participating. She just watched, arms crossed over her chest, face set in lines of disapproval. Max noticed that Ethan seemed be taking pains to avoid making eye contact with her.

Betsy came in from the back and stopped short, then approached Max.

"Hi, Cosmo. My goodness, this is horrible. What are they trying to do to that poor man?"

Max shrugged, but he wasn't feeling as casual as he tried to appear. "Extract their pound of flesh would be my guess."

Betsy watched for a moment, shaking her head in disapproval. "Grandma Cameron's known him forever," she confided. "She says he's not really a bad man. He just made a few mistakes."

"Her view's in the minority in this town. I take it you read yesterday's newspaper."

She darted him an anxious glance. "Not yet. Why?"

"Julie wrote quite a damning editorial."

Betsy groaned. "That girl! You'd think she'd never made a mistake herself, as hard as she is on other people. She's got it in her head that Mr. Turner is involved in the rustling, and she won't hear a word to the contrary."

"Yeah, and we all know Julie's such a great judge of character."

Their glances met and Betsy burst out laughing. "Right you are, *Cosmo.*"

Laughter loosened Max up. Enough, anyway, to admit that the role of observer sat uneasily on his shoulders. He straightened away from the wall. "What do you say we get him out of here?" he asked suddenly.

Her eyes widened. "I'd say great, but how?"

"Like this..." And leaning close, he whispered his plan in her ear.

IT WENT OFF without a hitch. Max had never given crooks much credit for brains, but Ethan Turner was quick on the uptake. Betsy had whisked him away "to take an important phone call," through the kitchen and storage room and out the back door of the café. Before anyone even knew he was missing, the Outlaw Grandpa was seated next to Maxwell Cosmo Mackenzie in Gene's Cherokee and being spirited away.

Except for one startled glance at his rescuer, Ethan betrayed no emotion. Max pulled into Cupid's only city park, on Lovers' Lane not far from Doc Kunkle's office, and maneuvered back behind a clump of scrub oak in full leaf. Turning off the engine, he grinned at the old man. Ethan returned a cautious smile.

"Cosmo Mackenzie." He stuck out his hand.

"Ethan Turner."

They shook hands.

"I brought us some coffee." Max produced a paper bag from the back seat.

"Much obliged." Ethan accepted the plastic cup and pried open the lid. "I knew a fella named Cosmo once." He frowned as if trying to remember. "I think his last name was...Topper?"

Max laughed. "Cosmo Topper was a guy in an old movie. He saw ghosts."

Ethan looked confused for an instant, then laughed ruefully. "And they say I'm the brains of the gang." He took a sip of coffee, then asked carefully, "And who might you be, Cosmo Mackenzie?"

All of a sudden Max was reluctant to tell him. "I might be the nephew of Gene Varner, editor and publisher of the *Chronicles*."

The old man went perfectly still. Then he let out a single sad word on a softly expelled breath: "Oh." He waited as if he had no other choice, as if he was accustomed to being without options. "I wondered why some stranger would go to any trouble for me."

Max felt like the worst kind of bastard. "Mr. Turner—Ethan—I'm probably the lousiest newsman in the world, but I'm not after a story anyway. I don't happen to think you've got anything to do with the horse rustling that's been going on around here."

"No?" So calm, so resigned, not yet ready to hope for understanding.

"It's been my experience that bank robbers rob banks."

"I did do that. Would your experience further suggest that horse rustlers rustle horses?"

Max shrugged. "I can't say I've ever known a horse rustler. But my guess is that rustling is a more... *personal* crime. Banks aren't people, they're faceless depositories of loot. Horses...well, I've already learned that people in Colorado take their horses real serious and real personal. You steal a man's horse, you not only hit him in the pocketbook, you hit him where he lives. It's like taking his dog or his wife, and then spitting in his eye."

Ethan smiled. "You're a smart young fella, Cosmo."

"Sometimes. Like now, I hope. Ethan, look me in the eye and tell me you know nothing about this gang of rustlers."

Ethan looked him in the eye. "I don't know sic'em about those rustlers," he said, "and I don't plan to. I just want to go home to the Lazy T and mind my own business." He cocked his head. "Think they'll let me?"

"I don't know. I'll help if I can."

"Much obliged."

"One more thing, Ethan . . ."

"Yep?"

"Is Beau involved in any of this?"

Ethan turned his head and gazed out the window at the tangle of greenery. A bluebird flashed past, and he followed its free flight with a revealingly hungry gaze. After a moment he sighed.

"I don't know what Beau's been up to since I been locked up," he said slowly. "All I can say is, if I find out he's been up to any meanness, I'll do everything in my power, up to and including hog-tying the boy, to put him back on the straight and narrow. I been locked up and it damned near killed me. I don't want that to happen to my grandson."

Max believed him.

But then, Julie had apparently believed him once, too.

Four days later, just when the commotion over Ethan Turner's release was calming down, two horses were stolen from a ranch south of town—and Julie went ballistic.

JULIE SLAMMED her notebook down on Gene's desk, braced her hands beside it and leaned forward belligerently. "This time, there's proof!" she exclaimed.

"What?" Gene glanced between Julie and Cosmo. "What proof? Proof of what?"

"Proof Ethan Turner's involved."

"You're kidding!" Gene fell back in his chair in surprise. "What?"

"A horseshoe nail!" Julie straightened, crossing her arms.

Gene frowned. "You lost me."

"It's simple. The rustlers left a calling card—a horseshoe attached to a gatepost with a gilded nail." She waited impatiently; when Gene didn't respond, she said, "Don't you get it?"

"Get what?" Gene looked equal parts confused and hopeful.

"Ethan Turner left a calling card, remember? He used to drop a lump of charcoal on his way out of banks after he robbed them."

Gene looked disappointed. "Aw, Julie, that's not much evidence."

"The heck it's not!" What was the matter with him? She'd seen the connection instantly. Gene was as bad as Marshal Deakins.

Gene appealed to Cosmo. "What do you think? Do you see any connection?"

"No."

Startled by his unvarnished negative, Julie twisted around and glared at him.

He added quickly, "I just don't see why a professional bank robber would turn to stealing horses. As far as your calling-card theory goes, Ethan's M.O...."

"M.O.? Cosmo, you've been watching too much television again."

He hunched his shoulders. "Sorry. You're right. Anyway, all the newspaper stories about the bank robberies at the time mentioned the lump of charcoal, so it could just be a copycat thing." He blinked. "Couldn't it? I mean, I don't know much about crime, but—"

"Cosmo, a crook is a crook, and the Outlaw Grandpa's a convicted felon." She sniffed angrily. "And don't think I've forgiven you for that little stunt the day he came back to town, either. How you could spend an hour alone with the guy and not dig out a single pertinent fact is beyond comprehension."

"I guess I just don't have your killer instinct," he said humbly. "But I'm learning. Really."

"Yeah, right." She turned back to Gene. "Look, I'll get right on this story." She started for the newsroom door.

"Let Cosmo help you."

"What!" She stopped short. "But—"

"He'll never learn if he doesn't get experience," Gene said patiently.

"Well, hell!" She glared from one to the other. "This isn't fair, you know. He's got no nose for news whatsoever."

"Yes, I do," Cosmo disagreed. "I just don't think we should print a story until we've got all the facts."

"All the facts?" She flapped her notebook in the air. "Left to his own devices, this guy wouldn't print the first story until the rustlers were caught red-handed, tried and convicted. He'll never make a reporter, Gene, never! Trust me on this."

Gene did not appear perturbed by her harsh assessment of his nephew's abilities. "Maybe, but if anyone can turn him around, it's you, Julie. I'm counting on you to do your best."

And dammit, she would. Not that it would do any good.

The guy was *hopeless!*

SHE DID GET ONE BREAK. Cosmo chose to stay in the office on the telephone, instead of trailing after her while she grilled Dwight Deakins. Even later, after she caustically pointed out to Cosmo that news seldom happened inside the newsroom, he kept at it.

A few days later, when Cosmo walked into the office and announced that the missing horses had been tracked to a meat-packing plant in Texas, you could have knocked her over with a feather.

"How'd you do that?" she demanded later, after she'd confirmed the information with the marshal. She struck her temple a glancing blow with an open palm. "I can't believe this! You knew before the marshal did."

"Luck," Cosmo said earnestly. "Blind stupid luck. I figured if I made enough calls, sooner or later one would pay off."

"Calls to where? To whom?"

"Cops, meat-packing companies, feed yards, auction barns—you name it, I called it. Gene's not going to like this month's phone bill." Cosmo rolled his eyes.

Gene leapt up from behind his desk and began to pace. "Phone bills be damned! I want that scum caught, and soon." He stopped short. "Why didn't I think of this before? We'll start a reward fund. Harry, over at the bank, will be glad to set up some kind of free account for us. The *Chronicles* will kick it off with..." He turned to Julie. "Whaddaya think, a thousand bucks?"

"Fantastic! I'll bet other businesses and organizations in town will contribute, too. Schoolkids can donate their milk money. Teenagers can hold car washes. We can turn this into the biggest thing that's ever hit town. We can—"

"Do you think that's a good idea?"

Both Gene and Julie turned toward Max, whose forehead was wrinkled with doubt.

"What's wrong with it?" Julie demanded.

"I thought inciting to riot was against the law."

He looked so confused when he said it that Julie had to laugh. "Watching TV again, Cosmo?" she teased. Turning back to Gene, she got serious again. "A good crusade is just what we need around here to get everybody pulling together again. I'll bet we can even get national exposure—the little town that refused to buckle under to the criminal element . . ."

She tossed Cosmo a mischievous grin. "Relax, Cos, I got this covered."

And that was how horse-thief mania *really* caught on in Cupid, Colorado.

THE TOWN WAS already in an uproar, but when the next issue of the *Cupid Chronicles* announced establishment of the reward fund, things really hit the fan. Max half expected kids to start turning in their parents and parents to turn in their neighbors. Even *he* got a few suspicious glances.

As if he'd know which end of a horse to halter. All he knew about equine creatures he'd learned from Gwendolyn. In other words, he considered them little more than big dogs you could ride—if you were desperate enough to want to.

Still, he wouldn't want anything to happen to Gwendolyn. Cutting across the parking lot on his way to the grocery store to buy her some apples, he heard his name called and stopped.

Marshal Deakins hurried up. "Yo, Cosmo, I got a bone to pick with you."

"Me?" Damn!

"Come on in my office where we won't be disturbed."

The grim-faced officer led the way, and Max, figuring he knew what this was all about, followed reluctantly. It had been a mistake, telling Gene and Julie the missing horses had been tracked. He'd thought he'd allowed plenty of time for Dwight to be notified, but according to Julie, such was not the case.

Dwight gestured Max into a Spartan office boasting whitewashed cinder-block walls and a portrait of John Wayne on the wall next to *Washington Crossing the Delaware*. "Have a seat and tell me *how in holy hell you knew about those horses before I did.*"

Dwight Deakins was not the pussycat Max had taken him for. Max tried playing dumb, playing lucky and playing indignant. Nothing worked. Finally Dwight stood up, leaned across the desk and stared hard into Max's eyes.

"Either you level with me or I will throw your butt in a jail cell and keep you there until you do."

"Hey," Max said, spreading his hands in defeat, "you've convinced me."

And that was how Max came to tell Dwight Deakins the whole story. Dwight listened intently; as the tale unfolded, an expression of satisfaction covered his broad face.

"I knew it!" Dwight slapped his thigh and leaned back in his chair. "There was no way Gene Varner would have a nephew as dumb as you and still claim kin. There had to be more to it. So you just called on your law-enforcement contacts, did ya."

"That's about it."

"Well, hotshot, unless you want me callin' you names at high noon on Main Street, we'd better get a few things straight."

Max, who did not find himself coming from a position of strength, raised one brow and waited.

"From here on, anything you find out you tell me first. Got it? I'm talkin' zero-tolerance here, boy. I do *not* want to be made a fool of in my own town. I've held this job for nineteen years and managed to keep my head above water. All I gotta do is hang on for another nine months, and I can retire with my reputation and the goodwill of the fine people of this community. So if you get any bright ideas of cuttin' me out..."

"Not a chance, Marshal. We're on the same team and I'm not after glory. I'm just having myself a good time while they figure out what to do with me back in Los Angeles. Honest."

"Yep," Dwight accused, "havin' a good time at the expense of us pack of hicks is what you mean."

"No way!" Max shook his head vigorously. "You small-town lawmen have my greatest admiration."

And curiously enough, while Max was congratulating himself for dodging the third bullet, he realized that was rapidly becoming the truth.

Dwight Deakins might be a country boy, but he was nobody's fool.

SCOTT HALE had not returned to Cupid to stay. He was living in Denver, so he said to Julie when he called her at the paper Thursday afternoon. But he'd be in Cupid this weekend, and he'd like to take her to the Hideout for dinner.

In fact, he insisted on it. "Nobody knows what's going on in Cupid like you do," he said, flattering her shamelessly. "We've got a lot of catching up to do, and you can fill me in on everything that's happened since I left. Please, Julie? For old times' sake?"

Julie told him thanks but no thanks and hung up.

He called back. "Gimme a break!" he said. "I thought we'd agreed to part friends."

"*I* agreed to part friends. You told me to—"

"Never mind what I told you," he interrupted hastily. "Time heals all wounds. It'd really mean a lot to me if you'd let bygones be bygones...."

As he did what he did best—talk fast—Julie's attention and gaze wandered to Cosmo. He stood at the file cabinet, blatantly eavesdropping. Today he had on a droopy Hawaiian sports shirt and baggy khaki pants, and she found herself wondering what he'd look like in a pair of good-fitting Wranglers—

"Julie? Are you still there?"

Flustered, she pulled her attention back to her caller. "Sorry, Scott," she said quickly. "My mind wandered."

"Jeez! You really know how to hurt a guy."

"I didn't mean to. It's just..." What? *I'm more interested in staring at Gene's nerd nephew than talking to you?* How had she ever thought she loved this man enough to marry him? Another horrible thought struck her; Ben had been right about Scott. He'd said from the very beginning that Julie's first love was a slug.

Scott was continuing in a cajoling tone, "You can make it up to me. Let me take you to dinner—just a simple dinner between friends, no strings attached. What time shall I pick you up?"

Julie stifled a groan. "How about I meet you there?" she countered. Then she'd have her own wheels and be able to leave whenever she took a notion.

"I guess, if that's the most I can get," he said grudgingly. "How about seven o'clock at the Hideout?"

"Seven at the Hideout it is. See you there." She was sorry she'd agreed to meet him before she even got the phone hung up.

"Big date?" Cosmo closed the file drawer.

"Not—" She bit off what she'd meant to say—*Not in a million years*—and substituted, "Not really." She hadn't had a date since Cosmo had come to Cupid. He probably thought she was the biggest wallflower in town—or perhaps even as big a nerd as he was. Did nerds, like water, seek their own level?

MAX THOUGHT it was pretty damned peculiar that the best-looking woman in town seemed to have no more love life than he, the biggest dweeb, did. *Perceived* dweeb, he corrected. He sometimes wondered if his disguise had taken *too* well, at least where Julie was concerned.

Still, he didn't like thinking of her out on the town with Hale. They shared a history, and the guy might want to renew old...acquaintances. Max just might have to do something about that—for Julie's own good of course.

Max didn't have any trouble talking Bob Mays into joining him for a bite to eat at the Hideout along about seven-fifteen that evening. Bob, Max had discovered, would climb the highest mountain if he thought he'd find somebody on top who'd listen to him talk sports.

Bob liked an audience. He didn't especially care if that audience knew zip about sports or anything else, as long as they'd let him talk.

And talk. The hard part was getting him to talk about anything interesting.

Like Julie. Max spotted her and Hale right away, in a booth on the right side of the room. He even managed to get a table nearby and seat himself so that every time she looked up, she saw him.

And every time they made eye contact, Max would smile and nod just to piss her off. After a while, it was fun simply to watch her try to pretend she didn't see him at all.

Max sipped his whiskey sour, wishing it was a nice cold beer. "So you say you've lived in Cupid all your life?" he asked Bob.

Bob blinked, cut off in the middle of a dissertation about local baseball. "Yeah, except when I went away to school."

"You must know all the Camerons."

Bob glanced around at Julie; subtle, he wasn't. "Everybody knows the Camerons. I went to school with Ben. Man, that guy's got a temper that won't quit. It's been better since he got married, but he's still a wild man if he gets going." Bob shook his head with apparent admiration. "Helluva ball player, too, but he never pursued it. Too busy out at the ranch, I guess. Good reflexes, you know."

"Julie's got a twin brother, I understand."

Bob nodded. "Jason. He's a lot more easygoing than Ben, but you get him riled and, whoa! Stand back! He's been following the rodeo circuit for a couple of years, doin' pretty good, I hear." Bob took a swig from his long-neck bottle of beer. "Then there's the oldest sister, Maggie, who married some rich guy in Aspen and isn't around much anymore. Julie's the baby of the family, in case you couldn't tell."

Max laughed. "I guessed. That guy she's with..."

"Scott Hale? He managed the local video store, but his old man owned it, along with a bunch of others. Never did like him—played third base for a while with the Cupid Arrows and couldn't hit for shit." Bob shook his head disgustedly. "He and Julie were engaged for a little while a few years back, but then, seems Julie's always engaged to somebody. Scott moved away after they broke up—don't know what he's doin' now. I gotta give that girl credit. Throws her heart and soul into everything she does, work or play."

"How many times has she been engaged?" Max asked, his disapproval strong.

Bob laughed. "A bunch. She's impetuous, know what I mean? Personally I think she's looking for a knight on a white horse. Once she gets to know these yahoos and discovers their feet of clay, she dumps 'em." He shrugged. "Or they dump her."

"Why in hell would anyone dump Julie Cameron?"

Bob cocked his head to one side. "Cosmo, old boy, you wouldn't by any chance be smitten with Miss Julie, would you? You're not her type, but I suppose stranger things have happened. I just can't think when."

"About Scott Hale—"

Max never finished his question because a commotion erupted near the front door. It was impossible to see who was talking, but the man's excited voice carried through the wide-open saloon.

"We got us an emergency here! Gene Varner's old mare, Gwendolyn, is missing! Looks like the rustlers got 'er!"

CHAPTER SIX

IT WAS AS IF someone had hollered, "Fire!" the way patrons emptied out of the Hideout en masse—and many *en drunk*. While they milled about in the parking lot, Max looked around for Julie. He spotted her on the fringes near the trees, Hale still at her side.

Johnny King appeared, weaving his way toward the pair. Max frowned.

"Where the hell did *he* come from?" he asked Bob, jerking his chin toward the swaggering little drunk. "I didn't see him inside."

Bob shrugged. "He was probably drinking in his pickup with Beau Turner or somebody. A habit left over from his underage days."

The crowd ebbed and flowed, concealing and revealing Julie and the two men. Max didn't like it. As a matter of fact, he didn't like Johnny King *or* Scott Hale anywhere close to Julie Cameron. By the time he'd shoved through to her side, Hale was gone, King looked fit to be tied, and Julie was visibly steaming.

Pleased with this turn of events, Max glanced around. "Where'd your friend Hale go?" he asked Julie.

"Who knows? Who cares?" Apparently remembering her manners, if belatedly, she nodded at Bob before adding, "Cosmo, you remember Johnny."

Johnny grinned, insincere but toothy. "How's it goin', Cosmo ol' buddy?"

"Never better," Max said enthusiastically. Johnny was swaying so much it was hard to get a fix on him.

Julie harrumphed. "I don't know how you can say that when Gwendolyn may be in the hands of rustlers," she scolded. "You know what that horse means to Gene."

"Dammit!" Johnny's face flushed dark red. "I keep tellin' you, this is a false alarm."

Max's antennae went up. "You think so?"

"Hell, yes." Johnny scuffed the toe of his boot in the gravel, his hands stuffed in his pants pockets. "That old mare busts out and wanders off whenever she takes a notion. Everybody knows that."

"She does have a mile-long rap sheet for pasture bust-outs," Max admitted.

Julie rocked back on her heels. "Cosmo, I've said it before and I'll say it again—you watch too many cop shows." She included Johnny in her censorious glance. "And what if you're both wrong? What if at this very minute she's in the back of a horse trailer on her way to—" she shuddered "—a slaughterhouse in Texas? How'll you feel then?"

Before anyone could reply, Tom Purdy went rushing past. "Posse!" he yelled. "We're formin' a posse! If them bastards took Gwendolyn, they're gonna rue this day! Meet at the pasture back of Gene Varner's house." And he was gone, spreading his call to vigilante justice.

Bob looked dubiously around their small circle, his glance settling on Max. "You going?"

Max shrugged. "I guess I got to. Julie shamed me into it. How about you?"

Bob shook his head. "Not me. I got a baseball tournament to cover tomorrow, so I'm heading home to get some sleep." With a wave of the hand, he turned back toward the building. "Good luck!"

Julie shook her head as if she couldn't believe Bob's lack of community spirit. "Well, I'm going. If you two—" her glance slashed at Max and Johnny "—want to wimp out, feel free."

Johnny let out a derisive guffaw. "You think I'd miss this? Hell, I'll ride that old mare home when we find her. I'll..."

They watched him stomp off to his pickup truck, still declaring his intentions. Around them, people were piling into vehicles and peeling rubber out of the parking lot for the short drive to the Varner house.

Max touched Julie's arm tentatively, and she gave him a hostile glance. "I'll drive," he said. "No need to take two cars."

For a moment it appeared she might refuse. Then she looked toward the "Y," where Main Street and Lovers' Lane intersected. Car lights were a blur as drivers took the turn toward Gene's house.

She gave in with a sigh. "Okay. There's sure to be a parking problem. It looks like everybody in town's going." She glanced at Max, her expression wary. "This has really spooked people. I wouldn't want to be in those rustlers' boots if they've really nabbed old Gwendolyn."

"I wouldn't want to be in their boots even if they haven't." Max took her elbow firmly. Giving her no chance to pull away, he steered her toward the Cherokee. Again he felt that pleasant tingle of awareness. The bones of her arm felt unexpectedly fragile, and he was suddenly aware of a surge of protectiveness. "Crime does not pay," he added, mostly in an attempt to take his mind off other, more dangerous thoughts.

"Honesty is the best policy," she said, her voice a little breathless although they weren't walking fast enough to warrant it.

"What goes around comes around."

"Nothing ventured, nothing gained."

Max reached past her and pulled open the car door. "In the end, everything is a gag."

She blinked, her long lashes feathery in the pale glow of a faraway street lamp. "Who said *that?*"

"Charlie Chaplin."

"Oh, you like old movies."

He nodded, suddenly not willing to trust his voice. She looked ravishing in the shadowy illumination, lush and mysterious in her beauty.

"Me, too," she whispered. "Maybe we do have something in common."

DWIGHT DEAKINS did his best to head the posse off at the pass, meeting them at Gene's house to assure them that Gwendolyn was *not* the victim of foul play. As proof, he pointed out the sagging wire at the back of her pasture and implored everybody to go home before they scared themselves, all the residents of Cupid, Gwendolyn and even the innocent little critters of the forest out of a year's growth.

It looked like good sense would prevail until Tom Purdy took matters into his own hands, shouting, "C'mon, boys, let's see for ourselves before we believe it! I'd walk through hot coals for old Gwendolyn. How 'bout you?"

After that the rush was on.

It took a couple of hours of crashing through the woods, into trees and into each other, but they finally found Gwendolyn. She was dozing in a formerly peaceful clearing a couple of miles away. When they burst in on her, she lifted her big head to give them a disbelieving glance, then settled back into drowsy indifference.

Soon some thirty or so horse hunters surrounded the old gray mare. The way they were congratulating each other, you'd have thought they'd actually *done* something, Julie thought. But what if Gwendolyn had truly been in danger? Julie shivered at the thought.

"Cold?"

Before she could reply, Cosmo laid his arm lightly across her shoulders, smiling down at her in the moonlight. It was the damnedest thing; she hardly recognized him. Although she could see him clearly in the glow of a full moon and a sky filled with stars, he looked like a different man.

He'd taken off his glasses, and somehow that made his face look leaner and harder. And his mouth... She stared. His lips quirked up in an almost amused line, as if he was only observing and not a part of this horse hysteria.

Fresh shivers ran down her spine, and she stepped away from him. "I'm fine. Thank heaven we found Gwendolyn. I was really worried—" She stopped short. What she really was, was babbling. This was only Cosmo Mackenzie, after all, not some... Hollywood hunk.

Johnny King pushed through the crowd. "Get outta my way," he croaked, tossing aside the liquor bottle in his fist. It crashed into the underbrush, and even Gwendolyn looked startled. "I'm a-ridin' that hoss home," Johnny announced, "just like I said I was."

Grabbing a handful of mane, he vaulted onto the mare's broad back. Even drunk, Johnny was a horseman. He glared down at the disapproving faces turned toward him. "Anybody got a problem with that?"

"I hope she throws you sky-high!" That was from Tom Purdy, and it elicited a murmur of agreement.

"In your dreams." Johnny kicked the mare into a shambling walk. "See you jokers in the funny papers."

Everybody stood around for a moment in silent disapproval until man and horse were out of sight. Then they began drifting in twos and threes back toward the bright lights of town visible at the bottom of the rolling forested hillside.

Julie glanced at Cosmo's dark form, feeling curiously ill at ease. "We'd better be going, too. It's getting late." She started toward the almost indiscernible trail the others had taken.

Cosmo fell in beside her. Glancing at him, she thought she saw amusement on his face.

"Do you have a law against drunk horseback riding in this town?" he asked.

Julie laughed. "Not that I know of. But maybe—" She'd glanced at him over her shoulder as she spoke, which caused her to stumble on the uneven ground. She felt his hand slide around her waist to steady her. Turning beneath that easy hold to face him, she looked up into his face with a kind of breathless resignation— or perhaps it was anticipation.

"Gee, Julie," he said in a husky voice completely unlike his own. "You're beautiful when you laugh...or yell...or..."

His lips touched hers, blotting out whatever else he'd intended to say.

HE HELD HER FACE between his hands and kissed her with an ardor held carefully in check. Her lips were sweet, as he'd known they would be, and compliant, parting beneath the slightest pressure from his. Fighting himself every step of the way, he slipped his tongue into her mouth with a clumsy indecisiveness completely foreign to him under normal circumstances.

She sighed and he sensed no resistance in her at all. Melting against him, her arms rose to slide around his neck. Her breasts pressed against his chest, her hips against his.

With a superhuman effort, he held himself in check. Cosmo, he thought; Cosmo wouldn't be greedy, the poor dumb schmuck. Cosmo wouldn't— Her tongue touched his, and another jolt of electricity shot through him. He had to cut this short, he realized with a touch of astonishment. As much as he wanted her, he knew he'd started something he didn't dare finish or he'd be finished himself, as far as Julie Cameron and his mission in this town were concerned.

But damn, she felt good pressed against him. There was a naturalness about her response, a sweet generosity in her kiss that caused his chest to tighten with some unfamiliar feeling—could it be guilt or remorse? God, he hoped so, seeing that as the least of several evils.

She didn't even know who she was kissing. She probably thought she was giving old incompetent Cosmo a break. Time to go back into his act. He started to lift his head to break the kiss, hesitated, reversed directions a couple of times and bumped his teeth against hers, finally rearing back and breathing hard.

"Wow," he mumbled. "Gosh, Julie, I don't know what came over me. I don't normally attack my co-workers, jeez, no! This is so embarrassing."

She clenched her hands at her waist and stared down at them. "Relax, Cosmo. I don't feel attacked in the slightest."

He couldn't see her face, but her voice sounded cool, almost detached. All that proved to him was her ability as an actress. With the taste of her lingering in his mouth, the faint scent of roses in his nostrils, he knew she'd been as caught up in the kiss as he had.

He knew—Max Mackenzie. Cosmo wouldn't have had a clue. "Is this what you call sexual harassment?" he asked with false anxiety. "I'm ashamed I did that. Please forgive me, Julie. I'm really, really sorry—"

"Cosmo," she interrupted pleasantly, "will you please shut up? It was a kiss, that's all. Blame...blame the moonlight." She glanced up at the guilty moon, which gilded her face silver, then back at her companion. "Get over it, okay?"

"Whatever you say, Julie. I really appreciate your understanding. I guess I just lost my head." He followed her down the trail, relieved that in the darkness he didn't have to worry about hiding his expression.

Maybe he'd just found a way to have his cake and eat it, too, he thought as he crashed through the brush beside her. Maybe all he had to do was end everything on a clumsy note.

BY THE TIME Max and Julie arrived back at Gene's, a dozen or more people milled around the yard. Gwendolyn stood patiently in their midst, Johnny still perched on her wide back. Suddenly Julie, who'd been telling Max the history of horse theft in the West, stopped short.

Max followed her gaze to the imposing figure of a cowboy standing off to one side of the cluster of people. He wore a black hat and boots, jeans and a plaid shirt, and he was tall and rangy.

Max felt his hackles rise. Was this another of Julie's romantic conquests? Another fiancé perhaps?

She gave a little cry of joy, and flew across the uneven ground to the stranger's side. He turned, saw her and scooped her up in his arms, enveloping her in a hug.

Jaw tight, Max ambled closer. When she came up for air and noticed him there, she struggled out of the arms that held her, smiling as if she couldn't stop.

"Jason," she said to the man still holding her, "I want you to meet Cosmo Mackenzie, Gene's nephew. He works—more or less—at the *Chronicles.*"

It took only a split second for Max to realize that this guy, who was acting as if he owned her, was Julie's twin brother. Max offered his hand and a sincere smile. "I've heard a lot about you. Nice to meet you."

"I ain't heard a damned thing about you," Jason replied. "Cosmo, you say?"

"Afraid so." Max shrugged, he hoped disarmingly. "I'm quite fond of your sister. She's taught me everything I know. About journalism, I mean."

"Is that right." Jason cast a puzzled glance at that sister, still cuddled against his side. "Will wonders never cease."

She poked him in the ribs. "So how long will you be home?"

"Just a day or two. I wanted to say hello on my way to Boise. Betsy told me where to find you." He glanced over her head at Johnny King, now sitting cross-legged on top of the gray mare. "It was worth the detour to see Johnny making an ass out of himself with that horse." He cupped his mouth with one hand and yelled, "Hey, Johnny, I'll give you a good price on an old stove-up plow horse we got out to pasture back at the Arrow. Oughtta be just about your speed."

Johnny looked up quickly, his face flushing. "That's all the Arrow's got, old stove-up plow horses!" he yelled back. "What the hell you doin' here, you dumb cowpoke? Thought they threw you outta Cupid years ago!"

"They tried, Johnny old pal, they sure as hell tried. But as you can see..." Jason grinned, an evil, challenging grin.

Julie cast a dark glance at Johnny, then tugged at her brother's sleeve. "Let's get out of here," she urged. "We've got a lot of catching up to do."

Max watched them go regretfully. He'd have liked a little more time with Julie but... He sighed. Maybe another opportunity would present itself in the near future. He sure hoped so.

In the meantime, he had a number of things to take care of, not the least of which was waiting until the crowd had cleared out so he could do something he should have done when he'd first arrived in Cupid—attach a bug to Gwendolyn's halter.

Just in case.

Gene set great store by that mare, and Max wasn't going to let anything happen to her on *his* watch.

LATER THAT NIGHT Julie lay in bed staring up at nothing and trying to find some justification for losing her head like that. It didn't make sense. Cosmo's kiss couldn't have been as powerful as she remembered. Strangely enough, even its awkward conclusion didn't dim the memory.

Am I losing my marbles? she wondered. Dweebs can't kiss. Maybe it was just beginner's luck.

ALSO LATER THAT NIGHT Johnny King drove out to the Turner ranch, the Lazy T, only about four hours late for the scheduled confab. He found Beau watching a tape of television cartoons while the boss dozed in a chair nearby.

When Johnny entered without knocking, Beau looked up with an absent grin. "Cartoons," he said needlessly, jerking his chin toward the flickering picture on the tube.

"Whaddaya think, I'm blind?" Johnny dropped into a chair with sagging cushions and a big ugly stain on one arm. He looked around with disgust. The Lazy T was a godawful mess, even by his standards. "Boss mad at me for bein' late?" He was spoiling for a fight, but kept his voice low.

Beau nodded, his attention glued to a cartoon featuring a shapely redhead singing some song about wolves. "You think that's really her singin'?" he asked after a moment.

"You idiot, it's a cartoon!"

"So?" Beau waited for an answer. When none was forthcoming, he shrugged and was reabsorbed by the animated action on the screen.

Johnny slouched in the chair, watching one man snore and the other stare at a kid's show. The booze was wearing off; his head throbbed and his hands shook. Worse, he was madder'n hell.

"Why the Sam Hill do we get blamed for every damned thing that goes wrong around here?" he grumbled. Beau glanced over, but Johnny was talking to himself. "We even get blamed for a damn stray horse. Tell me *that's* fair."

And that stupid reward started by the newspaper, and its stupid editor making the situation worse. Johnny would like to see Gene Varner get what he deserved and give folks something to *really* talk about at the same time....

He settled back in his chair, eyes closing while he mulled over his options. Maybe they could kill two birds with one stone, he thought drowsily. But maybe them uppity Camerons ought to come first, even before Varner. He knew there was a way.... He slept.

Beau watched his cartoon tape all the way through, then rewound and punched *play* again.

The more he thought about it, the more he was convinced she really was doing her own singing. Nobody could lip-synch *that* good.

EIGHT DAYS LATER on a Saturday morning, Julie went out to the front pasture to bring in Joey and Lisa Marie's pony.

Only the pony wasn't there. In its place was a great big horseshoe, attached to the gate with a nail the color of fool's gold.

BEN CAMERON paced the floor of Dwight Deakins's office, waving his fists and shouting. The marshal sprawled in his chair, unable to get a word in edgewise, while Julie tried to pretend she was a fly on the wall. Wearing two hats, she was beginning to discover, wasn't always easy. Sometimes the reporter and the sister got in each other's way.

Ben stomped to a halt in front of the desk. "So what are you going to do about this?" he roared, leaning over to bang impotent fists on the blotter. "My kids want their pony back!"

"Ben, if you'll just simmer down..." Dwight sighed. "This ain't helpin', you know."

"I don't give a flying—" Ben glanced at Julie and started over. "I want these thieves caught and I want 'em caught *now*. So what're you doing about it, Dwight?"

The marshal shook his head wearily. "We're doin' the best we can. We got a few leads."

"Yeah? Like what?"

"Now you know I can't tell you—"

A soft knock on the door interrupted him. The door swung open and Cosmo stuck his head through the opening. "I heard you yelling," he said, glancing at Ben. "Has something happened, Marshal?"

"Yes!" Ben roared.

"No!" Dwight shouted just as loud.

Cosmo walked inside and positioned himself beside Julie. She looked at him over her notebook. "Go away, Cosmo. I got this covered."

He smiled at her but made no move to obey. "Is it the rustlers?"

"Yes, it's the rustlers," Ben mocked. "Now they've gone and taken my kids' pony. A *pony!* What kind of scum would take a pony?" He appealed to the room in general.

"Maybe the kind of scum that doesn't like Camerons," Cosmo suggested softly.

Ben did a double take. "I don't have an enemy in the world," he said in a dangerous tone.

"I know it's hard to imagine," Cosmo conceded.

Ben went on, "But I will if I ever get my hands on those no-account—"

"Is this on the record?" Julie asked quickly.

"Hell, yes, it's on the record! It's time those bastards realized their days are numbered. Nobody makes my kids cry and gets away with it. Shootin's too good for the likes of—"

"Dammit, Ben, shut up!" Dwight heaved his bulk upright. "You can't stand in the office of the law and threaten people, even them that deserve it."

Julie turned to her brother. "Are you going to contribute to the reward fund?"

"Julie, that ain't a good idea," Dwight argued. "The town's already too stirred up."

"Damn straight I am," Ben snarled. "Hell, even Joey wants to donate his life's savings."

"Wow," Cosmo said, looking impressed. "How long's his life been?"

"He's nine," Julie offered. A beautiful thought struck her. "Hey, I've got an angle—we'll take a picture for the *Chronicles* of Joey at the bank handing over all his money. How much has he got, Ben?"

Ben frowned. "Who the hell knows? He spends his allowance almost as fast as he gets it. I'd say...maybe ten bucks. But it's not the goddamn amount. It's the principle of the thing!"

"It sure is," Julie agreed softly, ambition consuming her. "If we can't get a picture like that on the wire and printed coast to coast, I'm not the journalist I think I am."

"Gosh, Julie," Cosmo said at his most ingenuous, "Connie Chung isn't the journalist I think you are."

Only later did she realize that she didn't have a clue what he meant by that, but there seemed to be at least an outside chance it wasn't a compliment.

THE *CHRONICLES* photographer took the picture the next day: nine-year-old Joey and eight-year-old Lisa Marie Cameron tearfully thrusting thirteen dollars and twenty-seven cents at the embarrassed banker for inclusion in a reward fund that had slowly climbed to almost five thousand dollars, including Ben's five hundred. Afterward Julie let Max tag along with her while she did a quick "man on the street" piece.

Stopping Cupid residents at random, she asked each the same thing: "So what do you think we should do with those low-down scum-of-the-earth rustlers once we catch them—and we will!"

The first time Max heard the question, he waited until Rose Kunkle had given her answer: "Hangin's too good for a horse thief. I say, they oughtta be drawn and quartered! Make an example of them and then lock them up and throw away the key." Then he tried, as subtly as he could, to call Julie's attention to a slight bias in her presentation.

"Are you saying I'm not being fair and impartial?" she shot back at him.

"No, no, nothing like that," he denied hastily. "It's just—"

"Cosmo," she interrupted grandly, "let me do the reporting and you listen and learn, okay?"

What could he say but "Ohhhh-kay." After that, he stood it as long as he could before heading back to the office. Climbing out of the Cherokee in the parking lot, he saw Ben and Betsy Cameron disappear inside the marshal's office. On a hunch, Max followed.

Dwight was out, the secretary reported, but Cosmo could wait in the office with the Camerons if he wished.

He wished.

Betsy greeted him with a nervous smile. "How's it going, Cosmo? I guess you've met my—"

Ben waved away pleasantries. "Yeah, yeah, we've met." He turned his back on them to glare through the lone window in the room.

Cosmo looked at Betsy with a question in his eyes; she shrugged helplessly. Nevertheless, Cosmo asked, "Has anything else happened?"

Ben spun around. "It damn well better. Dwight's going to be up for reelection in less than a year, and if he's gonna stand a prayer, we'd better see some action."

Betsy looked so anxious that for an instant, Max flashed back to the first time he'd met her, in California. She hadn't liked conflict; he'd known it then, and she obviously hadn't changed. Her husband, it appeared, thrived on it.

How the hell had they ever gotten together? Max wondered. "The marshal's doing his best," he said soothingly. "Maybe it'd be better if we kind of, you know, let this die down a bit? Those rustlers have to be laying low, with all this talk about reprisals and so forth."

Ben's expression grew cold. "All I want is *justice*. So butt out, Mackenzie."

"Ben!" Betsy's hand flew to her throat; she looked appalled.

Ben patted her arm. "Calm down, honey. Why should you take offense when *he* doesn't?" His scornful glance flicked across Max like a whip.

Max was hanging on to his cool so tightly he heard a roaring in his ears. If there was one thing he hated, it was an arrogant son of a bitch who thought he had a lock on life. How'd that saying go? *Those of you who think you know everything irritate the hell out of those of us who really do.* Something like that.

Max had forgotten more than Ben Cameron would ever know about "justice." Without thinking, Max balled his hands into fists at his sides. "You *need* somebody to tell you how to handle your problems, Cameron," he said very softly and very pointedly. "Because as a problem solver, man, you suck."

Ben stopped short and stared; Betsy looked as if she'd been struck by lightning.

"Say that again." Ben took a menacing step forward.

Max, who'd weathered every crisis up to this very moment, felt his final shreds of control sliding away. "I said," he repeated with growing relish, "*as a problem solver, you suck*. Wanna make something of it?"

A fierce joy leapt into Ben's eyes, and he surged up on his toes. "You're damned right I do! Where? Here?" He looked around, realized they were in the marshal's office and shook his head. "Okay. Outside."

"After you." Max stepped aside, indicating the door with a flourish. The adrenaline pumped through him; after weeks of inactivity and false humility, he couldn't wait to get started.

"No!" Betsy darted between them, bracing her hands on her husband's chest. "You can't do this, Ben!"

"I didn't start it. *He* did!"

Max's palms itched. "To hell with who started it. I'm just interested in the finish." His muscles twitched; he could barely contain himself. He'd make mincemeat out of this guy!

Betsy burst into tears. "You can't," she sobbed, clinging to her husband, "because...because... I'm sorry, Max—"

"No!" Horrified, Max realized where this was leading. "Don't—"

"I've got to." Betsy squared her shoulders. "Ben, you can't, because he's a policeman, working undercover to catch the rustlers! If you get into a fight with him, they'll probably throw *you* in jail."

CHAPTER SEVEN

"YOU GOTTA BE KIDDIN'." Ben looked from his wife to Max and back again. "You expect me to believe Julie's nerd is a—"

Betsy banged Ben's chest with her fists, her pretty face exasperated. "He's *not* a nerd, Ben! He's working undercover for Gene Varner, trying to find out who's behind the rustling."

"You gotta be kiddin'," Ben said again, but without as much conviction this time. "I want to see some identification," he added more forcefully.

Max was steaming—at himself. He'd let Ben bait him, let him provoke a confrontation. This undercover stuff was quickly turning into one giant pain. "Take my word for it, turkey," he snarled. "You Camerons are starting to—"

"What in hell is going on here?"

They turned as one to find Marshal Deakins standing in the open doorway, his face an angry mottled shade of red. Stomping inside, he slammed the door. "No, don't tell me," he berated them, "let me guess. Now Ben and Betsy know, am I right? Who else, the town council? Will it be on the front page of the *Chronicles* next Thursday? Jeez!"

Max tried to tamp down his temper. "Now, Dwight—"

"Don't you 'Now, Dwight' me!" The marshal slammed a heavy ring of keys on his desk and whirled on Ben. "What do *you* want?"

"I want to know—"

"When there's something to know, you're on the list to hear it."

"But—"

Betsy grasped her husband's arm. "Ben, let's go. Don't you think we've done enough for one day?"

Ben looked from Dwight to Max. "Who else knows?" he demanded.

"That," Dwight said explosively, "is none of your danged business!"

"How'll I know who it's safe to talk to?" Ben let Betsy drag him a step closer to the door.

"*Nobody's* safe to talk to. You don't know nothin', got it? If you ever want your kids to see their pony again..."

"Okay, okay, I get the picture." In the doorway, Ben braced his tall body against Betsy's determined tugging. "But if I don't get some action soon, I may just have to take matters into—"

"Don't threaten me, Ben." Dwight looked completely disgusted. "And don't you go thinkin' about takin' the law into your own hands, either," he called after the retreating duo. Slamming the door, he turned his glare on Max.

"Shit," Dwight Deakins declared. "Your identity's turnin' into the worst-kept secret in town."

Max left Dwight's office a few minutes later, thoroughly ashamed of himself. He'd had no idea he'd been so close to an explosion. If Betsy hadn't been there, he might have killed Julie's brother.

Or been seriously damaged himself—the lean and rugged rancher didn't look like anybody's pushover. Still too worked up to put a good face on what had happened, Max walked between the newspaper office and the hardware store, emerging on Main Street. He wasn't ready to turn into Clark Kent just yet. Maybe...

A battered old pickup, feed sacks piled high in back, came slowly down Main, heading northeast. It took Max one quick glance to recognize the Lazy T vehicle, the same one that had carried Ethan Turner home from prison. On impulse, Max stepped into the street and hopped onto the running board. Bending down, he looked inside, across the tattered bench seat and into the startled blue eyes of Ethan himself.

"Buy you a cup of coffee?" Max invited.

Minutes later they sat in a corner booth at the Rusty Spur Café, ignored and avoided by everyone in the place except for Betsy Cameron's aunt, Nancy Wyatt. Nancy hustled right over with two mugs in one hand and the coffeepot in the other.

"Howdy, fellas." She plopped the mugs down and filled them. Her eyes, a paler blue than Ethan's but just as lively, surveyed the two men with overt curiosity. "You eatin' or just drinkin'?"

"Just—" Max couldn't get it out before Nancy went on.

"Because we got us some more of Betsy's peach pie, and it's to die for."

Max saw a yearning appear on Ethan's face, as if the old man wanted that pie badly but knew if he asked, it would be snatched away.

Prison must have been pure hell for him. "Two pieces of pie," Max said grandly, "and don't be stingy with the ice cream."

Nancy looked pleased. "Comin' right up."

Ethan looked ashamed. "I guess I don't fool you much, do I."

"I hope not," Max said. "Ethan..."

The old man sighed. "Now what? Something else happen?"

Max shook his head. "And I don't want it to. I just thought it might be time for a word to the wise." He shut up while Nancy served the pie, flaky crust bursting with golden fruit quickly obscured by melting vanilla ice cream. He picked up his fork. "Taking the Cameron kids' pony was not even half-smart. If Beau's involved in that, it'd behoove you to put a stop to it before the kid digs his hole any deeper. Because I *will* get to the bottom of this. That's a promise."

"I believe you," Ethan said softly, picking up his own fork. "Much obliged, Cosmo—for the pie."

And he dug in as if he'd never seen pie, or heard of horse rustling, before.

AFTER COSMO LEFT, Ethan sat in the booth alone, drinking Nancy's good coffee and thinking about what the big man had said. *Not even half-smart. If Beau's involved . . . it'd behoove you to put a stop to it . . .*

Who *was* that masked man? Ethan wondered. Not for a second did he believe Cosmo Mackenzie was the mild-mannered reporter he pretended to be.

Ethan put his empty mug on the table. Nancy was right there, holding out the coffeepot, smiling. Not everybody in Cupid was against him apparently. He shook his head and tried to return her smile.

Truth was, Ethan knew damned well what Beau'd been up to. He'd already tried to counsel his grandson on any number of occasions, but all he got for his trouble was a hard time.

That, and a strong hunch that the gang wasn't yet finished with the Camerons and the Straight Arrow Ranch. Should he have said something to Cosmo about that?

No. It was just a feeling. He couldn't go against his own blood over something that flimsy. He doubted he could go against his own blood ever. Beau was all he had left. Even his son, Beau's father, had taken off for parts unknown before his return home.

Rising, Ethan straightened the hat he hadn't removed. At the cash register he reached into his pocket. "What's the damage, Miz Wyatt?"

"Cosmo took care of it, Mr. Turner."

He frowned. "You sure?"

"I'm sure." She hesitated. "Mr. Turner... I know you've had a hard row to hoe since you got back to Cupid, and it must seem like the whole town's against you. But that's not so. Some of us are glad to have you home."

For a moment he just looked at her, letting her compassion warm him. Then he took off his hat and worried it between gnarled fingers. "Ma'am," he said at last, "I thank you."

WEDNESDAY NIGHT—press time—rolled around, but all was not well at the *Cupid Chronicles*. Computer problems had slowed production, and everything was running late. By the time Julie finally got out to her car about eight-thirty, she found the battery as dead as her vow to put Cosmo Mackenzie out of her mind.

Walking back inside, she met him coming out of Gene's office.

"I thought you were gone," he said, pushing his glasses back up his nose in that familiar dorky gesture that had somehow become curiously appealing.

"Obviously I'm not." Julie was tired, hungry and disgusted; she supposed it showed. Not a good start when you wanted a favor. "Look, my car battery's dead. I wonder if I could prevail on you to give me—"

"Sure."

"Wait and let me ask first!"

"Don't you want a ride?"

"Yes, but—"

"Sure. On one condition."

Julie groaned. "Which is?"

"That we go get something to eat first."

"Oh, I don't think—"

"Aren't you hungry?"

"Well, yes, but—"

"It's a long way to the ranch—not that I've ever been invited there."

She didn't like being put on the defensive. "That's purely an oversight," she said loftily, although that was far from the truth. "I've been meaning to have you out, but I've been so busy."

He looked hurt. "The fact remains, if I don't eat first, I'll have to drive all the way to the ranch and then all the way back to town, and by that time everything will be closed, and I don't know what's in the refrigerator at Uncle Gene's, and—"

"Okay, okay, I get the picture." She threw up her hands in surrender. "By all means, let's grab a bite to eat first."

"Gosh, Cosmo." Julie leaned back in the Cherokee with a satisfied sigh. "That was...fun." The realization that she'd enjoyed both the food and the company astonished her.

He gave her a quick sideways glance, and he might have been smiling. "I enjoyed it, too. Thanks." He hesitated a moment before adding, "But I still wish you'd lighten up on Ethan Turner. He's actually quite a nice old guy."

"Sorry. He's my prime suspect."

"What about his grandson?" Cosmo argued. "Beau strikes me as the kind of guy who'd be quite an asset to an outlaw gang—big and strong and dumb."

"Right, but he's a follower. Somebody else would have to give the orders, and I think that someone is Ethan Turner."

"I'm sorry, I just can't agree."

As Cosmo earnestly put forth his point of view, Julie found her attention subtly shifting from what he was saying to the man himself. The night was warm and moonlit, and as she'd noticed before, Cosmo seemed to change once out of the harsh light of day. Improve, actually.

Almost like a werewolf in reverse, she thought, stifling a giggle; the less light there was, the better the man looked. If she ever encountered him when it was pitch-dark...or if he ever got a decent haircut and some decent clothes...or took off those glasses...

God, she was thinking like a B movie with a gender switch: *Why Miss Jones, without your glasses you're beautiful!* Cosmo would never be beautiful, although with enough work he might achieve...passable. Of course, looks weren't everything.

Jarred by an unwelcome thought, Julie sat up straight in the car seat. She'd better get hold of herself before she actually acknowledged a certain...attraction to the square from California.

Cosmo drove across the little bridge over Horsethief Creek, which marked the southern boundary of the Straight Arrow Ranch. Following her directions, he drove slowly by the house, past pens and a small corral to the vehicle turnaround at the end of the road, then back the way they'd come so he'd be pointed in the right direction.

He killed the engine and turned toward her.

She hesitated, her hand on the door handle. "Thanks, Cosmo," she said too brightly. "I'll see you tomorrow at the off—"

"I'll walk you to the door," he cut in, sounding offended that she'd assumed he wouldn't. "My mother always told me... Well, never mind that."

Feeling vaguely uncomfortable, she waited for him to come around the Cherokee to open her door. Reluctantly she took his hand to step out of the vehicle, enjoying in spite of herself the feel of his fingers closing warm and unexpectedly strong around hers.

He helped her down, then shut her car door. But he didn't step away, and she found his body almost aggressively crowding hers back against the side of the car.

He lifted her hand and pressed it onto his shoulder, holding it there. "Julie," he said softly, "I find you... very attractive."

"Now, Cosmo," she said in a warning tone. She tried to pull her hand from his shoulder, but he wouldn't let her. There was no way she could escape his unwanted attentions, blocked as she was between the man in front and the car behind—if indeed his attentions *were* unwanted.

She licked her lips, trying to find a clue in his expression. Unfortunately the moonlight behind him threw his face into even deeper shadow.

He shuffled his feet with appealing shyness, managing to scuff the toe of one shoe against her ankle. Automatically she moved that foot out of his path, and when he leaned forward, his knee slipped easily between her thighs.

He didn't seem to notice, but *she* did. Before she could issue a rebuke, he slid his hand from hers to curve around her throat. Without meaning to, she turned her head to that side, effectively arching her neck into his hand.

Well, she wasn't going to have this! He'd taken advantage of her by moonlight once before. This was intolerable. She must say so in no uncertain terms. "Cosmo..." With horror, she realized that his name on her lips sounded more like a sigh of invitation than a rebuke.

"Yes, Julie?"

With a hand now on either side of her throat, he stroked up, his thumbs exploring her jawline, then her full lower lip. Struck dumb, Julie stood there like a post and let him, little tremors of exquisite sensation spiraling through her from the point where his hands touched her face to the point where his thigh pressed intimately between hers.

He leaned closer, while she stood there trembling like a doe caught in a beam of light. This unanticipated turn of events both shocked and enthralled her. Some deep instinctive knowledge warned her she was playing with dynamite, even while the rational side of her brain scoffed at such a notion.

This was Cosmo! Yet when he tilted her face up toward his and sighed, she felt a quickening of blood through her veins that couldn't be explained. "Oh, Cosmo," she groaned, her eyelids drifting closed even while she reached out to slide her arms around his waist.

"Oh, Julie," he returned, crushing her body back against the Cherokee, pressing his knee harder between her thighs. His hands cradled her face, and he dropped feathery kisses on her forehead, her eyes, her cheeks and, at last, her mouth.

Delightful as it was, it wasn't enough. Parting her lips, she slanted her mouth beneath his, cutting short the pecks and nibbles. He didn't need a second invitation to thrust his tongue into her mouth. The intensity of her pleasure rocked her.

Luck or skill or natural talent, this man could kiss! He also knew how to take his time, whether from ineptitude or sure and certain knowledge Julie could only guess. In fact, Julie had never been kissed so thoroughly in her entire life. Sensual heat built in the pit of her stomach, pulsing through her body in languid waves.

He lowered his hands, and one sought the firmness of her breast. Until then, she hadn't known how she'd ached for that touch. He curved his other hand around her thigh and lifted it, until she automatically curled her leg around him, clutching the back of his thigh with her calf. He sank into her, his hips pinioning her own, and she felt his arousal burn its hard length into her stomach.

The evidence of his physical reaction scared her, shocked her...thrilled her. But this was insane! She had to call a halt to the proceedings, and she would—just as soon as he stopped kissing her...and kneading her breast...and moving his lower body more deeply and snugly into the receptive cradle of hers. If only he'd give her a few seconds to catch her breath! But he showed no sign that he was growing weary of this assault on her senses—

The front door of the house banged open and a figure charged out onto the porch, stopping short at the edge of the top step. Cosmo reacted more quickly than Julie had ever imagined a person could, yanking himself away from her, whirling and in the same instant shoving her behind him as if for protection.

"What is it?" she gasped, trying to push him away so she could get a little air into straining lungs. He was crushing her. She couldn't breathe, couldn't see, had no idea what was going on. "Cosmo, you're suffocating me!"

"Sorry." He edged forward barely enough to give her room to breathe. "What the hell's—"

"Get in the house and stay there!"

The voice was unmistakably Ben's. Julie shoved with all her strength, finally stepping out from behind her savior just in time to see Ben rush past, heading toward the west pasture.

Moonlight glinted off the barrel of the shotgun in his hands.

She fought to follow, but Cosmo wouldn't turn her loose. "Ben," she screamed, "what is it?"

"I don't know. Rustlers maybe. Stay out of this."

Only then did Julie become aware of the sound of pounding hooves in the near pasture, as if the horses were stampeding. But saddle horses didn't stampede without a reason, and if the reason was rustlers...

"Oh, my God! He's got a gun!" She grabbed Cosmo's arm. "We've got to do something!"

"I'll do something, just as soon as you get into the house and promise to stay there!" He gave her a not-very-gentle shove toward the front steps.

"I want to help!"

"No, dammit! With Ben running around in the dark with a shotgun, you could get hurt, and for sure, you'd get in the way."

She couldn't believe this blunt and bossy individual was the Cosmo she knew. "You can't give me orders," she declared. "Who do you think you..."

But he was gone, a shadow moving swiftly down the path after Ben.

MAX HEARD a blast from the shotgun, closely followed by another.

That was what he got for losing his head over a woman. While he was hitting on Julie Cameron, horse thieves had been literally next door helping themselves. Some big goddamn expert he'd turned out to be.

Rounding a clump of trees, he came up against a six-foot wooden fence. Without so much as slowing, he vaulted over the top rail. The pasture lay before him in shadowy darkness. Several horses thundered past; across the way, he could see a truck and trailer at the very edge of the trees, several dark figures converging on it.

"Steal *my* horses!" Ben's voice, but where was he? "Let's see how you like—"

The shotgun boomed again, and Max dropped into a crouch. Ben darted out of the shadow of the fence and took off running toward the truck and trailer. Apparently he never took his gaze off his target and thus didn't see anything or anybody else.

Two leaping bounds hurled Max into the outraged rancher's path. "No, you don't," Max commanded, grasping the shotgun with both hands. "I think you've already done enough damage tonight."

"Let go, you..." Ben grappled for control of the weapon. "They're getting away!"

Sure enough, the roar of a truck engine cut through the night air, closely followed by the screech of tires.

Closely followed by a cry of pain.

Ben froze, both hands still gripping the shotgun. "Dear God," he said in a suddenly horrified voice. "What have I done?"

What he'd done was shoot the Outlaw Grandpa. Max, who reached the old man first, knelt in the grass beside the slender form. "How bad you hit, Ethan?"

Another groan, and Ethan struggled to sit up. "I... Not bad."

"Think it'll do you any harm if I carry you inside?"

"Reckon not." A pause, then, "Did *you* shoot me?" Ethan sounded puzzled and more than a little hurt by that possibility.

"Nah, it was Ben Cameron."

"I mighta knowed."

Ethan slid a wiry arm around Max's neck and gritted his teeth. Max stood up, lifting the old man easily.

"Do I hafta go inside the house? Can't you just drive me to the doc or somethin'?"

"You know better than that, Ethan. We don't even know if it's safe to move you, and then there's the law to get involved."

"Reckon so."

Max carried the old outlaw toward the house, slowed only by the unevenness of the ground. Ben still stood where Max had left him, Julie beside him now. She stepped forward, as protective of her stunned brother as Max had tried to be with her.

"Wh-who is it?" she whispered.

"Ethan Turner."

"Is he...?"

Ethan spoke for himself. "Sorry to disappoint you, missy, but it looks like this old fool's gonna live."

"Thank God." Her shoulders slumped.

Ben flung up his head. "You, Ethan? *You?* Julie's been right all along, then."

Max strode on past, not liking the direction this conversation was headed. Over Max's shoulder, Ethan strained to get in the last word.

"Me, nothin'! I didn't come to rustle. I just come for a little neighborly confab. You cain't shoot a man for that, leastways not and get away with it!"

Max might have found that easier to believe if this little visit hadn't occurred right around midnight.

GRANDMA TENDED Ethan's wound in the kitchen under Max's watchful but again disguised eyes. Ben, haggard and shaken by what he'd done, hovered nearby while Betsy sought to calm him. Julie stood just inside the door, wringing her hands, her agitated gaze swinging from her brother to the injured man.

Grandma pulled the wet towel away from Ethan's shoulder. "Praise the Lord, the boy was only loaded with bird shot," she said. "It's just a flesh wound, Ethan. Take more than that to kill an old goat like you."

Ben let out his breath in a gusty sigh, but his grandmother wasn't done with him yet.

"Call the marshal, Benjamin."

Ben's eyes narrowed and a muscle worked in his jaw. "Yeah," he said, "you're right. This doesn't change anything."

Walking to the telephone on the wall, he dialed. Not a sound disturbed the leaden quiet of the kitchen. He straightened. "That you, Dwight? This is Ben Cameron at the Arrow. We've got us an emergency out here. I caught me a rustler red-handed." A moment spent listening, and then Ben nodded. "Yeah, he's right here in my kitchen. I shot the son of a bitch and—"

Ben blinked and hung up. "I guess he'll be right out," he reported to his awed listeners.

THE CAMERONS TOLD Max he didn't need to wait; they told him the marshal could contact him the next day for anything he might have seen or heard. Max, of course, wasn't buying it. He'd found it difficult but not impossible to resume his mantle of mild-mannered nerd after the rush he'd gotten when the lead started flying hot and heavy. Now he watched and waited.

First chance he got, he slipped outside to look around. Sure enough, the old rattletrap Turner pickup was parked out on the edge of the public road that ran past the Straight Arrow. Back inside, Max sidled up to Ethan.

"It'd be a good idea," he whispered in his ear, "if you leveled with the marshal when he gets here."

"I'm gonna tell the truth, the whole truth and nothing but the truth." The old man glared at Max.

"Which is?"

"I just dropped by to talk to my nearest neighbors. I... I wanted to know if Ben would help me...move some cows. That's it, move some cows."

"Yeah, right, and you were on his land and heading away from the house toward a truck and trailer of unknown origins when you got waxed. This is me you're talking to, Ethan. You came out here to warn your grandson not to do what he and his buddies were already doing.''

Ethan shot Max a sour look. "You got a big imagination there, son. I'll deny—''

A pounding on the front door announced the arrival of Marshal Dwight Deakins, who walked into the center of the room and glared at all and sundry.

"Okay, folks,'' he announced, hitching up his gun belt. "Who wants to tell me what the hell's going on here?''

The upshot was, Marshal Deakins arrested Ben, drove Ethan into town to see the doctor and then arrested him, too. Max hung back at the Straight Arrow to comfort the women—those who needed it, anyway.

Which included everybody except Granny Cameron. She stood back watching with narrowed eyes while he offered awkward support to Betsy, who was terrified, and Julie, who was furious.

"I'm sure this is just a technicality,'' he soothed, although he wasn't sure of that at all. "They'll both be out by noon tomorrow.''

Julie glared at him. "Oh, Cosmo, what do you know about it? I don't *want* them both out by noon tomorrow!''

"Julie!'' Betsy stared at her sister-in-law. "You can't mean that!''

"Not about Ben of course.'' Julie patted Betsy's shoulder. "But if Ben has to stay in jail a day or two in order to make that rustling rap stick on the Outlaw Grandpa then it's—"

"Now how," Max interrupted, "do you figure that?"

"Simple." She gave him an ingenuous look. "Ben's in the right, naturally—"

"Naturally."

"—and if he spends a day or two in jail, he'll end up a hero." She clasped her hands together in apparent ecstasy. "Poor but honest rancher jailed for defending his own."

Max groaned. "That sounds suspiciously like a headline."

Betsy burst into tears. "I don't want a hero. I want my husband," she sobbed.

Julie seemed to come back down to earth with a guilty start. "And you'll get him," she promised. "Don't worry, Betsy. I'm here to help you."

Suddenly Betsy's wet eyes grew wide. "I'm calling Chase!" she cried. "He'll know what to do!"

Max watched her rush into the kitchen. "Who's Chase?" he asked.

Julie looked disgruntled, as if she couldn't understand why Betsy would need anybody else. "He's an old friend of Betsy's from California," she said absently. "He's married to my sister, Maggie. They live in Aspen."

Max heard the word "California" and stopped listening.

GRANNY WALKED Max to the car a few minutes later. When they got there, he opened his door, then hesitated. "I've been looking forward to meeting you, Mrs. Cameron," he said, pushing his glasses back up on his nose. "Julie mentions you often."

Granny laughed. "She talks about you a lot, too."

He didn't know quite how to take that. "Uh...that's nice. I...I guess I'd better be on my way." He climbed into the driver's seat and rolled down the window. "If you need me..." Damn, he shouldn't have said that.

"Now why," she asked calmly, "would I need an unemployed insurance agent from California?"

"Dumb thing for me to say." He hung his head on the outside chance she could see anything in his face. "I am employed, though."

"Yep, but at what?" Suddenly she laughed and stepped back. "Run along, Cosmo. I got me a sneakin' suspicion I ain't seen the last of you."

He drove away gladly, dead certain she had a sneaking suspicion all right—and equally sure she hadn't leveled with him about what it was.

CHAPTER EIGHT

NEWS OF THE ARRESTS shot through Cupid like a bolt of lightning. By noon the following day, small knots of men and boys lingered grim-faced outside the Outlaw Grandpa's jail-cell window, talk of the "get a rope" variety rampant.

Because the jail contained only two cells, Ben and Ethan were being held side by side. That meant that, although the two exchanged not a single word, Ben heard everything Ethan heard, and vice versa.

So both quickly became aware that Ben was being hailed as a hero for shooting a rustler—Ethan.

Only by now, Ben wasn't too sure of anything, including the righteousness of his cause. Hour after hour, he and Ethan Turner sat, separated only by a wall of bars; hour after hour, Ben wallowed in his own remorse over actually shooting another human being. Ethan just sat with his face toward the wall and kept his own counsel.

Granny came to visit, and the first thing she said was, "If I've told you once I've told you a hundred times, that temper's gonna get you in a peck of trouble someday, Ben Cameron. Looks like this is the day."

But then she hugged him—Dwight had opened the cell door and let her come inside, rules be damned.

"Kids upset?" Ben asked around the tightness in his chest and throat.

"They don't know nothin' about it," she assured him. "Before they do, you'll be outta here." Her voice rose. "How's it goin', Ethan? Doc patch you up all right?"

"Right as rain," the old crook replied. "Much obliged for your interest, Miz Cameron."

"You wasn't tryin' to make off with any Arrow hosses, were you, Ethan?"

"No, ma'am, I surely wasn't."

Etta May Cameron turned back to her grandson. "See? This is all a big mistake. I bet if we all set down and talked it over, we'd find a way outta this mess."

Maybe they would have, if the door leading to the marshal's office hadn't crashed open to allow the dramatic entrance of Julie, breathing hard and waving a newspaper in the air.

"Special insert to the *Cupid Chronicles!*" she declared, thrusting a single sheet through the bars of Ethan's cell. "Read it and weep!"

ETHAN READ IT and lost his temper, stomping around his small cell with a lot of "dagnabbits" and "goldurns"—an apparent attempt at self-censorship due to the presence of women.

Ben read it and couldn't really blame his jail mate for being upset. The story wasn't too bad, but the editorial, also written by Julie, was incendiary.

The upshot: *Honest and stalwart rancher jailed for trying to protect his own in the best tradition of the Old West; is there no justice left in America?* The editorial stopped short of inciting to riot; *just* short.

"And," Julie boasted, "best of all, I've already got it out on the news wire. Unless I miss my guess, newspapers all over the state will pick this up. State? The West! The country! Maybe even the world!"

If Ben had been able to reach her, he'd have boxed her ears.

He was still in a foul mood a half hour later when Betsy arrived, Maggie and Chase Britton in tow. Again Dwight opened the cell door and, after admonishing them to mind their manners, let the family go right on in.

Ben held Betsy in his arms, trying to soothe her while meeting his brother-in-law's level gaze. "There was no need to call the family home, Betsy," Ben said in a tight voice. "If Jason shows up, I'll know I'm in real trouble."

"Is that in doubt?" Chase raised his brows. As usual, he looked prosperous and perfectly turned out. "I'm getting you a lawyer, Ben. We'll have you out of here in no time."

Ben shook his head. "I don't want a lawyer."

Maggie glared at her brother. At thirty-six, she was the oldest of the four Cameron siblings and mother-hen bossy. Ben had thought when she married Chase last November, she'd boss her new husband and leave *him* alone.

"You need a lawyer," Maggie said.

"Why? I shot the old goat. I don't deny it."

Chase looked exasperated. "Oh, man, you haven't told the authorities that, have you?"

Ethan gripped the bars, pressing his face between them. His white mustache bristled with indignation. "He sure has. Me, too. He done it all right."

Maggie smiled. "Oh, hello, Mr. Turner. I didn't see you there."

Ethan dipped his head. "Howdy, Miss Maggie."

Betsy looked up from her husband's shoulder, swallowing tears. "I hope you're feeling better, Mr. Turner."

"Shore am, little lady. Kind of you to—"

"What the hell's going on here, a ladies' social?" Ben hadn't meant to roar, but that was what he did. "That old thief was stealin' horses from me. I lost my head and shot him."

"And now you need a lawyer," Chase inserted smoothly. "I'll see you get the best money can—"

"Don't bother. I won't talk to him." Ben wasn't shouting any longer, but he was dead serious. "I lost my goddamn head. Even if he *was* stealin' from me—"

"Which I wasn't," Ethan cut in.

"Even if he was, I had no call to shoot him." Ben closed his eyes for an instant, hanging on to Betsy. How had he ever survived before he had her to hold on to? "I'm ready to pay my debt to society. I don't need any damned lawyer to do it, either."

They all started talking at once, but Ben just closed his ears. He was a man who did what he had to do.

MAX SAT in Dwight's office, a newspaper page crumpled in his hand. "I tried to stop this," he said. "I really tried."

The marshal sighed. "When Julie Cameron gets the bit between her teeth ..." He shook his head. "So, whaddaya make of this mess, Max?"

Max glanced around uncomfortably. "Call me Cosmo."

"Sorry. So whaddaya make of this mess, Cosmo?"

"Ethan had no legitimate business in that pasture at midnight."

"Then you think the old guy's guilty."

"Not of attempted rustling."

"What, then?"

"Of trying to call off the raid. I think his grandson is one of the gang."

Dwight nodded slowly. "That occurred to me, too."

"Unfortunately we don't have anything on Beau— yet. You notice he hasn't even visited his grandpa?"

"Yeah, I did." Dwight frowned. "Who else you think's involved?"

"Johnny King or maybe Scott what's-his-name. Then there's Tom Purdy. I've been snooping around, and Tom's spent a lot of money out at his place lately.

Could be legit, but I haven't tracked that down yet. Or it could always be somebody we haven't even thought of, somebody at least smart enough to come in out of the rain.''

"Well, hell, that narrows it down some." Dwight banged a heavy fist on his desktop. He jerked his chin toward the door leading to the cells. "There's a way outta this, you know."

"Yeah," Max agreed. "I'm not sure they'll go for it, though. You want to do the honors?"

"You do it," Dwight said quickly. "What I don't know I can't be hung for, can I? I'm pretendin' I don't know sic'em about any of this."

"About what, Marshal?" Max pulled a notebook from his shirt pocket. "All I want is a statement for the paper."

Max grinned. So did Dwight.

BEN WAS SICK with remorse, just as Max had expected him to be. The rancher had lost his temper and done something stupid; his sense of fairness meant he felt obliged to pay the price, regardless of the provocation.

Max squatted next to the narrow cot on which Ben sat with his head propped in his hands. "Never shot anybody before, I take it," Max said.

Ben's head bobbed up; he looked pasty beneath his tan. "Never." He swallowed hard. "Did . . . you?"

Max thought about the best answer to give. No details; just enough to keep Ben from feeling any worse. "Yeah. The last one—"

"More than *one?*"

Max nodded. "The last one was just before I came here. The department's looking into it now. Even cops can't go around blasting the populace, generally speaking."

That earned him a wobbly smile.

"You got a lawyer yet?"

"No. My brother-in-law wanted to get me one, but..."

"Let it wait a bit, okay?" Max rose. "If we reach the point where you need one, I'll make sure you know it. We might still be able to wriggle out of this mess."

Ben shook his head. "I don't want a lawyer. I'm not trying to get away with anything. I did what I did and I'll pay the price."

Looking down at the bowed head, Max felt an unexpected rush of sympathy. In a more perfect world, maybe that would work. In this one... "I repeat, if you need one, I'll tell you."

Over in Ethan's cell, Max ran into new stumbling blocks. "Just tell me the truth," he urged the old man. "Why were you really in that pasture last night?"

"I went there to talk to Ben Cameron. Didn't know the danged fool would meet me with a shotgun."

Bluster, nothing but bluster. "Can the bullshit. You're lucky to be alive and you know it."

Ethan's bravado evaporated. "Reckon you could be right."

"Hell, you know I am. But what if Beau had been on the receiving end of that shotgun, instead of you?"

"Beau?" Panic flared in the blue eyes, then was quickly shuttered. "My grandson's got nothin' to do with this. I tell you, I went to the Arrow to—"

"—warn Beau you were onto him, maybe threaten to go to the authorities if he—"

"I'd never sic the authorities on my own flesh and blood."

Max saw the flushed cheeks, heard the tremor in the voice. Shit, now he was feeling sorry for the old guy. "Ethan, I know about Beau. Dwight knows."

"You're guessin'." Ethan's blue eyes looked watery.

Max felt like a heel but pressed on. "I'd guess you've been trying to hold the boy back."

"I ain't talkin'."

"You don't have to if you'll listen. What's going to happen to Beau if you're not around to talk sense into him? He got mixed up with this while you were in the slammer, but now the heat's really on. If you're not careful, you'll be back there before you know what hit you."

Poor old guy hadn't thought about that. He just wanted to keep his grandson out of jail, even if he had to take a load of shotgun pellets himself. Max figured just one more little push ought to do it. "If Beau came forward of his own accord and confessed . . ."

The quick glitter of resentment in Ethan's eyes told Max he'd gone too far, too fast.

"Beau's got nothing to do with this." Ethan turned his head away.

Max sighed, knowing he'd lost that one. "Forget Beau, then, and think about yourself. How about a deal? You don't press charges against Ben, and maybe he won't press charges against you."

Ethan turned back. "He'd go for that?" His gaze swept past Max to settle on Ben, lying on his cot with his arms behind his head and his gaze steady on the two men in the next cell.

"Go for what?" Ben rose from his bunk and walked to the bars between cells. "I don't make deals with horse rustlers."

Ethan reared back. "And I don't make deals with...with trigger-happy gunmen!"

And Max apparently wasn't going to be able to make deals with anybody.

MAX MET Grandma Cameron and Julie's twin, Jason, in the parking lot.

"Now what?" Grandma asked, lingering while Jason charged ahead into the jail.

Max cocked his head. "You got a stubborn grandson in there, Mrs. Cameron."

"Call me Granny," she suggested.

"Thanks, don't mind if I do. You got a stub—"

"I know it. What's it about this time?"

Max shrugged. "I had this idea—dumb, I guess. It's really none of my business..."

"Why, lands alive, the boy's protestin' too much," she said. "What're you up to, Cosmo?"

This was one shrewd old lady. "Nothing. It just occurred to me that if Ethan refuses to press charges against Ben for shooting him, and Ben drops rustling charges against Ethan..."

"You don't really think Dwight would let 'em go, do you?"

Max did his best impression of an open book. "Looks to me like he'd have to. Maybe Ethan *did* stop by to talk to Ben, and maybe Ben was cleaning a shotgun, and maybe the shotgun just happened to go off. Accidents happen."

"You know," Granny mused, "you could be right. You're mighty quick about local affairs and the law for a fella from outta town, Cosmo—or whoever you are."

Max felt the loop slip over his head. "You know who I am, Granny. I'm Cosmo Mackenzie, Gene's nephew. I'm a former insurance agent and an ace reporter in the making."

"Yep, and I'm queen of the May."

The party line wasn't working very well on Grandma. "Julie knows," Max said. "She'll tell you I'm just a simple—"

"Julie don't know sic'em when it comes to men and a whole lot of other things, too. And you don't know sic'em about insurance."

"You're right, Granny, I wasn't very good at it. That's why I decided to chuck the insurance game and come work for Uncle Gene."

"Not very good at it? Ha! Accordin' to Cupid's one and only insurance agent, you wouldn't know insurance if it hit you up alongside the head. On the other hand, you seem to know plenty about crime and jails and the criminal element."

She stepped back, right there in the parking lot, and looked him up and down. Max wanted to squirm but didn't.

"Everything about you's as phony as a two-dollar bill, Cosmo Mackenzie. I may be an old lady, but I ain't blind and I ain't stupid. You come clean with me, or I'm callin' your bluff."

And she drew a deep breath as if preparing to shout God only knew what at the top of her lungs.

So what could Max do besides came clean? And when she promised, with that twinkle in her eye, to keep his secret, he knew he'd dodged—what was it now? The fifth bullet?

GRANDMA CAMERON flat played hell with the inmates of the Cupid jail. She lit into both Ben and Ethan without fear or favoritism. By the time she got through with them, they were ready to promise just about anything to get away from that razor tongue.

After that, it was mostly a matter of paperwork.

"I never saw anything like it," Jason confided later to Julie as they stood in the *Chronicles* parking lot with

Cosmo. "It was like...hell, like she was programmed or something. She accused them both of overlooking their duty to their families out of stupid pride..."

"What do you suppose that meant?" Julie wondered aloud. She hadn't been happy to hear about what had happened at the jail, not happy at all. Outraged was more like it. She glared at Cosmo, who'd hailed it as the best of all possible outcomes. "Betsy was upset, of course, but—"

"Will you shut up and let me tell you?" Jason gave her a scathing glance, then frowned. "Hell, now I forgot what I was about to say."

"Ben should've held out," Julie said grimly.

"Held out for what?"

"He should've rotted in jail, if that's what it took to put that crooked old geezer away forever and break this crime wave."

"Jeez, Jewel—"

"Don't call me Jewel."

"Easy for you to say, Julie," Cosmo cut in. "You've never been in jail. It doesn't look like much fun to me."

"I should be so lucky. Haven't you heard about all the journalists who go to jail, rather than reveal their sources? It means instant celebrity."

"Ha!" Jason snorted. "I think I've heard of maybe one."

"There've been more, and I would love to be among them—my reputation would be made. They could lock me up and throw away the key and I'd never talk." She slid her arm around her brother's waist, hugged him and changed the subject with lightning speed. "So how long will you be home this time, Jason? I've missed you."

"A few days. Long enough to make sure Ben's got his head on straight again."

Cosmo put in his two cents' worth. "That could take more than a few days."

The back door of the *Chronicles* building opened, and Avis stuck her head out, spotted the trio in the parking lot and called, "Cosmo, telephone."

"If you'll excuse me . . ." With an awkward nod, he turned and hurried inside.

Jason watched, shaking his head. "Weird," he said. "That guy is really weird. Jeez, Julie, you sure know how to pick 'em."

That earned him an elbow in the gut.

THE PHONE CALL was from, of all people, Chase Britton. "There's something I'd like to talk to you about," he said pleasantly. "Maybe you can meet Maggie and me at the Spur for a cup of coffee."

"Gee, I'd love to, but I'll be busy here for at least . . . oh, at least a couple of hours, maybe longer." Max had heard something in the man's tone he didn't like. "Maybe another time."

"A couple of hours, huh? I'm disappointed." Chase Britton's pleasant tone didn't waver. After a brief but pregnant pause, he added, "I'd appreciate it if you could make time for us *now*. It's important or I wouldn't insist . . . *Max*."

Damn. "Give me five minutes."

NANCY WYATT POURED coffee for the three of them before departing with a smile. Chase added a spoonful of sugar to his cup while Maggie and Max eyed each other like natural adversaries.

Max shoved his cup away. "Okay," he said, "I'm here. Talk."

Chase nodded. "Happy to. It's like this, Mr. Mackenzie. I've had my doubts ever since Julie started talking about you."

"Julie talks about me?"

Maggie pursed her lips. "Not in glowing terms. Get that satisfied smirk off your face."

Max smoothed out his features. "Sorry." To Chase he added, "You were saying?"

"I'm saying," Chase went on with a smile as pleasant as if he was about to pin a medal on Max, "that you're a fraud. It just so happens I'm from California myself."

A horrible thought struck Max. "Aw, hell. Chase Britton. You're the guy with the restaurant in...Beverly Hills?"

"Used to, anyway. I relocated to Aspen several years ago." Maggie's hand lay on the table, and Chase covered it with his. "I left California not long after Betsy's first husband died. But I still have contacts there, Mr. Mackenzie. And when I called those contacts, they snooped around and discovered . . ."

Everything, as it turned out; everything that was public knowledge, at least. Britton even knew that Max's mother lived in Simi Valley, that he was divorced, that he'd been involved in several high-profile cases, that although he'd received a number of awards and citations, this wasn't the first time he'd been investigated for the use of force some might call excessive.

The guy was cool, Max admitted, watching him explain. Chase Britton showed neither approval nor censure, although his wife did. Maggie was becoming quite agitated, and Max didn't know why.

Chase finished talking and looked at Max expectantly.

"So what's your point?" Max asked. "I'm one of the good guys."

"That issue has yet to be decided," Chase replied. "Apparently there are those in your own department who consider you a trigger-happy jerk."

Max felt his gorge rise but held himself in check. "I wouldn't doubt there's a waiter or two in your restaurant who'd bad-mouth the boss, given half a chance and guaranteed anonymity."

"That's possible." Chase laughed. "Although highly unlikely and beside the point. You want to tell us what you're really doing in Cupid?"

"No, but I guess I will." While he talked, Max could see Chase relaxing, but not Maggie. Reaching the conclusion of his tale, Max turned to her. "You've still got a problem with this. What is it?"

She leaned forward, speaking intently. "I don't want my sister to get hurt."

"Julie?" Max was taken aback. "Look, I made a vow that there'd be no gunplay. I didn't even bring a weapon with me." He held his arms wide. "Want to search me?"

She gave him a look brimming with disgust. "Oh, boy, maybe you're as dumb as she thinks you are."

"Julie thinks I'm dumb?" Somehow he'd thought she was revising that opinion.

"Well, *I* think you're dumb, and I'm warning you..."

Chase slipped an arm around her shoulder and squeezed. "Maggie, you can't warn a cop."

She ignored him. "Watch me. I'm warning you, Mr. whoever-you-are, once my sister knows how you've been conspiring behind her back—"

"You're not going to tell her, are you?"

"The hell I'm not," Maggie retorted. "She has a right to know."

"Not if you ever expect the Cameron kids to get their pony back. Not if you want to see that gang of rustlers stopped for good."

"Oh, come on now. I'm sure there are others who know about your little charade. Betsy, for example."

"You two talked to Betsy?"

Chase shook his head. "We haven't had a chance yet, but we plan to."

"Don't," Max said. "The less talk about me, the better. It won't be much longer now. Let me wrap up the case, and then you can tell anybody and everybody... although..."

Even Chase was frowning. "You're real hung up on secrecy," he observed.

"It's the publicity," Max admitted. "I don't want it or need it. Same with the credit, assuming there'll be any when this is over. Let Marshal Deakins have it. I'm doing this as a favor to my uncle, and it's all unofficial. I'll admit, once I arrived and got into it, I started having fun..."

"That's the part that worries me," Maggie said darkly.

"Hey, enough people know about me that I'll be a sitting duck if anything goes wrong. I don't have any more authority here than any other private citizen. Once this is over, I'm outta here."

"So," Chase said slowly, "you're asking us to forget everything we know and let you break the case so you can go back to L.A. and pick up where you left off. Right?"

Max's gut tightened; it had been stated somewhat baldly, but accurately. "You got it." He looked from one to the other. "What's the harm, if you keep quiet?"

Chase and Maggie exchanged glances. "What do you think?" Chase asked her finally. "It doesn't sound unreasonable to me."

Maggie bit her lip. "I don't like it."

"Maggie, he's on our side."

"Is he?" She cocked her head and stared at Max. "Okay, I'll give you this much," she said. "I'll reserve judgment. But if I think for a single minute that you're up to anything that'll hurt Julie . . ."

It was more than just a threat. There was nothing friendly in those probing brown eyes.

Chase Britton must be a helluva man to handle *that* one, Max thought.

So NOW just about the entire Cameron clan knew, Max explained to Gene that night when his uncle finally got in from a Chamber of Commerce dinner at the community center.

"They'll keep their mouths shut," Gene predicted. He patted his stomach. "I don't know where they got the food for this shindig tonight, but it wasn't enough to satisfy a hummingbird. I think I'll fix me some of that microwave popcorn. Want any?"

"Sure." Max had devoured a dried-out pork chop and some leftover beans for dinner. He followed his uncle into the old-fashioned kitchen, still talking. "I hope you're right about the Camerons. Julie and Jason are the only ones who don't have a clue. I don't know him, but *she'd* never be able to keep her mouth shut. Julie seems to think secrets are un-American. She wants everything splashed all over the paper, preferably the front page."

"Give her a break. It's her job."

"Yeah, well . . ." His next words just kind of popped out. "When this is all over, I want to be the one to tell her."

Gene closed the microwave door and started punching buttons. "Good idea. She'll be major pissed at being left out, but not like if she heard it from someone else."

A cold chill shot up Max's spine and his scalp tingled. "You got that right." He shivered. "Do you think—"

The telephone on the wall jangled and Gene answered. He listened for a moment, then he said, "Thanks, Charlie," and hung up.

"Gwendolyn's loose again," he announced. "That was Charlie at the Hideout. One of the boys is riding her back home."

Max almost hated to ask who. He'd attached a bug to the old mare's halter after her last unauthorized excursion, but it had been a makeshift job; he'd snugged it up inside the band beneath her heavy forelock. No one was going to find it. No way.

Nevertheless, he had to ask. "Which boy?"

Gene grinned. "Speak of the devil," he said with a shrug.

CHAPTER NINE

JASON CAMERON stood beneath the bare bulb suspended above the door to Gene's barn, which was really little more than a large shed behind the house. The tall cowboy was grinning ear to ear, his hat shoved back and his thumbs hooked in the belt loops of his jeans.

"Well," Gene said uneasily for the second or third time, "thanks again for bringing her home, Jason. Where'd you say you found her?"

"Outside the back door of the Hideout, eatin' lettuce out of a trash can. She made quite a mess."

"I'll see it's cleaned up," Max said quickly. "We wouldn't want old Gwendolyn to wear out her welcome."

"No problem." Jason kept right on grinning. "While a bunch of us guys argued over who'd bring her home, she cleaned it up herself—ate everything in sight, including a coupla things she may regret."

"That's Gwendolyn." Gene shook his head and sighed. "Well, thanks again. If that's all, I hear a bag of popcorn calling me."

With a wave of his hand, he departed. Max lingered, waiting for Jason to say...something. He didn't, just stood there and kept on grinning.

His expression was making Max nervous. "Guess I'll go in, too," he said cautiously. He took a tentative step away. "Unless there was something else you wanted to say?"

"Maybe just one little ol' thing." Jason straightened, releasing the belt loops. Offering one hand palm up, he slowly uncurled his fingers to reveal a black object no bigger than his thumbnail. His grin grew wider still. "Care to tell me why old Gwendolyn was wearin' this bug?"

Jason crossed his arms over his chest and waited . . . still grinning.

"SO WHO'RE YOUR SUSPECTS?" Jason lifted his mug of coffee and drank, his curious gaze intent on Max and his elbows on Gene's kitchen table.

Max considered how much more he should reveal; Jason already had the basics—bullet six or seven, Max had lost count. "I'd rather not say," he hedged.

Jason nodded, and Max was struck again by the strong family resemblance among all the Camerons. Jason had the same black hair as his sisters, but his eyes were Ben's gray, not Julie's brown. At twenty-six, Jason carried himself with a bone-deep authority, yet without a hint of arrogance or pomposity.

"Julie thinks Ethan Turner's behind it," Jason said suddenly. "He burned her once, you know."

"Yeah, I know." Max frowned. "Julie tends to shoot first and ask questions later."

"Yeah, I guess so." Jason cocked his head, his expression open and cheerful. "She gets on your nerves, I take it."

"No, no, nothing like that." This guy sure could jump to conclusions. "I just don't like newspaper people much, for starters. Had a few brushes with the media back in California."

"If you say so." Jason leaned forward. "But you do think you're gonna catch these rustlers."

"Damn straight. No two-bit backwoods—" Max bit off his hostile words, realizing they could be taken as a more general criticism than he intended. "Sorry, but I'm pretty ticked off about this. I should already have 'em behind bars by now."

Jason nodded as if he understood. "Any chance the rustlers might get violent?"

"I doubt it, or at least I did, before Ben turned vigilante. Seems to me the rustlers have just been picking up a little pocket change and maybe—" the thought jelled as he spoke "—maybe evening up a few old scores."

"Interesting theory." Jason sat back and picked up his mug again. After a swallow, he said, "What about the animals being stolen? The kids' pony, old Poco, for instance. Think he's in a dog-food can on a shelf at some grocery store?"

"Nope. I think he's hauling some other bunch of kids around on his back—for one reason, because slaughterhouses buy by the pound. A pony would probably be worth more alive than dead."

Jason's solemn face brightened. "I sure hope you're right. The kids are crazy about that animal. Figure we'll ever see 'im again?"

"Could be."

"Makes sense what you said about Poco avoiding the slaughterhouse because he's too little to bother with."

"Maybe, but I doubt that's the real reason Poco's alive—if he is. I think the rustlers took him to make a point."

"Which is?"

"That the gang can take any animal they want, including one highly valued by the mighty Camerons. Think of it—right from under Ben Cameron's nose. Then when Ben started making threats and throwing his weight around, they came right back in his face, only the second time, old Ethan Turner got in the way. The gang didn't get what they were after, but at least they had the pleasure of seeing Ben in jail."

"Yeah," Jason muttered, "they made their point all right. You figure Ethan's in the clear?"

"I figure Ethan's not a rustler. There's a big difference."

They exchanged hard-eyed glances. *This guy could be my friend,* Max found himself thinking. *Hell, he hasn't even warned me about Julie yet.*

Jason took a final gulp of coffee and stood up. "About Julie..."

"Sheesh. You, too?"

"Others been on you, have they?"

"You could say that."

"She doesn't like being wrong. If you can prove she is, she'll admit it, but circumstantial evidence won't do the trick. She's my sister and I gotta love her, but she's also one stubborn female." Jason's infectious grin resurfaced. "That's the only reason she hasn't figured you out."

"Figured *me* out?"

"Sure. She had you pegged for a know-nothing dweeb before you ever hit Colorado. Hell, she even wrote to me about you."

Max felt his ears getting hot. "And said what?"

"That you were everything she expected—and less." Laughing, Jason headed for the door. "Don't worry, I won't say a word about your free-lance crime-fighting gig. Just don't get my sister messed up in anything that could hurt her, because if you do—" he paused at the door and gave Max a pleasant smile "—I might have to take matters into my own hands."

Tapping the brim of his hat with two fingers, Jason stepped through the doorway. Max sat alone at the kitchen table, brooding.

Jason might seem more easygoing than his older brother, but underneath that laconic cowboy charisma lurked the heart of a warrior.

Kind of made Max wonder how Julie's former boyfriends had escaped with their lives.

IT TOOK A WHILE, but things in Cupid finally calmed down. Ben had suffered through his fifteen minutes of fame; he'd been swamped with telephone calls from news media across the country, all looking to embroider Julie's handiwork.

Ben refused to talk, a sensible course of action for those sincerely seeking to avoid the limelight. And he was. All he wanted was to discover the fate of his kids' pony. He'd already found another pony for them, but it wasn't the same.

Whatever had become of old Poco, the Camerons wanted to know.

So did Max. To that end, he put in hours on the telephone, drove miles across the mountains, talked to innumerable lawmen and horsemen and anybody else who might be able to give him a lead.

He did that until, all of a sudden, he realized Julie wasn't stepping on his heels any longer. In fact, her attention—and perhaps her affection—seemed to be otherwise engaged.

Scott Hale was back in town. And word was, he was dating Julie Cameron again.

JULIE GLARED at Scott from her seat at a small round table at the Hideout. "If I let you sit down, it's with the clear understanding that this is not—repeat, *not*—a date. We ended all that nonsense years ago."

Scott pulled out the other chair and sat, his slickly handsome face assuming a petulant expression. "Yeah, I know. It's just...did you ever think that if we'd gone ahead and gotten married the way we planned, we'd probably be living in Denver and have a kid or two by now?''

Julie shuddered. Have Scott's child, be tied to him forever? It was too horrible to contemplate. "*You* broke our engagement if you recall—and we both know why.''

"Damn, Julie!'' His long-lashed blue eyes looked hurt. "That's cruel. Yeah, I broke the engagement, but it was your fault. If you'd've just let me—''

"I wouldn't sleep with any man to keep him, Scott,'' she said quickly, "not ever. I told you at the time you were putting too much pressure on me.''

"It was an honest mistake,'' he whined. "I thought you were just playing hard to get.'' He stared down at the scarred wooden table. "How about the other guys you were engaged to? Did you sleep with them? Maybe that's why they all dumped—''

"That's enough!'' Julie surged to her feet, feeling her cheeks burn with anger and embarrassment. Bracing her hands flat on the table, she leaned forward. "If you wanted to have lunch with me just so you can dredge up old arguments...''

"No way,'' he denied. "Sit down. Please.''

Still she hesitated. "I can buy my own hamburger, you know.'' It was a warning.

He took it as such. "I promise not to bring it up again if you'll just— Look, here comes our waitress. Sit down and let's order.''

She sat reluctantly. They ordered, then kept up a strained conversation until the waitress plunked down two burger baskets—old-fashioned red plastic ovals each overflowing with a king-size hamburger and big golden brown steak fries.

Scott reached for the catsup. "The Hideout's fries are about all I missed when I left this burg—except you of course." He dumped on a big blob of the red sauce. "I never was too crazy about the other people around here."

"They returned the sentiment." Julie remembered how violently her brother Ben had opposed her relationship with Scott. "So what brings you back now?"

"I've gone into the TV-satellite business. I'm scouting out new locations for stores."

"For your father," Julie guessed.

Scott didn't look happy. "Yeah."

"I guess you travel a lot, then."

"Some. Say, Julie, how's Ben getting along since he got out of jail?"

She gave him a testy glance. "Who told you Ben was in jail?"

He laughed. "Nobody. I read about it in the paper."

"No kidding." That pleased her; she knew her stories had gone on the news wire, but she didn't know how many papers had published them.

"So has Ben calmed down?"

"Pretty much, but that doesn't mean he's any less interested in catching that outlaw gang. Did you know the reward is up to almost ten thousand dollars?"

Scott looked stunned. "You're kidding!"

She shook her head. "In fact, Ben's been kicking around a few ideas. He thinks there might be a way to set a trap..."

She forgot what she'd been about to say, for around the low wall shielding the front door of the Hideout walked Cosmo Mackenzie, Lorrie Anderson at his side. He saw Julie and waved.

Scott leaned forward. "Go on," he said, looking only mildly interested. "Ben thinks he can outwit the gang of rustlers, does he? Your brother always did have a high opinion of himself."

She pulled herself together. She hadn't seen much of Cosmo lately; he'd been traveling for Gene, although she couldn't imagine for what purpose. The fact that he was with another woman now certainly wasn't what threw her, was it?

Although she was definitely thrown. She licked her lips and tried to regain her concentration. "Ben thinks...well, since the rustlers have already hit the Arrow twice and the second time didn't turn out too well..."

Cosmo marched right up to their table. Julie frowned, hoping to discourage him, knowing that to him, a hand grenade would be little more than a subtle hint.

His smile was artless. "Hi, Julie. Fancy seeing you here."

"Yes, fancy," she said.

Cosmo glanced at Lorrie, who was also smiling. "Julie and I work together, you know."

"I know. Hello, Scott. You back to stay or just visiting?"

"Visiting!" Scott looked disgusted. "Don't let us keep you."

Cosmo pulled out a chair and sat down. "You're not. Lorrie's meeting Tom for lunch—"

"Oh, Julie," Lorrie broke in, "I'm so excited! Tom and I are finally getting married!"

"That's wonderful! Congratulations to you both."

"Of course, we want you to be there. Cosmo, too."

"Just tell me when and where."

"Sunday, right here at the Hideout. We're inviting the entire town." Lorrie giggled. "Know what Beau said when he heard? 'Be here or be square!' That guy cracks me up."

Cosmo touched her elbow gently. "Tom just walked in the back door, Lorrie."

"Oh, thanks." She wiggled her fingers in a departing wave. "Nice talking to you, Cosmo, and remember what I told you. See you all Sunday at the wedding, I hope."

Julie watched Lorrie walk away. "What did she tell you?" she couldn't help asking Cosmo.

"Nothing really. We—"

Scott leaned forward. "Julie, you were about to tell me Ben's—"

"—we were just talking about Cupid and all the nice people here—"

"—plan to—"

"—and she said—"

"—catch the—"

Julie threw up her hands. "Stop, you two. You're both talking at once and I can't understand either one. Scott, Ben's plan didn't amount to anything. I was just trying to make conversation."

Scott appeared ready to blow his top. The skin beneath his golden tan looked blotchy, and his lips were pressed in an angry line. He glanced at Cosmo before speaking directly to Julie. "Why don't you tell your shadow here to run along?"

"Scott! Don't be rude."

"Rude! You call that rude? *This* is rude" He glared at Cosmo. "You, Cosmic clown, shove off. You're not wanted here, savvy?"

Cosmo frowned. "Are you talking to me?" He tapped himself on his yellow-and-orange-flowered chest, but he didn't make a single move to leave. "I haven't had lunch yet."

Julie glared at Scott, then turned to her co-worker. "Never mind, Cosmo. Scott's the one who's going."

"Like hell I am!"

"If you don't, I will."

Their glances clashed; he looked away first. "Well, hell, Julie," he muttered, "I see it's still got to be your way or the highway. You Camerons may have been here since the Ice Age, but it doesn't make you a damn bit better than the rest of us."

The silence was long, and into it Cosmo said softly, menacingly, "I think it does." Julie looked at him in astonishment as, almost in slow motion, he rose from his chair, his green gaze through the silly round glasses locked on Scott.

Who cut and ran.

MAX ATE his burger and fries with a fastidious clumsiness that earned a smile from Julie. She reached out with her paper napkin, and he gave a start, aware of the surprisingly delicate wrist revealed by her rolled-up chambray sleeve. Julie always seemed so sturdy, so aggressively strong. He looked at her questioningly.

"Here," she said, gently touching the napkin to his face. "You've got catsup on your chin."

He caught that delicate wrist with his hand and held her still for just a moment, savoring the feel of her. Something electric seemed to pass through him, originating where his skin made contact with hers. "Thank you," he said at last, his voice husky.

She laughed uneasily and slipped her wrist from his light hold. He noticed that she unconsciously rubbed the spot he'd touched with her other hand.

"Cosmo," she murmured, "about what happened the other night..."

He realized instantly that she was referring to the kiss they'd shared. He let out his breath in a gusty sigh. "I knew you were mad at me about that." He figured Cosmo would believe that; Max didn't. Anger had been the farthest thing from her mind, as it had from his.

"Oh, no, I'm not mad at you at all."

"But you've been avoiding me ever since." Which was more or less true; if not avoidance, she'd stopped following him around so she'd know what he was up to.

"N-not really. I've been busy. What with Ben in jail, and everybody coming home..."

"I don't think your sister, Maggie, likes me."

"I...wouldn't say that exactly."

"Jason's an all-right kind of guy, though. You knew he brought Gwendolyn back the other night."

Her eyes widened. "He didn't mention it. She got out of her pasture again, did she?"

Max nodded. "Has Jason moved on?"

"Yes. He's in...Wichita? And then he's going on to someplace in Oklahoma, I think he said. It's really hard to keep up with his schedule."

"You miss him."

"Yes."

They sat for a moment in uneasy silence, and then Max said, "If you're waiting for me to apologize for what happened, I don't think I can."

"You don't need to. It was...temporary insanity."

Temporary? He didn't think so. "Whatever. I'm not trying to cop a plea."

She made a wry face. "I love it when you talk television."

She moistened her shiny pink lips with the tip of her tongue, and Max had to grit his teeth. He'd never seen this vulnerable side to her before. It made her more appealing than ever.

"This is embarrassing," she went on, "but in a way, I'm glad we're talking about it."

"You are?" She didn't look glad. She looked confused—and sexy as hell with her shirt unbuttoned low enough to show him the shadow between her breasts. Her cheeks were bright and her eyes sparkled. He almost wished he'd waited to pursue the subject when they were alone.

No, dammit! He'd deliberately chosen a public place to avoid any further weakness on his part. He'd decided quite rationally to stop making moves on Julie Cameron. Gene was right; there was too much at stake—including Max's own peace of mind. When he left Cupid, it would be alone and under his own power, not run out of town on a rail for seducing the darling of the Cameron clan.

That darling nodded, her thick hair tumbling around her shoulders in dark silky waves. "I like you, Cosmo," she said suddenly.

She looked so surprised that he laughed, which brought a brighter stain of color to her cheeks. "I like you, too, Julie."

She shook her head wearily. "You don't understand. You came to Cupid prepared to like everybody, but I had no intention of liking you back. I didn't even intend to give you a chance."

"I knew that."

"You did?"

"Julie, I'd have had to be an idiot to miss it. You're not very subtle."

"Oh." She looked disappointed, but then she rallied. "So okay, I like you, but not like...that."

"Like what?"

"You know, like what happened the other night. Making out."

"Making out?" *Don't laugh,* he warned himself, looking at that vulnerable face and struggling to keep his own straight.

She lifted her chin. "There can never be anything between us, Cosmo. I'm sorry. I don't want to hurt you, but you need to know. You're new here, and I suppose you expect to stay for...well, the rest of your life, for all I know. While I..." She sighed. "The time has finally come for me to test my wings—no more excuses. There's a lot of things in this world I haven't tried yet. As Grandma is so fond of saying, I'm not getting any younger."

His throat was dry; it was almost as if he really was this nerd named Cosmo who'd set his heart on a beautiful butterfly who had just announced her intention to fly away. "What are you trying to tell me, Julie?"

"That I'm planning to send out résumés, Cosmo. So as you can see, even if I wanted any kind of personal relationship with you, which of course I don't, there simply wouldn't be time."

She rose, dropping her crumpled paper napkin on the table. "I wouldn't want to hurt you, in case you'd...you know, hoped for more."

Stunned, he watched her walk out of the Hideout.

He hadn't given her credit for that kind of honesty. Apparently he hadn't given her credit for a lot of things.

THE CAMERON PONY turned up three days later on a dude ranch on Colorado's western slope. When Julie relayed the news to Jason next time he called home, he didn't seem surprised.

"That's what Cosmo predicted," he said.

The hair prickled on the nape of Julie's neck. "Cosmo *Mackenzie?*"

"You know another Cosmo?"

"Don't get smart with me, Jason Cameron. You're saying Cosmo expected to find Poco alive and well and living in western Colorado?"

"I mean, we were kickin' it around, and he said he didn't think the pony had been sent to the meat packers and would eventually turn up. No big deal. It's not like he's psychic or anything. It was just a lucky guess. So, I bet the kids are tickled . . ."

They went on to speak of other things, but after she'd hung up, Julie couldn't get Jason's remarks out of her mind. When Ben and the kids came in from the barn where Poco had been reinstalled like equine royalty, Julie sidled up to her older brother.

"Getting that pony back was like a one-in-a-million shot," she said. "Did Dwight happen to say how he did it?"

"It wasn't Dwight. It was—" Ben stopped short, eyeing her askance.

"Who?"

"Well, Cosmo, if you must know."

Julie's heart sank. "I can't believe it! The guy doesn't know the western slope from the Front Range!"

"You're probably right," Ben readily agreed.

"What happened exactly?"

Ben shrugged. "Dwight didn't go into detail. He just said something about Cosmo spotting a pony resembling Poco while he was passing through Grand Junction on some errand for Gene. No big deal."

"Yeah, sure," she muttered. "The man's got more luck than brains."

"So what if he found one lousy pony? That doesn't make him Dick Tracy."

"He also tracked those other horses to a meat-packing plant."

Ben raised his brows. "Even a blind pig finds an acorn once in a while. Me, I don't intend to look a gift horse in the mouth. Joey and Lisa Marie have their pony back, and I'm grateful to whoever's responsible." He looked thoughtful. "Reckon I oughtta tell him so."

FINDING BEN CAMERON on his front porch at seven in the morning was enough of a shock to Max, but when the rancher stuck out his hand he was floored.

As Max shook the hand, he realized he was completely unprepared for a visitor. No goofy glasses, no

Hawaiian shirt, no pomade on his hair. Stupid to answer the door this way; it could have been anybody.

But it was only Ben, who already knew. "Wanna come in?" Max invited, opening the screen door and stepping aside.

"Nah." Ben shuffled his booted feet. "I just wanted to say thanks to the person responsible for gettin' my kids' pony back. Dwight says it was you."

Max groaned. "I asked him to keep my part in this quiet."

"Yeah, well, I don't think he intended to tell me. And then I sorta let something slip to Julie, and she jumped on it like a duck on a june bug."

Naturally. "Tell me you didn't—"

"I didn't." Ben grinned. "When I suggested that even a blind pig finds an acorn once in a while, it seemed to satisfy her."

"It would."

"I just wanted you to know I almost blew it, so you can protect yourself—and that I'm grateful to you." Ben hesitated, looking distinctly uncomfortable. "I've learned some hard lessons, Mackenzie."

Max followed the rancher to the edge of the porch. "Which are?"

"To keep a lid on my temper...and not judge a book by its cover." Their gazes met, and for the first time they really connected. This time it was Max who put out his hand, and Ben who took it. "If there's ever anything I can do for you..."

Max watched Ben climb into his pickup truck and drive away, thinking there might, indeed, be something the man could do for him someday.

Depended on how much influence he had with his sister...

JULIE WAYLAID Cosmo the minute he walked into the *Chronicles* office. "Playing detective again, I hear," she accused.

His eyes were as wide and ingenuous as usual. "Not really. I was passing by—"

"I don't want to hear it!" She glared at him. "I already dragged it out of Dwight. Listen, Cosmo, I'm getting sick and tired of you sneaking around behind my back to beat me on my own stories."

"Sneaking? Gosh, Julie, I wasn't sneaking. I hoped you'd be proud of me."

"That'll be the day. What I want to know is, how'd you get that sheriff on the western slope to even talk to you? I've tried for years to ingratiate myself with him, then you come along and all of a sudden—"

"I don't know." Cosmo looked embarrassed. "Maybe he just doesn't like women."

She shook her head and advanced on him. "That's not good enough. I want to know—"

"I honestly don't have any idea what you're talking about." He glanced down at his wristwatch and his face registered alarm. "I'd love to stay and chat, but I've got an interview."

"A *what?*"

"Interview. For a story, you know."

He edged toward the door and she followed. "With who? What story?"

"John Wyatt's going to take me out to his favorite fishing hole. Did you know he's really into hunting and fishing?"

"Of course I—" She gasped. "John Wyatt is Betsy's uncle. You're poaching! John's practically my kin. You can't come in here and—"

"Have you ever done a story about him?"

"No. It never occurred to me."

"Finders, keepers," Cosmo said, slipping out the door without further ado.

Which was a good thing, for Julie was ready to throttle him. To find herself competing with a rookie was too much, too blasted much! Maybe . . . maybe it was time to get serious about her job search.

CHAPTER TEN

SINCE HIS ARRIVAL in Cupid, Max had grown accustomed to dropping by the Rusty Spur frequently for a cup of coffee and a slice of Betsy's delicious pie. That was where he'd met John Wyatt last week, not too surprising since Nancy Wyatt spent most of her time there. This was fine with John, who spent most of *his* time with a fishing pole or a rifle in his hands. As Nancy remarked to Max, "If we can eat it, John'll drag it home."

"You ever do any huntin'?" the lean and sun-browned man had asked Max.

"Not for anything I could eat," Max admitted with a grin.

John cocked his head, considering Max's comment with deliberate care. "Funny," he said at last. "You've got a shooter's eye."

Max gulped. "That *is* funny," he agreed, placing his glasses more firmly on his nose.

"How about fishin'? Ever try that?"

"Only for compliments." *Stop that, Max. This is no time to be a wise guy.*

John laughed. "I don't usually cotton to tenderfeet, but I like your style, boy. If you ever decide you want

to take a gander at the great outdoors, I'm your man."
He looked thoughtful. "As a matter of fact, I'm goin'
out tomorrow if you'd care to tag along."

"Sounds like a story to me." Max, who had about
as much interest in the stalking of furry creatures in the
wilderness as he did in oral surgery, made a frame with
his hands and recited, "Local Mountain Man Shows
Ropes to Poor Deprived City Boy."

"Sounds like a story to me, too," John said.

On sudden inspiration, Max inquired, "You ever do
any hunting or fishing on the Turner place?" He'd
been looking for an excuse to get in there. Maybe John
would provide it.

"One of my favorite fishing spots is away back on
the Lazy T," John admitted. "It's kinda hard to find
if you don't know the way. Funny you should mention
the Lazy T. I haven't been there in a coon's age."

Max felt a prickle of premonition. "That wouldn't
be where you're heading tomorrow," he asked with a
feigned nonchalance.

"Well, it could be. I stayed away while Ethan
was...gone. Just didn't seem right to use his land when
he couldn't. But he's no fisherman or hunter, either, for
that matter. Neither's his boy or grandson. He's been
real neighborly about lettin' me use it, and my pa before me. Yep, if that's what you'd like to do, we could
check out conditions on the Lazy T tomorrow."

"John," Max said with heartfelt sincerity, "I can't
think of anything I'd like better."

And that was how Max found himself seated in a pickup truck beside Betsy Cameron's uncle on a crisp and beautiful autumn day.

John broke the comfortable silence. "If you want to look over there to the left, you can see the Straight Arrow headquarters."

Max looked out the window. He'd been so deep in thought he hadn't even noticed his surroundings. Now he saw that they were driving along the summit of the forested rise behind the Arrow ranch house.

He caught his breath in appreciation of the view: red roofs framed by evergreens and a mountainside just coming alive with the fluorescence of aspen, the changing colors of leaves shimmering in the sunshine. The scene was like something you'd find on a post-card. Suddenly he felt as if he'd never really looked at Colorado before.

As a Southern Californian born and bred, the variations of the seasons were a mostly foreign concept to Max. He looked at his guide in astonishment. "The leaves are changing colors," he said. "Is winter coming already?"

"It's only the last day of August," John said, "but around here the line between seasons gets pretty blurred." He glanced at Max's light windbreaker. "I should've made you go back and get a heavier jacket. You out-of-towners have no idea how quick the weather can change on you."

"I don't own a heavier jacket," Max admitted with a laugh. "Never needed one."

"Then you better get one, and quick, because you're gonna need one here. Winter can hit in these mountains in the blink of an eye. But as I was sayin', I didn't mention your needin' a jacket because I got stuff you can use in an emergency."

"What kind of an emergency?" Through the trees, Max saw a deer bound away through the trees, moving with incredible grace. He found himself holding his breath until the deer was out of sight.

"Emergencies—all kinds. It could snow or hail or rain or blow or any combination thereof. We could get stuck in a ditch or run afoul of a bear or—"

"A bear? Nah!"

"Yep." John grinned broadly. "I guess nobody ever told you about Betsy and the bear."

"Betsy Ross—I mean, Cameron?"

The slip earned Max a quick curious glance. "When Ben and Betsy were courtin', they went on a picnic way out in the middle of nowhere, them and their two kids. Next thing they know, Lisa Marie's calling them to admire the teddy bear she's found. Only it ain't a teddy bear, it's a black-bear cub. The old sow comes chargin' out of the trees, and for a few minutes there it must've been nip and tuck." ·

"So what happened?"

"Maybe Ben grinned that old bear down like Davy Crockett. Whatever he did, nobody got hurt, but it sure put a crimp in their courtship, I can guarantee you that." John shook his head for emphasis. "I don't know what would've become of that boy if Betsy had packed up and moved back to California.''

Like I'm going to do one of these days, Max realized with a twinge. That knowledge didn't make him as happy as it should have.

They drove past a weathered piece of board tacked to a fence post, indicating that the Lazy T was straight ahead. Around the next bend in the narrow dirt road, John pulled to the side and stopped.

''Wanna hop out and open that gate for me?'' he requested. ''Then you can wait'll I drive through and close it again, if you don't mind. I doubt the Turners have any stock back there, but you never open a gate in this country without closing it.''

If the previous road had been primitive, this one was little more than a two-rut path through trees and brush. Climbing higher through alpine forest, Max found himself staring with fascination at these unfamiliar surroundings. This was truly a wilderness, broken only by occasional clearings and meadows.

And over it all hung a sky bluer than any he'd ever seen. Even the air smelled different, redolent of pine, fresh and clean and heady as wine.

They rounded a bend, and at that point even the track played out. John stopped the vehicle and slipped the key from the ignition. ''From here on out, it's shank's mare,'' he said. ''We've still got a ways to go, so we'll get a chance to see what you're made of, son.''

Max was curious about that himself.

THE TWO MEN sat on boulders above the creek, looking down at rushing blue water or up at a bluer sky. An animal John identified as a pine marten darted weasellike in and out of boulders along the shore. Its long slender body undulated on stubby legs, making it look like a furry streak of lightning.

Off to one side, two chunkier-looking balls of fur Max couldn't identify watched anxiously. Suddenly one let out a series of high-pitched shrieks, which cut through Max like nails on a blackboard.

"Wow!" he exclaimed. "What's that?"

"Some call it a whistle pig. Guess you can figure out why." John rested his forearms on denim-covered knees. "Technically they're yellow-bellied marmots, also known as groundhogs or woodchucks."

"How much wood would a woodchuck chuck—that kind of woodchuck?"

"One and the same. You never saw one before?"

"In a zoo, maybe, but everything looks different out here, even the animals. Gosh, it *feels* different, even *smells* different."

"That's because it *is* different." John took a deep breath, savoring it as if judging the finest perfume. "You kept up real good on the trail," he said suddenly. "Didn't bitch, didn't moan. You could make a first-class outdoorsman, son, if you ever wanted to."

Max felt a rush of pleasure so intense it was almost annoying. For some reason, praise from this man meant a great deal more than it should have. After a moment Max asked, "Who taught you to appreciate all this, John?"

"My pa." John looked out over the sylvan scene, a faraway expression on his weathered face. "Comin' out here to this particular place over the years has been kinda like chasing my childhood, I suppose. God knows it's not got the biggest fish and it's not the easiest spot in the world to get to. Sometimes I find a new favorite and stay away for years, but I always come back. When I do, it's almost like payin' my respects to my pa."

He looked around suddenly, catching Max's gaze. "Most folks don't learn to love the outdoors unless someone who already does is willin' to take 'em in hand and show 'em. I was lucky to have a pa to teach me. If he'd lived a hundred years earlier, I think he would've been a mountain man."

"A fur trapper, that sort of thing?" Max was thinking of his own father, who'd taught him to hold his liquor and take nothing for granted.

John nodded. "By the time I was two or three, I knew how to bait a hook and pull in a fish. At five or six, I was as comfortable out here as I was at home."

He pointed west. "There's an old line shack over there a few miles where me'n Pa used to camp. He taught me to live off the land, to build a fire and cook what I caught. I still have gear stored here and there, just in case I take a notion."

He was deep into his memories now, and Max was content to listen. He felt a sense of timelessness here that mocked civilization's omnipresent need to hurry.

"When I got older," John rambled on, "Pa taught me respect for firearms, just as he'd already taught me respect for the land. It's because of him that I won't kill anything I can't eat."

He chuckled, a richer and more mellow sound than any that had come before. "I loved that man and God knows I respected him, but every time I have to let a big cat or a bear go on by, I wanna cuss him good. I got a hunch that if I killed anything just for the sake of killin', he'd know. That's why you won't find any stuffed critters on my walls, but you'll find plenty of good eats in my freezer."

Listening to John talk about his father made Max think again of his own father. He'd also taught his son about firearms, but he'd left a different legacy: "Do unto others as they'd do unto you, only do it first. Don't shoot unless you have to, but when you shoot, shoot to kill."

A light touch on his arm made Max blink, and he found John looking at him with curiosity. Max cleared his throat. "Is your father still alive?" he asked.

"Nope. Is yours?"

"No."

"Want to talk about it, son?"

It was the *son* that did it. Every time John called him that, Max felt himself soften just a little bit more. He stared down stoically at the little stream rushing past below, wondering where it had come from and where it was going. Wondering where *he* was going.

That stream had been here before him and would be here after, as would these mountains, this sky. A sudden and unexpected sense of peace settled around his shoulders, and he lifted his head and spoke easily. "My old man was a cop. He was shot to death in the line of duty a long time ago."

"That's a hard thing." John nodded, his expression filled with compassion but not pity.

"Yeah, well—" Max shrugged and stood up "—I don't want to sit here and get maudlin. Isn't it about time we headed back?"

"I'm ready if you are." John rose more slowly, stretching as if his muscles had stiffened up on him. "Kinda nice to find a young person interested in all this," he added.

Tromping through the brush behind the smaller man, Max realized that John had him pegged; he *was* interested.

Or maybe he'd be interested in anything John put before him. Maybe he just wished he'd had a father like John Wyatt. Maybe—

"What's that?"

John stopped so short Max almost ran up his heels. He'd been carried away with his own roving thoughts, instead of paying attention, a bad habit he seemed to have developed from breathing this thin mountain air.

"What? Where?"

John pointed. "Over there."

Max peered through the screen of aspen, hearing nothing except the rustle of wind through the leaves. After a few moments of concentration, something began to come into focus. "A truck," he announced, feeling a prickle of excitement. "Maybe somebody's dumping stuff back there."

"Let's go take us a look-see."

John turned off the trail and Max followed, belatedly remembering why he was here. Together they stepped into a small clearing and looked around.

Max bit off a triumphant exclamation and glanced at his companion. There was only one good explanation for a beat-up old horse trailer without a license plate, a fire ring with the charred remains of many fires and a multitude of horse tracks—at least Max took them for horse tracks. The bare earth in the little clearing was plenty churned up.

John picked up a short metal rod. "Rustlers." His eyes widened. "This is a running iron."

Max looked at him blankly. "What's a running iron?"

"It's a branding iron without a stamp on the end." John indicated the plain rod. "It's used to draw a brand sorta freehand, if you get my drift."

"Rustlers," Max agreed softly.

John nodded. "'Course there're honest uses for it, but not a helluva lot. We better high-tail it out of here and go straight to the marshal's office. Julie Cameron must be right—Ethan Turner really is behind that rustler gang."

"Don't be too hasty." Max didn't want to call anybody; what he wanted was to catch the whole gang redhanded. "There could be another explanation. Why don't we..." Max let his lame words trail off.

John's stare said he didn't buy any of it. His sigh was almost an anticlimax. "Okay," he said, "let's put our cards on the table. Who *are* you?"

Max, well aware that his cover story was wearing thin, started talking. This man's good opinion was important to him, and Max explained, rationalized, almost pleaded.

He won the day when John agreed to keep his secret. Still, Max realized that at the rate he was dodging bullets—was that eight now?—it was going to take a miracle to catch the crooks before the crooks caught on.

It was going to take a miracle, but maybe finding this place would turn out to be just that.

"BUT I DON'T WANT to go to the Hideout," Julie wailed.

Jason gave her a rakish grin. "Come on, Jewel. I'm only going to be here for twenty-four hours. We won't stay late."

"You just *got* here, Jason. You must be tired from the drive. Let's stay home and watch a movie or something. John Wayne, Clint Eastwood...your choice."

"My choice is the Hideout, with you or without you." He hitched up his jeans and reached for his Stetson. "You comin' or not?"

She grumbled but went with him. Just because she'd heard Cosmo and Bob Mays making plans to eat there after the softball game was no reason to miss out on time with her brother.

"—BUT I LOST OUT to my partner in the last go-round," Jason finished up solemnly.

Tom Purdy, who'd muscled through to the front of the crowd surrounding Cupid's own rodeo pro, whacked the tall cowboy on the shoulder. "You'll take him next time, partner." Tom raised his voice. "Another round for Jason and his sis."

"Nothing for me," Julie protested. They'd been at the Hideout for a couple of hours, and the drinks just seemed to keep coming. "In fact—" she looked at her brother, at the half-closed eyes and the way he seemed to sway even sitting down "—I think Jason's had enough, too. It's time we thought about heading home—"

"Yeah, cut and run. You Camerons are good at that." The sneering voice came from the back of the crowd, a voice with edges almost as fuzzy as Jason's.

Jason grinned and managed to get bleary eyes open practically the entire way. "Is that my ol' pal Johnny King slinking around at the back of the pack like the yeller dog he is? Come on out, Johnny, and look us in the eye."

A couple of cowboys laughed; several others moved aside to let Johnny through. He stumbled forward drunkenly.

"Calm down, Johnny." Scott Hale spoke anxiously, Beau Turner at his side.

Julie hadn't even noticed Scott in the crush. Everybody in the saloon seemed intent on getting as close to Jason as possible, which made it hard to see who might be lingering at the back.

Usually Julie enjoyed the attention her twin generated when he came to town. Bull riders were bigger news around here than baseball players. Although Jason hadn't reached the top rank of riders yet, he was improving his position all the time. He'd missed the National Finals Rodeo in Las Vegas last December by less than a hundred dollars. If he could maintain focus this year, avoid injuries and keep up the pace, he should have his best shot yet at the big time.

Julie wished him nothing but well, although she'd seen recent changes in him that disturbed her. It was beginning to look as if the only things in the world he cared about were rodeo, drinking and chasing women. Since they'd arrived at the Hideout tonight, he'd eyed every woman in the place boldly and explicitly. He'd tossed back who-knew-how-many beers and gotten tipsy in little more time than it took to tell.

Now he was squaring off with an inebriated Johnny King. Julie didn't like the way this was shaping up.

Johnny's glare included Scott. "Shove it, Hale. This is between me'n the big man here."

Beau's eyes widened. "Johnny, you don't mean that. You can't talk that way to—"

"Shut your trap." Johnny leaned forward abruptly, stopping what could have been a fall by planting his fists on the table. He lifted his head, almost eyeball to eyeball with the leaning tower of Jason. "I never did like you, Cameron."

"I know." Jason blinked and grinned. "I never liked you, either, but my mama taught me not to pick on folks lit'ler than me."

"She did, did she? Well, I know a way to cut you down to size."

"You do, do you?"

"I sure as hell do." Johnny straightened to a weaving upright. "Let's you and me step outside and I'll damn well show ya."

"Helluva good idea."

"Jason, don't!" Julie grabbed his forearm and tried to hold him in his chair. "You're both drunk as skunks. Somebody's liable to get hurt."

Jason patted her hand, then looked up at Johnny as if inviting him into a conspiracy. "Women."

"Yeah," Johnny echoed, "women."

Jason stood up. Since Julie wouldn't release him, he pulled her up, too. "Wait right here, honey." He shoved her back down into her chair and put one big hand on top of her head to hold her there. "I got business to take care of, and then I'll be right smack—back, I mean. Get me another beer while I'm gone, will ya?"

"Jason!" But she was helpless; laughing onlookers held her in her chair, others flowing like an avalanche around Johnny and Jason, sweeping them to the door.

She saw Scott just before he was swallowed up in the crowd, Beau still dogging his heels. Everyone was laughing, jostling for position, thinking it all a big joke. Didn't they realize the damage two drunks could do? she wondered, beginning to feel genuinely frightened.

There was no one she could call on for help. *Oh, Cosmo, where are you when I need you?* she wondered, trying to struggle free of the hands holding her in her chair.

SOMETHING WAS GOING on at the Hideout. The parking lot was so crowded with cars and people that Max had to drive around in back to find a place to leave the Cherokee. Jesus, they were even arriving on horseback; several saddled horses were tied among the trees. The Hideout was obviously the place to be tonight.

Gravel crunching beneath his feet, he walked around to the side of the building where the greatest concentration of people seemed to be. Everybody milled about in a state of great excitement. Before Max could work his way closer, he noticed Scott Hale and Beau Turner in a huddle beneath the trees at one side of the lot. Walking toward them, he heard Scott swearing, heard Beau say, "But, boss, I don't know what I'm supposed to do."

Scott glanced up and saw Max. "Hail, hail, the gang's all here," he said sarcastically.

Beau looked from one to the other, confusion on his pug-nosed face. "We gotta *do* something," he said helplessly.

Max glanced around, feeling cool and uninvolved. "Do something about what? I just got here."

Beau looked at Scott as if giving him a chance to answer; when he didn't, the big man said, "Johnny and Jason."

"Johnny King and Jason Cameron?"

"Yep."

"And?" It was like pulling teeth, Max thought, still only mildly interested.

"And they been lookin' for a showdown since they was kids."

"So now they've found one, I take it." Max started to move away, intending to go inside. "What's the big deal about—"

"Look out! He's got a gun!"

The shouted warning knifed through the buzz with ease, sending good ol' boys—and a few girls—diving for shelter. A woman screamed; a man swore. Max dove for the cover of the nearest pickup truck, then looked quickly around. It was easy to spot the two combatants now; they were the only ones upright.

But just barely. Max had never seen men weave like that without falling on their faces. Drunk, he thought; drunk and armed and dangerous.

Somebody could get killed.

Somebody like Julie, who rounded the corner at a dead run, dark hair streaming out behind her. Her attention was directed at her brother. Without looking right or left, she headed straight for him.

Her path took her right past the pickup where Max crouched. Without warning, he stepped out and grabbed her on the fly. His arm jammed into her waist and she doubled over, gasping. She fought him, but he dragged her back behind the pickup.

"Let go! I've got to stop—"

"A goddamn duel," Tom Purdy, hiding at the front end of the same pickup, yelled. Eyes wide, he glanced at Max. "I heard 'em—they're talkin' twelve-gauge shotguns at ten paces!"

Max felt Julie go rigid with fear. He looked down to see her staring at him with an expression of terror.

"Do something!" she pleaded, grasping the lapels of his avocado-green-and-gold shirt. "Jason's drunk as a skunk. He doesn't know what he's—"

"One!"

By the time Max and Julie managed to get sufficiently untangled to peer over the bed of the truck, the count had reached five. Johnny and Jason marched away from each other with unsteady steps, their shotguns held barrel up in front of them. Jason faced the vehicles parked at the back of the lot while Johnny's path led toward the street.

The sound of running feet and excited voices brought a roar from Johnny. "You folks stay outta our way and you won't get hurt. I don't plan to shoot nobody except that idiot, but I will if I have to."

"Shut up and keep walkin', Johnny," Jason bellowed. "Seven— Get outta the way, Hale!"

Scott Hale was peering over the hood of a car directly in Jason's path. "Call it off, fellas!" he shouted. "This is stupid. You'll both end up in jail."

"Eight!" Johnny yelled.

"No, seven!" Max stood up suddenly, disgusted to find himself offering a new target for those two idiots. "Hale's right," he hollered. "Marshal Deakins is on his way now, and if you don't want to wind up behind bars—"

"Eight!" Johnny tried again, glancing over his shoulder. "Mackenzie, I'd almost just as soon shoot you as I would that—"

"Five!" Julie shrieked, popping up beside Max. He tried to shove her back down, but she stepped quickly aside. "Jason, if Johnny doesn't kill you for this, I promise you Ben will! Don't do it!"

Jason hesitated, his boots scuffling in the gravel. "Get down, Julie, before—"

"Nine . . . ten!" Johnny whirled and fired, buckshot from the first barrel of his shotgun blasting up a spray of gravel.

Jason fell toward the trees, his own gun barrel rising. He fired. Leaves shredded above Johnny's head, but he came on, walking deliberately toward his adversary. The second barrel of his weapon discharged with a deafening roar. Gravel, tree bark, paint from a dozen cars flew through the air.

But what the hell had become of Jason? Johnny stood alone in a silence so total the call of a canary would have sounded like an explosion.

Which was why everybody in the parking lot heard the weak groan with such horrifying clarity.

CHAPTER ELEVEN

PANDEMONIUM ERUPTED. People began screaming and rushing every which way in an attempt to get out of the line of fire; from the heart of town, a siren wailed. Somebody really *had* summoned the marshal, Max realized, leaping around the end of the truck to race toward the spot where he'd last seen Julie's brother.

He could only hope somebody would have the presence of mind to grab Johnny King. Jason was his first concern. Pushing people aside, he started into the trees and brush at the edge of the parking lot. On his third step, his heel crunched down on something other than grass or leaves or twigs.

"Son of a bitch!" The voice was strong and outraged. "Will you get your big foot off my hand?"

Max jumped back. "Jason, is that you? Are you hurt?"

"Hell, yes, I'm hurt! You just broke my damn finger!"

The brush parted and Jason crawled out on hands and knees—or rather *hand* and knees, for he cradled the other hand to his chest. There was no sign of his shotgun.

Max squatted. "What the—"

"Jason!" Julie hurtled past and threw herself at her brother, slamming him sideways. "I thought he'd killed you!"

"Get off me, dammit!" Jason tried to struggle free. "Johnny didn't hurt me near as much as you two."

An ominous chill slid down Max's spine. "If you're okay, Jason, then who groaned?" he wondered aloud. Rising, he turned—and found himself face-to-face with Johnny King.

The other half of the dueling duo was being restrained by two burly cowboys, one of whom also carried the shotgun. Like Jason, Johnny seemed considerably more sober than he had five minutes ago.

"Lemme go," he snarled, trying to shake free. "This is a private quarrel. Nobody got hurt, so why the hell are you guys—"

A scream split the air, followed by a somewhat hysterical female voice. "Quick, over here! I think they've killed Scott Hale!"

Johnny broke free of his guards. "Not me!" he yelled. "I didn't shoot nobody!"

"Grab him," Max instructed, aware of Marshal Deakins's white car pulling into the lot. "Jason, stay where you are—don't move. Julie, you go inside and call Doc Kunkle."

Without waiting to see if his commands were followed, Max strode toward the small knot of onlookers, pushing his way through. Lorrie sat on the ground behind a pickup truck, cradling Hale's bloody head on her lap. His eyes were closed and he wasn't moving.

She glanced up and saw Max. "Cosmo!" she cried. "He's bleeding! You've got to do something!"

"Take it easy, Lorrie. Everything's under—"

A shout, followed by the sound of running feet, brought Max swinging around. His glance darted over the crowd, caught by sudden movement near the farthest line of trees—way back where the horses were tied.

A figure flew through the air and landed on the back of the nearest horse. Clinging like a burr, the man leaned down and jerked the reins free of the tree limb around which they'd been wrapped. The horse reared, its forefeet flailing the air and driving back the two men trying to get close enough to apprehend the fugitive.

For fugitive he was: Johnny King, riding the animal like a man possessed.

"Holy shit," someone muttered in awe. "He's makin' his getaway on a *horse.*"

And he was, kicking the animal into a gallop and heading straight for the street. At the last minute, a pickup truck pulled across the exit—somebody who apparently had the presence of mind to see what was going on, Max thought.

"That's it," someone said almost regretfully. "Nice try, but he'll have to pull up now."

Johnny obviously didn't have any intention of pulling up; instead, he spurred the horse forward. A stunned "ohhh" escaped the onlookers; the horse pushed off with a powerful thrust of his hindquarters, forelegs bending under gracefully while the rider leaned over the animal's neck.

It was the prettiest jump anybody in Cupid, Colorado, had ever seen: Johnny King and Slim Talley's bay gelding, Macho, sailing up and over the bed of that pickup truck as if they'd sprouted wings. They came down on the other side—"light as a feather," someone announced in an admiring voice—and took off down Main Street at full tilt.

This time the sound from the crowd was a satisfied "ahhh!"

Max heard Jason's voice at his shoulder: "That little asshole can *ride!*"

"Yeah," Max agreed, "but he can't shoot worth diddly and neither can you, Cameron. You better hope Scott Hale lives, or you two dumb bastards will be up on more than felony stupid charges."

Disgusted with himself for being impressed by what he'd just seen, Max turned to greet Marshal Deakins, who was stomping and swearing his way out of his police car.

MAX SAT in Dwight's office, listening to sounds issuing from the cell area in back. It gave him enormous pleasure to hear the hell Julie was giving Jason, who was locked up tight in the same cell his older brother had so recently occupied. Maybe they should just declare it the Cameron Family Cell and put a plaque over the door.

Dwight took off his hat and tossed it onto his desk with a sigh. "Damn, what a night. One in jail, one runnin' from the law, one in the hospital. No rest for the weary."

"Will Hale be all right?"

"Doc says so. Says he'll be laid up a few days, that's all."

"Any way you can keep him laid up a little longer than that?"

Dwight looked interested. "Whatcha got in mind?"

"Just—"

"Cosmo!" Julie appeared in the doorway, her tear-streaked face appealing. "How can I ever thank you?"

Oh, boy, did he ever know a way. "For what?" he said calmly.

"For risking your life to save my brother." She took a couple of steps, then glanced at Dwight. "Did you know that? Cosmo's a hero. Those two miserable drunks were walkin' and countin', and Cosmo stands up from behind a pickup truck just as calm as you please and gets them all...confused. When the lead started flying, he saved my life, too, by pulling me to safety. Then he was the one who found Jason."

"I broke your brother's finger, Julie." Max hunched his shoulders and avoided her glance. "Doc had to put a splint on it."

She laughed, but she sounded on the verge of hysteria. "Doc should have put a splint on his *head*. Don't try to be modest, Cosmo. So you stepped on Jason's finger—big deal." She knelt by his chair. "I'll never be able to thank you enough." She caught his hands in hers, squeezing hard.

Over her shoulder, she explained earnestly to Dwight. "It's like they say about some 110-pound woman lifting a car to save her baby. You know she can't really do that. You know it's impossible. But the adrenaline starts pumping, and people do things they'd never be able to do if they had time to think."

Max tried to extract his hands from hers, feeling like a total jerk. "I didn't do any more than anyone else, honest. I'd love to take all the credit, but I hardly even remember what hap—"

"Shh." She touched his lips lightly with one forefinger, her smile misty. "That makes it all the more special. None of us knew what was happening, but you're the one who rose to the occasion. I'll never be able to thank you enough. Never!"

And lifting her hands to cup his face, she leaned forward and kissed him lightly on the lips.

By Saturday morning, the verdict of public opinion was in: boys will be boys. Scott Hale wasn't going to die, so maybe the law could just forget about the antics of those throwbacks to the days of the wild West. Johnny King and Jason Cameron were just two high-spirited Cupid boys who'd added a new chapter to local legend.

Max was not so forgiving. When boys were dumb shits, they should expect to pay the price. And the appropriate price, in this case, might have to cover considerably more than that little altercation at the Hideout.

Beau had called Scott "boss." It could have been a slip of the tongue; it could have been meaningless. But what if it wasn't?

What if Scott Hale was the only thing holding that crazy Johnny King back? Now that Hale was incarcerated in Doc Kunkle's mini-hospital, there was no telling what Johnny might do.

With Gene in Denver for the day, Max made the trek across Lovers' Lane at least a half-dozen times in an attempt to talk to Hale. Each time there was a reason he couldn't: Hale was sleeping, he was eating, he'd just taken a shot for pain and didn't feel up to it, the doctor was with him. Rose's list of excuses seemed endless.

Max did get a chance to talk to Dwight's deputy guarding the door but found out nothing except that Hale's only visitor had been Julie Cameron, who was still in there. Damn. Sympathy and guilt could be powerful motivators. Maybe he'd just wait for Julie to come out.

JULIE SAW COSMO and stopped short. "Oh, hello. What are you doing here?"

"I came to see how Hale's doing." He nodded toward the door she'd just closed.

She sighed. "He's in a lot of pain. Doc picked a ton of buckshot out of him."

"That's too bad. I...guess he's pretty mad at Jason and Johnny."

He held the door for her, and she led the way to the parking lot. "Not as mad as I expected, especially after I groveled." She made a face. "He seems to blame Johnny mostly. Have they caught him yet?"

"Not that I know of, but they're looking. Uh...did he mention Beau?"

"Beau? Why would he mention Beau?"

"I don't know." Max shrugged. "They're friends, aren't they?"

"I suppose. No, he didn't mention Beau. But he made me promise that if they bring Johnny in, I'll let him know right away." She reached her car and turned to face him. "Cosmo, about what happened at the jail last night..."

He gave her a blank look, which annoyed her considerably. If he didn't even remember the way she'd literally thrown herself at him and proclaimed him a hero, who was she to remind him? In the clear light of day, she realized she'd made a fool of herself.

She'd been overwrought, and with good reason. Jason was more than a brother. He was her twin.

This morning at the breakfast table, Ben had remarked grimly, "Maybe a couple of days in jail are just what he needs." Betsy had shared Julie's outrage at the remark, but Julie knew that Ben's own sojourn in the pokey had had a profound effect on him. She knew for a fact that he'd been working harder to control his temper ever since, as evidenced by the relatively calm manner with which he'd accepted the news of Jason's disgrace.

"About last night?" Cosmo gave her a verbal nudge.

She sighed. "Oh . . . yes. I just wanted to apologize for falling apart that way."

"You didn't fall apart, Julie." He gave her a long enigmatic look.

"I feel otherwise, though. So I do apologize, and I do want to thank you for everything you did." Taking a deep breath, she squared her shoulders. "But I also want you to understand that nothing's changed."

He blinked. "Nothing's changed? Like what?"

"Like nothing. I mean, like anything. You're still a thorn in my side at work, and we still disagree on just about everything. And we still can't be more than friends. Not even good friends, just casual friends." There, she'd said her piece.

"No problem." He spoke cheerfully, as if she'd just given him good news. "I could never hope to be more than friends with someone who was once Miss Cupid, now could I?" He started to turn away, adding almost as an afterthought, "Don't forget about the wedding tomorrow."

"Wedding?"

"Lorrie and Tom are tying the knot at the Hideout, remember? Before he left for Denver this morning, Uncle Gene said he wants us to cover it for the paper."

"Both of us? Since when does it take two people to write—"

"You handle the words, I'll handle the pictures." Cosmo held an imaginary camera to his eye and snapped an imaginary photo with his forefinger.

"But—"

"Don't worry, Julie. Like you said, I won't presume upon our friendship—or lack of same."

With one last smile, he trotted across the street to Gene's house, leaving Julie more disgruntled than ever. Cosmo sure wasn't very broken up to learn he didn't stand a chance with her.

JULIE STOOD beside Max, her notebook in one hand and a pen in the other. "Covering a wedding, even one in a honky-tonk bar, is not my idea of a hot news story," she groused.

Cosmo shrugged. "While I, on the other hand, find the photographic opportunities almost limitless." He held up the battered office camera.

"Yeah, right. I'll have to be sure to thank Gene for this one. Is he back from Denver yet?"

Max shook his head. His uncle had called to say he was staying over with a friend, another newspaperman, and wouldn't be back until evening.

"Coward," she muttered. "I'll get him for this on Monday."

Max figured she would, but he had nothing to reproach Gene for. Actually Max had enjoyed the show so far. Lorrie had married her cowboy in a ceremony at once tacky and touching. Now bride and groom were sharing the first dance while most of Cupid ringed the floor and cheered them on.

Most of Cupid—but not all. The hairs on the nape of Max's neck prickled. Everybody was here except Jason, who was still in jail; Scott, still in the hospital; Johnny King, still on the lam; and Beau Turner.

Without Scott Hale to stop them, what was the most outrageous thing Johnny and Beau might do?

Movement on the other side of the dance floor caught his attention, and he focused on Ben and Betsy. She smiled and waved; Ben gave a nod of acknowledgment.

And suddenly Max was certain: The gang was going to hit the Cameron ranch again. The pony caper hadn't worked out, since the animal had been recovered. On the second raid, Ethan had gotten shot and the gang had to take it on the lam without anything to show for their trouble.

Max edged away from Julie, who promptly noticed.

"Just where do you think *you're* going?"

He assumed an innocent expression. "Men's room. Be back in a couple of minutes."

Without waiting for her response, he headed for the facilities, veering toward the front door only when he figured he was out of her sight. But when he rounded the stuffed buffalo and the low wall screening the front door, he stopped short.

Julie Cameron stood there, a shark's smile on her face. "Goodness gracious," she cooed, "did you lose

your way to the men's room? It's back there, Cosmo."
She pointed with a flourish.

His grin felt sheepish. "I was almost there when I got
the insane urge to...to take a drive."

She stared at him, her disbelief obvious. "A drive."

"Sure. It's so crowded in here that it's...it's making me feel kinda sick."

"Sick. Honestly, Cosmo, do you expect me to believe that? You're up to something."

He widened his eyes. "I don't know what you're
talking about."

"Oh, please. I'm talking about the duel, about the
rustlers, something like that."

"You got me all wrong, Julie." He slung the camera strap over his shoulder. "I've got plenty of pictures, so I'm just going for a drive."

"Fine. I've got plenty of notes and I'm going with
you." She stuffed her notebook and pen into her
shoulder bag and indicated the double doors with a
sweeping gesture. "I do trust you, Cosmo, almost as
far as I can throw you."

"And we're not even good friends," he marveled.
"Julie, you're...really something."

He did not specify *what*.

FOR A MAN who didn't know where he was going,
Cosmo drove the Cherokee with considerable purpose. Glad to be out of the crowded saloon, Julie
leaned back against her seat with a sigh and looked out
the window.

What she saw brought her upright again. "My God!" she exclaimed. "Is it fall already? The aspen are turning."

"Yeah, kinda pretty."

"Not pretty, gorgeous." She watched the saffron-yellow gilt of aspen leaves flash past on the mountain-side. "I love this change from summer to winter," she went on dreamily. "How do people stand living where there's only one season?"

"You mean like California?" He gave her a knowing smile.

"Well, yes."

"We forget what we're missing. Or maybe we never knew."

"Which one applies to you?"

"I never knew. I was born and raised in Southern California. I grew up thinking Christmas decorations belonged on palm trees, that pink and yellow stucco was the norm for houses and that grass stayed green year-round."

"That's really sad."

"Do you think so?" He shrugged, his gaze steady on the road ahead. "Strange, coming from someone who recently announced her intention to move there."

"For professional purposes only," she said quickly. "I just want to see if I can cut it on a big newspaper. I mean, I *know* I can. I just want a chance to prove it. You know what they say..."

"No, what do they say?"

"When you're old and gray, you regret the things you didn't do, not the things you did that didn't work out."

"You might not like being a little fish in a big puddle," he suggested.

She raised one brow. "Who says I would be? Forever, I mean. I suppose I'd have to start at the bottom, but I could work my way up." After a moment she added, "How about you? Do you miss California?"

He shrugged. "I don't know. I don't think about it much. Now that you've brought it up...I guess I don't."

She felt a little thrill of pleasure, although why she should take his reply personally she couldn't imagine. "You've never mentioned—do you have family there?"

"A mother."

"No brothers or sisters?"

"No."

"Father?"

"I had one of those once."

"What did he do?"

"Die."

"Oh. Oh, Cosmo, I'm so sorry. Was it very long ago or...?"

She stopped talking, realizing he was no longer listening to her but staring ahead intently. Following his gaze, she saw the end of a horse trailer disappearing around a curve in the road. They had just come up to the turnoff to the Straight Arrow. Cosmo stepped down hard on the accelerator. The Cherokee surged ahead.

"What is it?" she asked, feeling the first faint stirrings of uneasiness. "Slow down, will you? These roads are treacherous."

"I'll be careful," he promised, but instead of driving slower, he drove faster. "That horse trailer on the road ahead . . . "

Again the elusive trailer whipped around a curve and out of sight. Julie licked her lips. "What about it?"

"Have you ever seen it before? It's not a Cameron trailer or anything, is it?"

She peered ahead, seeing movement through the trees where the road switched back. "It's definitely not from the Straight Arrow," she decided. "Have I seen it before? If you've seen one rickety old horse trailer you've seen them all."

He took a curve on two wheels. Julie gasped and made a grab for the armrest. "Cosmo, slow down!" she begged. "You're driving like a bat out of—"

"Hang on, Julie. I've got a feeling about that rig."

On the basis of a "feeling," he'd scare her within an inch of her life and maybe kill them both? He sent the Cherokee careering around a corner. Through her window, all she could see was a sheer drop straight down. With a helpless little moan, she closed her eyes and hung on.

"Open your eyes!"

At his shouted command, she did. How had he known they were closed unless he looked? And to do that, he'd have to have taken his gaze off the narrow ribbon of road ahead of them . . .

His profile looked grim. "Try to get the license number on that trailer, will you?"

"What for? Wait a minute, are you saying . . ." Digging around in the shoulder bag on the floor at her feet, she came up with her pad and pen. "Does this have something to do with the rustlers?"

"Maybe. I've seen that trailer before, somewhere it didn't belong. Can you see the license plate? Do me a favor and write down the number."

She leaned forward, squinting, trying to make out the letters and numbers on the green-and-white Colorado license plate. "I'm trying, but trees keep getting in the way. Cosmo! Will you slow down before you get us both kill—"

The Jeep skidded around a curve and struck a patch of soft earth and gravel that had washed down from the hillside. Her scolding ended in a scream. With Cosmo fighting the wheel, the vehicle skidded around in a circle, coming to rest at the very edge of a precipice.

Julie opened her eyes cautiously. The Cherokee pointed back the way they'd come. Turning her head an inch at a time, she forced herself to look out her window—and screamed again. There was nothing between her and eternity, nothing at all except a sheer drop hundreds of feet to a faraway valley floor. Even looking at it made her dizzy.

And nauseous. "C-Cosmo," she whispered, "I think I'm going to be sick."

"Maybe I can still catch them," he said, as if he hadn't even heard her. "You wouldn't know of any shortcuts?"

"I said I think I'm going to be sick! Will you... kindly pull up enough so that I can—"

"This road eventually connects with I-70, right? And once those guys hit the highway, they can go east to Denver and on to Kansas or—"

"Cosmo!" She grabbed the sleeve of his baggy shirt, her stiff fingers clawing. She couldn't remember ever being so scared in her life. "If you don't pull this car back onto solid ground, I won't be responsible for my actions!" she shouted. "I'm hanging off the edge of a cliff over here!"

He looked at her finally. "Oh, sorry," he said, pushing his glasses back up on the bridge of his nose. "I didn't realize."

He drove slowly forward. Julie could have sworn she felt the right rear wheel spin in thin air before catching on the dirt of the shoulder. He pulled up to a point where the cliff on the passenger side rose straight up, instead of plunging straight down, then stopped again. He turned to her with a smile.

"I'll bet you're wondering what that was all about," he said brightly.

All she could do was groan and slump back in her seat.

HE TOLD HER as little as he could get away with: that he'd been heading to the Arrow purely on a hunch, that he'd seen the old horse trailer—or one much like it—on the Lazy T when he'd gone there with John Wyatt.

Her eyes lit up at that. "Aha!" she said triumphantly. "I told you Ethan was involved."

"Or Beau. Or Johnny." He shrugged. "Let's go see if anything's missing at your place."

Nothing was. Granny and the kids led them through the barn, sent the dogs to fetch the horses in the near pasture, and everything was accounted for.

"I don't get it," Max admitted on the drive back to town. "I'd have sworn..."

"I know you would," Julie said gently, "but obviously your hunch was wrong this time. May I add one more thing?"

"Sure, Julie." He didn't like her tone.

"Don't get involved in any more high-speed chases, okay? Leave that kind of thing to the cops. Because, Cosmo dear, you are beyond a doubt the *worst* driver in the world. Trust me on that."

"You called me dear." He brought it to her attention to irritate her and was surprised by the shiver of pleasure he got out of it himself.

"What?" She blinked those big brown eyes. "I certainly did not."

"You did. You said, 'Cosmo dear.'"

"I did not! And even if I...I slipped and did by mistake, the rest of it was the important part. Promise me you won't go speeding around mountaintops in the future, because, Cosmo—"

"Dear," he prompted.

"*Cosmo,* you're an accident looking for a place to happen."

They wrangled about it all the way into town. At First Street, Max turned right.

"Where do you think you're going?" Julie carped.

"I want to go by home to see if Uncle Gene's back." First Street curved into Lovers' Lane; Gene's was the last house before it curved back and became Eighth Street at the opposite end of town.

Sure enough, Gene's old sedan was in the driveway.

"Okay," Max said, "I'm satisfied. I'll just drop you off at the Hideout—"

A shout made him bring the Cherokee to a halt. Both Max and Julie turned to see Gene appear on the covered porch, then run down the steps waving his arms. Max pulled over to the curb.

The publisher was in a highly agitated state. His cheeks were more florid than usual, and what hair he had stood on end.

Julie cast Max an alarmed glance, then leaned out the open window. "Good grief, Gene, what is it? You look like the world's about to come to an end."

"It is." He put his hands on the door and leaned down so he could talk to both of them at once. "They've got Gwendolyn!"

Max's gut clenched painfully. "Take it easy, Gene. We've thought that before, but she's always turned up. She's just busted out again."

"No. If she turns up this time, it'll probably be in a can of dog food." Gene thrust his arm through the window, his hand fisted. He uncurled his fingers.

On his palm lay a horseshoe nail the color of fool's gold.

CHAPTER TWELVE

GWENDOLYN WAS GONE and this time there could be no doubt she was in the hands of the rustlers. The gilded nail had secured a horseshoe to the gate, the calling card of the gang of half-wit cowboys who'd outsmarted the big bad L.A. policeman.

The mare's halter, complete with bug, still hung on a nail in the barn, where it had been since Jason had discovered the bug.

Marshal Deakins had arrived, and it was all Max could do to keep his cool. He'd been so sure the rustlers would hit the Straight Arrow again for revenge. They'd gone after revenge, all right, but it was revenge against the man who'd started the reward fund and made Cupid almost too hot to handle. Nor would the gang feel kindly toward his nephew, the troublesome nerd—especially if the gang consisted of Johnny, Beau and Scott, as said nephew suspected.

Max and Julie had, in all likelihood, seen the trailer bearing Gwendolyn away to some unknown but indisputably horrible fate. His mistake had been in believing the trailer had come from the Arrow Ranch, when in fact it had come from town, and in letting Julie's fear keep him from continuing the chase.

If he had it to do over again, he'd make a different choice. He forced himself to glower at her. "We should've kept going," he said. "We would've caught them, and Gwendolyn would be safe and sound in her own pasture."

"No, Cosmo *dear,*" she said in a sweetly mocking tone. "Gwendolyn would still be in a heap of trouble. The only difference is, you and I would be dead at the bottom of some cliff. I don't really see how that would help her, do you?"

"Don't fight, kids," Marshal Deakins advised. "We're all on the same team, remember?"

As word of Gwendolyn's horse-napping got around, the town went wild, and Julie was right there to egg them on. With her little notebook in hand, she appeared to enjoy whipping up the populace.

Unfortunately the rustlers weren't going to be apprehended through the license number she'd written down. Dwight checked it out, and the plate had been stolen over on the western slope. Nor did questioning the suspects—at least those who could be found—help.

Dwight made a trip to the Lazy T, returning to tell Max that Beau was nowhere about, and Ethan, although he acted nervous, denied knowing anything.

"Said he hadn't seen Beau or Johnny King, either, not since before the duel at the Hideout," Dwight reported.

"Did you believe him?" Max asked.

"About Johnny? Yep. About Beau? Nope."

Max nodded. "I finally got to talk to Hale this morning. He's denying everything, too, but he's mighty nervous about something."

Dwight laughed. "The only one we can be sure of is Jason Cameron. That boy's still locked up, and he ain't too happy."

"Jeez, you don't suspect Jason!"

"Nah, but he's better off out of the way until we get a handle on this situation."

"That's the truth." Max stood up, prepared to leave. "You know, I think I'll take a look around the spot where John and I found that trailer. At least I'll know if it's been moved."

"You say that's on the Lazy T?"

"That's right."

"You got permission to wander around back there?"

Max grinned. "John Wyatt's had permission for thirty years or so, and he gave it to me. Hey, Marshal, this is just a little fishing expedition."

Dwight grinned. "Okay, but if push comes to shove, I'll deny I know anything about anything." He followed Max outside, then paused to look up at the sky. "I'd be careful, was I you. We might be in for a touch of weather."

"I'll be back way before anything can blow in," Max said confidently.

"Spoken like a true Californian." Dwight hitched up his gun belt and made a great show of looking around. "Where might your little shadow be? I don't recall the last time we spoke without Julie hoverin' around or tryin' to eavesdrop.''

A big grin split Max's face. "She's been sticking to me like glue, but I sent her on a wild-goose chase. Told her I thought I saw Ethan drive into town, and she took the bait. She's out looking for him now. By the time she realizes her mistake, I'll be long gone."

"Just make sure you let me know what you find out." Dwight glanced at his wristwatch. "I want to have another little talk with Scott Hale, and then I think I'll drop by the Arrow and talk to Ben about gettin' his baby brother out of stir." He punched Max on the shoulder. "We'll talk first thing tomorrow."

They parted, Max heading for the Cherokee and Dwight for the squad car. They drove away in opposite directions.

IT HAD SEEMED like a good idea at the time. Now, cramped and stifling beneath a wool blanket on the back floor of the Cherokee, Julie had to wonder.

Where was Cosmo going, anyway? She'd known he was up to something the minute he claimed to see the Outlaw Grandpa drive past; didn't he think she knew the difference between a Ford truck and a Chevy? But she'd played along, having realized the hard way that Cosmo's hunches could sometimes be valuable.

He'd had phenomenal luck in locating stolen horses. If he got lucky again, she was going to be there to see it—and report it. So she'd slipped into his vehicle and made herself as comfortable as she could and waited. And waited...

Now, what seemed like hours later, she had to wonder where in Cupid County there could be roads this bad. At last the Cherokee halted—so abruptly that at first, she thought he'd run into a tree. She could hear him moving around in the front seat, hear the jingle of keys, finally the opening of the car door. The vehicle shifted with his weight as he crawled out.

The door slammed with a solid thunk. Julie lay there, unconsciously holding her breath. After a few moments, she slipped from beneath the wool blanket and cautiously raised her head to see where she was.

Her mouth fell open. The Cherokee was parked in the middle of nowhere, in a small clearing surrounded by firs and pines. Behind lay a sort of track; ahead lay no road, no track, nothing.

Except Cosmo, just disappearing into the trees. With a little gasp of alarm, Julie struggled to her feet and grappled for the door. One thing she didn't want was to be left here all alone.

She crawled out of the car into an autumn nip that made her shiver. She turned up the corduroy collar of her bright red barn coat and casting an anxious glance at clouds scudding across an innocent blue sky, hurried after Cosmo.

AN ERECT FIGURE on horseback paused at the edge of the trees to watch. Ethan Turner, too, glanced at the sky, then at Julie Cameron hurrying to catch up with Cosmo Mackenzie.

What were they doing on Lazy T land, anyway? If they expected to nab that no-account Johnny King at the old line shack, they were in for a big surprise.

Not that Ethan had time to worry about them now, what with Beau running wild. That boy was on the verge of serious trouble, and he had to be his grandpa's number-one priority.

The girl disappeared into scrub oak, scraggly at this time of year. For another minute or two, Ethan waited. Heck, he thought finally, they'll probably get out before the weather turns. Jabbing his boot heels into the shaggy sides of his horse, he rode on.

"COSMO! WAIT UP!"

He couldn't believe it; he damn well couldn't believe it. Slowly he turned to watch Julie Cameron hurrying toward him through the underbrush beneath the tall pines.

How stupid could he get, letting her hitch a ride in the back seat? If she'd been an L.A. gang member, he could be dead.

Shoving his hands deep into the pockets of his double-knit trousers, he waited with his chin sunk deep into the collar of his jacket, feeling thoroughly depressed.

Still a good ten or twelve feet away, she uttered a self-righteous "Aha!"

"Aha, what?" he asked.

"Aha, so you thought you could get away from me, did you?"

"I was hoping." He ignored her and continued down the faint trail.

She fell in behind him. "Where are we?"

"China."

"Very funny. I mean, really."

"On the Lazy T. I'm going back to the spot where John and I saw what we took to be a rustlers' camp."

"A rustlers' camp!" She grabbed his arm and dragged him around to face her. Her eyes glowed more amber than brown. "Why didn't you tell me?"

"So you could tell the world? No, thanks." He blinked; was that a snowflake settling onto her cheek? Glancing up, he saw a few more flakes floating down.

"Cosmo, that's what newspapers do—tell the world. We *work* for a newspaper, so that's our job. Oh, I can't believe you didn't tell—" She stopped suddenly, her gaze, too, lifting toward the sky.

A snowflake landed on her full pink lower lip. Her tongue darted out to lick it away and she frowned. "It's snowing."

"Is that what this white stuff is?" Slipping his arm from her grasp, he continued on down the trail.

"The temperature is dropping," she called after him.

"No, it isn't. It's just getting colder."

"You're in fine form today. Am I to assume you're not happy to see me?"

"You mean now or ever?"

"Now, naturally."

"Then you assume right. I'm not happy to see you." He walked faster.

"That still doesn't give you the right to run off and leave me," she complained.

He could hear her heavy breathing behind him as she struggled to keep up with his deliberately fast pace. "You could wait in the car."

"I'm...not sure I could find...the car." Her words ended on a wail of alarm. "Cosmo, I think we're walking into a blizzard! Stop for a minute so we can get our bearings straight."

"My bearings are straight." He walked faster, although now he had to lower his head against the snow whipping into his eyes. His ears felt cold enough to snap off.

"M-maybe we should go back to the car while there's still time," she pleaded. "Wait! I can't see you!"

He turned just as she plummeted forward, smacking into him hard. He caught her in his arms and she clung to him, shaking.

"Cosmo, I think we're in serious trouble here."

"No, we're not. It's early October. How much snow can we get in October?"

"In the Rocky Mountains? How does forty inches sound?" Her teeth chattered, perhaps from cold or perhaps from fear. "Do we have much farther to go?"

"No." He hoped it was true. "But we're not headed for a house or anything, just an old horse trailer and—" And then he remembered; John had waved a hand and said there was an old line shack nearby. "Uh, what's a line shack?"

"A l-line shack? It's where c-cowboys used to bunk when they were riding fence lines. A line shack means shelter. What are w-we waiting for?"

"Nothing, I guess." Snow swirled around her face and he brushed it away. Then he gave in and drew her against his side, his arm going around her protectively. Together they walked into the swirling snowstorm.

THE HORSE TRAILER was there all right. With a bare hand, Cosmo flicked aside the snow while Julie read the license plate.

"Oh, my God," she said, feeling faint. "It's the same one we saw on the road the other day."

"Let's look inside." He pawed at the tall door in back, trying to get it open with hands that looked numb and clumsy with cold.

"Can't we find the line shack first?" she asked plaintively. "I'm freezing, Cosmo. Neither of us is dressed for this kind of weather."

For a moment she thought he'd ignore her plea, but then he smiled. In the fading light of day, he looked so completely different that she gaped at him. He looked . . . wonderful, in fact. Handsome and strong and—

"Sure," he said. "I'm sorry. I'll get you safe inside and then take a look around out here."

"And then?" She hated to ask.

He seemed surprised. "And then we'll walk back to the Cherokee and go home. Look, it's letting up already." He held out a bare hand as if testing for rain. Snow piled up on it so quickly he had to brush it away before he could take her arm.

Together they hurried through the blinding snow. Julie's head was down; curiously enough, she trusted him to know where they were going. Which was probably stupid, she berated herself, since every year people got caught by weather in these mountains and occasionally killed by weather in these mountains. And here she was, putting her life in the hands of a nerd from California. She should have her head examined.

"There it is!"

At his shout, she lifted her head and saw the most beautiful sight in the world: shelter from the storm. They hurried forward together, Julie still nestled against his side beneath his protective arm.

"JEEZ," COSMO SAID, looking around. "This really is a shack."

Julie laughed, feeling almost weak with relief. "Which must give you a clue how it got its name." In the faint light coming from the door, she saw a lamp on a nearby table, a packet of matches nearby. With hands still trembling from cold and fear, she managed to strike a flame and touch it to the wick.

The sudden brightness made her blink, that and the black smoke rising from the chimney. Coughing, she adjusted the wick and replaced the glass globe. "Someone's been here," she said, "and recently."

Cosmo was looking around with an odd expression on his face. He took off his glasses and dried the lenses with his shirttail. "I wonder..."

And then it struck Julie, too: wood stacked haphazardly beside the fireplace, empty cans and packages littering the floor, empty booze bottles. "My gosh," she whispered, her wide-eyed gaze settling on Cosmo's face. "Johnny King's been hiding out here, I'd stake my life on it."

"You just could be right."

"What if he comes back? He might have a gun, and we'd have no way to defend ourselves. What if—"

"Calm down, Julie. He's not going to come back in the middle of a blizzard." Max crossed to the fireplace, beside which was a stack of wood, then knelt and thrust a hand into the charred remains of previous fires. "Cold as a well digger's— Cold," he announced. "Do you know how to get a fire going?"

"Sure." She smiled at his ignorance. Although still trembling in the chilly room, she was no longer frightened. At least they'd found shelter. And as far as Johnny King went, she wasn't really afraid of him. She'd known him all her life, for heaven's sake.

"Good." Cosmo gave her a grin that was almost...devilish. "While you light a fire, I'll take a look at the rustlers' camp before it's covered with snow."

"Covered with snow! You said it was about to let up."

"And you believed me?" He shook his head pityingly and slipped back out the door.

By the time he returned, Julie had a fire roaring in the fireplace, a pot of coffee bubbling off to one side. She'd also opened a box of crackers and found a can of squirt-cheese. Along with a couple of cans of beans, she figured they wouldn't starve to death.

Cosmo entered with a blast of cold and snow. Slamming the door, he stomped across the uneven wooden floor, slapping his hands together to restore circulation. He shook his head like a wet dog, flinging snow and water around the room.

Including in Julie's face, for she'd stepped forward to offer assistance. "Here," she sputtered, brushing away dampness on her cheeks before reaching for his coat. "Let me help you."

"Thanks."

His lips looked blue, but he managed to smile. Once the coat was off, he jumped up and down and flapped his arms to get the blood moving again. At last his gyrations brought him around, and his gaze settled on Julie.

His eyes opened wide. "What're you wearing?"

"Somebody's old flannel shirt." She looked down at herself, at the length of leg exposed beneath the curved hem that reached midthigh. Her feet were bare. Beneath his intent perusal, she curled her toes into the floor.

"I was wet," she protested, as if he'd offered a criticism. She indicated her clothing spread neatly over the woodpile. "Once I got the fire going, the snow started melting and..." She frowned. "You're wet, too."

He looked down at himself. "There was so much snow blowing that I stepped in some kind of puddle before I even knew it was there."

Looking at him, she saw it was true. His ugly double-knit trousers were wet to the knee, at which point a gaping three-cornered tear exposed the skin beneath.

"It also appears you ran into some barbed wire," she said.

He looked impressed. "How'd you guess?"

"I didn't guess, I knew. Come on, Cos, you'll have to get out of those wet things before you catch your death."

He shifted his feet uncomfortably. "I don't think so."

"You're being silly," she said matter-of-factly. "We're adults." She gestured. "There are some odds and ends in that cardboard box, and you can help yourself. Once our stuff is dry, we can change and head back for the—"

The expression on his face stopped her cold. "What is it?" she asked.

"We won't be going anyplace for a while, Julie. I'm sorry." He stared down at the floor, but his gaze seemed to slide inevitably toward her bare toes.

"What do you mean, you're sorry?" Striding to the door, she hauled it open. Snow and wind met her charge, hurling her back into the room and flinging the door against the wall.

Cosmo moved quickly and slammed the door closed again. "That's what I mean, I'm sorry," he said. "Looks like we're stuck here." He raised his brows. "It is kind of pretty, though, isn't it?"

She clenched her hands into impotent fists. "This is awful! I'm marooned in a blizzard in the middle of the Rocky Mountains in a shack with a guy who thinks snow is *pretty*. I'm doomed!"

"In that case," Cosmo said, "I think I *will* get into something a little more comfortable. If we're doomed, I refuse to go in wet underwear."

"And I refuse to go—" Julie clamped her lips together, horrified at what she'd been on the verge of revealing: that she refused to go a virgin.

For that was her darkest secret. Julie Cameron, the butterfly of Cupid, Colorado, the belle of every ball, engaged to be married several times, had never slept with a man.

She'd always justified this quite simply: she was saving herself for the man she married. Now she wondered if that man would ever come along—and if he did, whether she'd be alive to enjoy it.

This was the second time in the past couple of days that she'd found herself in danger. The first had been on that narrow twisting mountain road, hurtling along the abyss in a car driven by the very same individual who'd led her to this snow-marooned shack in the middle of nowhere.

He might not know it, but people died in blizzards all the time. They got lost and froze to death or starved to death, or fell off a mountain or some other damn thing. Julie was too savvy to fall off a mountain, but what about her companion, the erstwhile Cosmo Mackenzie of sunny Southern California? He was apt to do just about anything.

If he did, Julie realized gloomily, she was apt to do it with him. Up to and including...

She turned quickly. He stood in the corner of the little room, his back to her while he fumbled with the ugly double-knit trousers.

His *bare* back, his broad shoulders, his smooth skin ridged with muscle that rippled beneath the flickering lamplight.

Julie's eyes widened in disbelief, then closed tightly. How fast could you get cabin fever? she wondered. That, or something, seemed to be afflicting her mind already, for Cosmo no longer looked like the hapless nerd she knew him to be.

Which reminded her of the old cartoon about two shipwrecked sailors floating around on a raft; after a while, when they looked at each other they no longer saw what was really there. They saw big barbecued steaks and juicy hamburgers and...

Mouth dry, she turned away, knowing she'd just made up her mind. Julie Cameron did not intend to die of starvation when there was a big juicy hamburger within reach.

But maybe before she crossed the Rubicon, she'd take one last look at that weather.

THEY SAT BEFORE THE FIRE and drank their coffee in a silence that sizzled. Julie cocked her head and looked at Cosmo, who had struggled into the only clothing he could find: ragged jeans a delectable size too small and a faded plaid shirt with long sleeves that didn't quite reach his wrists. His hair, wet with melted snow, had dried to black silk. On a sudden impulse, she reached out and snatched his eyeglasses off his nose.

"Hey!"

He lunged for the glasses, looking alarmed, but she held them out of reach. "You don't need them at the moment," she said. "There's nothing to read. I just want to see how you look without them."

"You've got no right to take a guy's glasses," he grumbled, squinting at her. But after a moment, he settled down again, turning slightly away to peer into the fire with a brooding expression.

While she peered at him as if he was a total stranger. How could a man hide so many natural assets under hair pomade and eyeglasses and double knit and un-fashionably styled hair? How could a woman fail to see past all that to the man beneath: a strong and hand-some face, a body that was—her thoughts turned again to hamburgers—yummy.

Yet this was still undeniably Cosmo, the same man she'd scorned week after week. Which led her to an in-evitable conclusion: Cosmo hadn't changed; *she* had.

She saw him now in a whole new light and was ashamed of how shallow she'd been before.

A gentle sigh escaped her lips. Who'd believe it? Julie Cameron was—she fought the phrase that sprang to mind—*in love*. She was in love with this...man. She'd never let herself call him a nerd again, even in her thoughts. What he was, was inappropriate, although not nearly as inappropriate as her growing feelings for him.

At twenty-six, she'd been in and out of love with alarming regularity, but this time was different. For one thing, she was willing to admit to herself that, before, she *might* have been attracted, at least initially, to good looks or a healthy bank account or a promise to take her away from Cupid, Colorado, to more cosmopolitan surrounds.

None of that applied to Cosmo. He wasn't handsome, except when seen through the eyes of love; he wasn't rich and, in fact, had just given up California, the apogee of Julie's dreams. Yet to her dazzled eyes, at this moment he was, if not a knight in shining armor, at least capable of making her remember advice she'd once given Maggie during a particularly unsettled point in her sister's life: *Life is uncertain. Eat dessert first.*

Now Julie was psyching herself up to take her own advice, despite years of "saving herself" for the man she loved enough to marry. Obviously that man was an insurance-salesman-turned-newspaper-reporter, because at the moment, she wasn't planning to save a damned thing.

Now all she had to do was figure out some subtle way to get that message across to Cosmo.

THEY SAT BEFORE THE FIRE and drank their coffee in a silence that sizzled.

Looking at her in profile, Max was struck again by the elegance of arched brows and high cheekbones, tender lips and graceful throat.

And the rest of her wasn't too bad, either, judging by what the faded old shirt revealed. He had a gut feeling she didn't have anything on beneath it. Putting down his cup, he slid his hands under his thighs to keep from grabbing her.

Julie Cameron was a babe, a fact he'd acknowledged from the start. But over the weeks they'd worked together, he'd gotten to know and appreciate her particular brand of allure in a way he'd ever done with a woman before.

For one thing, Julie had bought into his nerd persona hook, line and sinker. She didn't trust him and made no bones about considering him an incompetent lout.

Okay, an incompetent lout who knew how to kiss. His mouth tilted in a wry smile when he thought about it. She'd been putty in his hands—until he'd decided to back off.

He sucked in a deep breath, resolving to do the right thing now—or more importantly, not do the wrong thing. Gene had warned him that Julie wasn't the kind of woman you played around with. She deserved better. She might not be the sweet young thing he frequently found himself thinking she was, but he sensed a vulnerability in her that scared him. All those broken engagements aside, Julie Cameron wasn't the tough cookie she herself seemed to believe.

She sighed and stretched, never taking her gaze from the flames leaping in the fireplace. He'd never seen her like this before, as tense and tightly strung as a cat. She must really be upset to be stranded in this ramshackle cabin with him. Of course, he hadn't invited her to stow away in the back seat of his car, but...

She whipped her head around, and her gaze locked with his. *Here it comes,* he thought. *This is where she gives me hell.* He braced himself to take it like a man.

"Cosmo," she said in a voice like black velvet, "I've been trying to think of a subtle way to say this but—" she swallowed hard "—to hell with subtlety. Let's make love."

And she lunged for him, her arms surrounding him and her momentum carrying them both over sideways.

CHAPTER THIRTEEN

MAX WRAPPED his arms around Julie's lush body and rolled onto his back. Her sudden and unexpected assault had knocked the breath out of him. Before he could regain it, she began showering kisses on his face, his neck, any part of him she could reach.

"Dammit, Julie!" He tried to hold her off, turning his head aside and clamping his hands around her waist.

Which was a terrible mistake, he realized when one hand touched not the fabric of her shirt but bare skin. He groaned; louder when one of her knees slid between his thighs and pressed up against an already raging erection.

Then she found his mouth with hers, pressed her breasts into his chest and wiggled against him, on top of him, around him. Not being made of steel, he found himself sliding one hand up beneath her shirt, the other down to squeeze her naked bottom.

He heard her gasp and then she was lifting her hips, opening her thighs to him, urging him to take what she so freely offered. He thrust inside her with his tongue, his fingers. She moaned, writhing above him, driving him wild with the pressures of her body upon his. Surprised by the intensity of his response, he was still un-prepared when she managed to release the snap of his jeans. His penis, unencumbered by underwear, sprang free.

She closed a hand around it, skimming the length of his erection as if measuring it, then muttering against his mouth an impressed, "Oh, my goodness!"

He was so excited he could barely think. He grabbed her bottom with both hands, lifting her, bringing her forward. "Goodness...has nothing..."

Pressing her onto her back, he crouched above her, the tip of his penis touching the moist cleft between her thighs. She caught her breath, then finished his thought for him. "...to do with it."

He lowered himself slowly, prolonging the agonizing torment of suspense. Covering her hands with his, he pulled her arms wide. For a moment his weight rested on his knees while he looked into her eyes with a silent question: *Are you sure?*

Her lips curved into a smile at once triumphant and...secretive?

Before he could wonder at that, she slid her knees wider apart and pulled him down, at the same time lifting her hips to meet him. He sank into her easily and naturally, until—

Too late he knew. Son of a bitch, she was a virgin! But before he could feel more than that flash of outrage, she began to move against him and his body took over....

THE FIRST TREMOR caught her by surprise; the second lifted her, sent her head back on the arching column of her neck. Sensual heat began where their bodies joined, expanded and spread through her, hot and slow and delicious. She gave herself up to it entirely, and to the man who'd introduced her to this heart-stopping pleasure.

The man whose body beneath hers suddenly tensed, then exploded in its own series of fierce shuddering movements. Julie, completely sated, fell onto his chest, absorbing the little shocks still shaking him. After a moment he, too, stilled, except for the deep rise and fall of his chest as he breathed.

After waiting so long, the reality of what had just happened stunned her. It had been so right. On other occasions, she'd come close to succumbing but had always pulled back, although she'd never been quite sure why. Now she knew why; she'd been waiting for the right man, just as she always told herself in her romantic dreams. At the moment she didn't have a shred of doubt that she'd found him.

The room was warm, and Cosmo held her gently but firmly. Her eyelids fluttered down, her breathing steadied. Just as she was beginning to drift off, he spoke in a tone resonating with shock.

"You were a virgin!"

Her eyes popped open and uncensored words popped from her mouth. "Nuts. I hoped you wouldn't notice."

"What kind of an idiot wouldn't— Don't answer that." He rolled her over beside him and sat up, shoving his hair back with both hands, then zipped his jeans. There wasn't much he could do about his shirt, which hung open with all its buttons missing. "God, Julie," he said with a helpless groan, "what have I done?"

"Nothing I didn't want you to do." She, too, sat up, straightening her shirt and pulling it down around her hips. "Cosmo, don't you understand?"

He looked wild-eyed. "Understand what?"

Smiling, she stroked his cheek. "That I love you."

"You love..." He grabbed her wrist and pulled her hand away from his face, then released her to fumble his glasses out of his shirt pocket and prop them on his nose.

As if that would protect him. She almost laughed.

He cleared his throat. "You don't love me," he said in a raw voice. "You couldn't. I—I'm not your type."

She nodded. "Strange bedfellows, as they say. I guess I'm not your type, either, but here we are."

He licked his lips, apparently at a loss. "Love." He shuddered. "I was married before, Julie. It didn't... work out."

She felt a little stab of shock that he'd committed so completely to some other woman. "Wh-what happened?"

He shrugged. "She said I put my work first."

Insurance? It didn't seem possible. She smiled. "Was it true?"

"Yes." He looked surprised, as if he'd only just now acceded to his ex-wife's point of view. "So you see, you can't possibly love me. I'm . . . not worthy."

"Probably not, but there's no other explanation for the way I feel."

"Yeah. Yeah, there is." His gaze went directly to her cleavage, generously revealed by the shirt unbuttoned to her waist.

"Not for me," she said with perfect confidence. "It's not that I think my virginity is the greatest gift in the universe or anything, but it was too important to give to the first joker who wanted it. Don't you see, Cosmo? I gave it to you and I'm not even sorry! In my book that's love."

He closed his eyes and groaned. "In my book it's insanity. And I didn't even . . . use anything."

"You mean like a condom?"

"Yeah, like a condom. I'm really sorry, Julie. You . . . caught me by surprise."

"I forgive you."

"You *like* living dangerously?"

She laughed. "No." She pressed one palm flat against his chest, relishing the feel of his skin. "But it was my fault as much as yours. I should've known this would happen sooner or later."

"How could you know? I didn't. I'd made up my mind to keep my hands to myself . . ."

His voice sounded strangled, but his movements were quick and efficient as he slid her shirt off her shoulders and pulled it down her arms. She gasped, looking down quickly at her naked breasts, then back up at him.

He tossed the shirt aside, leaving her kneeling naked before him.

He grinned. He groaned again. "Despite popular opinion, I don't do stupid dangerous things as a rule," he said, tearing off his own shirt, "but your logic overwhelms me."

"Oh?" She licked her lips and waited, eager to see the scratchy denim fall.

He stood up and kicked out of his borrowed jeans, revealing strong well-formed legs. "I may hate myself in the morning," he muttered, "but what the hell. You only live once." He reached for her.

MAX WAS IN SHOCK. Trying to figure it all out, he lay awake long after Julie had fallen asleep in his arms. Which was one of the reasons he was having so damned much trouble putting this into perspective. Every time he looked at her, he forgot what he'd been thinking about in a burst of...what was it? Sympathy? The poor kid was worn out. They'd made love every way but standing up, and when she challenged him on that, they'd tried it and damned if it hadn't worked.

But now in the wee hours of the morning, they lay tangled together in exhaustion on a narrow bed with the fire burning low and a blizzard howling outside. While she slept as blissfully as a baby, Max was sweating bullets.

He'd never slept with anyone except his wife, Tina, and look how that had worked out. It had taken him a helluva long time to learn how to *sleep* with her.

Not to be confused with *going to bed* with a woman, or *having sex* with a woman; those things he'd done, both before and after his marriage. But with the single exception of Tina, he'd never spent the entire night or allowed anyone to spend the night with him. It wasn't his style. It smacked of commitment, and the c-word had been excised from his vocabulary. Tina had made him forget for a while, but then she'd left, and it had nearly killed him.

If any woman could make him forget the bitter lessons he'd learned from his marriage, it was Julie. She was like quicksilver, bright and beautiful and honest. She said exactly what she meant and refused to let anything or anybody sway her. Would she be that loyal in love?

She shifted in his arms, murmuring words he couldn't understand. Her lips settled, soft and warm, against the side of his neck. Damn, she felt good, her body flowing smoothly against his as if it belonged there.

But how could it? She didn't even know who he was. When she found out, there'd be hell to pay, and Max knew who'd get the bill. Nevertheless, he had to tell her. Tomorrow...

He slept, but not peacefully.

"HELLO-O-O, THE HOUSE!"

Max sat bolt upright in bed, trying to focus his foggy

brain. "What the hell?"

Julie rolled into the impression left by his body and moaned. "What is it? Don't leave me." She wiggled her fingers and smiled a drowsy smile. "Lay back down and let's talk about it."

"I know you're in there!"

Now it was her turn to sit up, which she did, clutching the blanket across her breasts and beneath both arms. "Oh, my God! Who *is* that?" Her horrified eyes sought reassurance from him.

"Sounds like Ethan." Max leapt out of bed and made a dive for his own clothing, still spread out atop the woodpile where he'd hung everything to dry. The fire had burned to embers; he'd have to throw on more wood before it went out entirely.

Stepping into his trousers, he glanced at Julie. "You might want to put something on."

"Oh, Lord! It looks like we're saved whether we want to be or not."

She came out of the bed, a creamy flash of breast and thigh and belly that made his mouth water and his knees weak. Damn that Ethan Turner.

Max dragged his shirt on over his head and shoved his hair back with both hands, looking around for his glasses. He spotted them on the table and grabbed them. "You ready?"

She paused in the act of pushing her shirttail into her jeans. "No. No, I'm not." She bit her lip. "There are things I wanted to say..."

"They'll have to wait." Thank God, because he wasn't sure he was up to hearing them.

"All right." She looked disappointed but blew him a kiss.

He felt like a heel but reached out with one hand to catch the kiss, anyway.

"SORRY TO DISTURB you folks." Ethan stared down at the floor, at the hat in his hand, anywhere but at Cosmo or Julie or the rumpled bed. "I saw your car yesterday but didn't see no need to disturb you until..." He chewed on his lip beneath the snowy mustache.

"Something's happened." Cosmo indicated one of the two chairs in the room. "Sit down, Ethan. We'll get you a cup of hot coffee and you can tell us."

"I'll set, but there's no time for coffee." He crossed to the table, scattering snow from coat and boots. He sat down, started to say more, stopped, tried again and stopped. "Damn," he said softly. "Pardon my French, ma'am, but it sticks in my craw, turnin' traitor to my own kin."

Julie stopped short in the act of dipping coffee into the fire-blackened pot. Her heart sank. Whatever was coming was bound to be bad.

Cosmo, sitting facing the old man, leaned forward. "Johnny was hiding out here," he suggested gently.

Ethan nodded. "Yeah, he was. I didn't find that out until yesterday, though. When I asked Beau about it, he denied it at first, then got real hot under the collar and went roarin' out. By the time I got here, him and Johnny was long gone. It took me all night, but I finally figured out what they're up to."

Cosmo's gaze met the old man's and held. "And that is?"

"They're gonna bust Scott Hale outta the hospital whether he wants to go or not. My guess is, he don't. I'm afraid the mood they're in, somebody could get hurt." Ethan sighed and turned his head away, but not in time to conceal the tears rolling down his leathery cheeks. "I seen the handwriting on the wall, Cosmo. I reckon you always knew I would."

"I hoped, Ethan."

Julie looked at Cosmo, surprised by the depth of caring in his voice. He really liked the old guy, she realized. Liked him and believed him.

And so did she. Despite all her reasons to be suspicious, she could no longer doubt. Max had been right about Ethan all along, while she'd been blinded by her own bias.

She went to him now, kneeling beside his chair so he'd be forced to look at her. "Mr. Turner..." She bit her lip. "I think I owe you an apology."

"Don't do that," he said, his expression pained. "I done you dirt once, and I'm right ashamed of it. Don't get your knees all dirty for me."

"Don't worry about my knees." She smiled and patted one old veined hand. "I thought you were guilty, but I see now I was still mad about...you know.

I'll do everything in my power to make it up to you, including printing it in the newspaper."

He shook his head, looking very tired and very old. "No need for that. I'm the one owes the apology, not you. My only excuse is, I was scared and—"

"Please, you don't have to say anything else. Just tell me how I can make this up to you."

"Just help me keep Beau from gettin' hurt. That's all I want."

Hot tears burned the back of Julie's throat. "If I can," she promised. "I owe you that, at least."

ETHAN HAD RIDDEN IN leading two saddled horses, so it was a simple matter for the three of them to ride out again. Simple for everybody, that is, except Cosmo. When he said he'd never been on a horse in his life, Julie hadn't believed him.

Watching his struggle to climb on, she did.

They rode out through sunshine so brilliant its reflection off the spun-sugar world was nearly blinding. Chilly at first, Cosmo and Julie soon warmed up as the temperature rose and snow began to melt. The ground turned mushy beneath their horses' hooves. The biggest hazard wasn't the cold, it was snow mounded on tree limbs. Suddenly shaken loose by their passage, great wet clumps showered down on the unwary time and again.

Finally they arrived at the Cherokee, which was barely visible beneath the snow. Swinging off her horse,

Julie checked a moan. How could she, an experienced rider, be so stiff and sore after riding only a few...

A wave of heat swept into her cheeks. She wasn't stiff and sore from the ride, at least not *that* ride. Last night was the reason she could barely move. She'd used muscles she hadn't even realized she had.

Cosmo dismounted with an appealing clumsiness, handing the reins to Ethan. "I'll see you later in town," he promised. "And don't worry. I'll make sure nothing happens to Beau."

"*We'll* make sure," Julie chimed in with a warning glance at Cosmo. If he thought he was going to dump her now, he had another think coming.

HE KNEW SHE WANTED to talk, but he also knew he couldn't, not under these circumstances. What he had to say was too important to simply blurt out. So he kept her so scared with his driving she couldn't open her mouth except to shriek or utter little moans of terror.

First he needed to get to Cupid and foil the snatch from Doc Kunkle's hospital. Then he'd figure a way to let Julie Cameron down gently.

For that was what he'd have to do. She might be bright and beautiful and sexy as all hell, but he'd been that route before.

They entered Cupid from the sweeping curve on the northern edge.

"We'll go straight to the hospital," Max said, glancing at her where she clung to the armrest like a lifeline. "If everything's all right there, we'll head for the marshal's— *What in hell?*"

He stepped on the brake, and the Cherokee fishtailed on slushy blacktop, coming to a rest against a wooden barricade across the road. Looking past it, he saw the Rusty Spur, its parking lot empty except for three police cars at the curb.

He threw open his door and jumped out. Julie did the same.

"Stay here," he ordered curtly. "I don't know what's going on, but it could be dangerous."

She came around the car and walked straight into his arms. Before he could stop himself, he was kissing her and she was kissing him, and he knew that everything she'd said last night she meant. She leaned back in his embrace to look up at him.

"How sweet of you to care," she teased. "Thanks, but don't start thinking you can boss me around."

"Julie, I don't want—"

—to stand here talking like a fool while she darted around the barrier and sprinted into the trees overhanging the road. Swearing, he took off after her. Whatever was going on in front of the café, he didn't intend to let her walk into the middle of it.

Not if he could help it, anyway.

JULIE AND COSMO hunched behind the cop car with Dwight Deakins, trying to catch their breath. She still had no idea what was happening, but from the look of things, it wasn't good.

More cops hovered behind other cars, some with guns drawn. Across the street she saw several other men trying to keep back a crowd gathering near the drive-in restaurant and gasoline station on one corner, the real-estate office on the other.

· Dwight ignored Cosmo to glare at her. "Just what in hell do you think you're doin'?" he berated her. "You could get killed, girl."

"By who?" She started to raise her head enough to look around, and he yanked her down.

Cosmo settled back on his haunches, forearms resting on his thighs. "Spill it, Dwight. What's going on?"

"Hostage situation," the marshal said grimly, patting the firearm on his hip. "Johnny King and Beau Turner are holdin' a half dozen or so folks in the Rusty Spur. Nobody's been hurt at this point, but you never know what those two crazy bastards might decide to do next."

"Well, hell," Cosmo said in total disgust. "How'd it come down?"

"They tried to spring Scott Hale out of the hospital, and he didn't want to go. He started hollerin' and carryin' on, which brought Rose Kunkle on the run. King knocked her down—"

"She's not hurt!" Julie interrupted, horrified.

"No, fortunately." Dwight shook his head. "But she screamed so loud Johnny and Beau thought she was. They dropped Scott on his head and lit out of there. Rose called my office and the dispatcher called me. I was drivin' in from the north—" he indicated the road with its barricade and the Cherokee on the other side "—and wouldn't you know it, them two maniacs came roarin' up the street headin' right at me. Well, I changed their minds about that real fast, threw a coupla slugs at their tires. Nothin' any sane man could do but get out and surrender."

"Only," Cosmo guessed, "they're not sane. They ran into the Spur and hollered stick 'em up."

Dwight looked pained. "Somethin' like that."

Cosmo appeared to be on the verge of an explosion. Cosmo, in fact, hardly looked like Cosmo at all. Taking off his glasses, he shoved them into his pocket with a muttered oath, his expression savage.

Without warning, he turned to Julie. "I want you out of here," he said in clipped tones. "This is no place for a woman."

She glared at him; he could at least have said, *no place for the woman I love.* "You can't boss me around, Cosmo Mackenzie."

"The hell I can't."

Their gazes met and locked, and she felt her defiance wilting but was too stubborn to give in.

"Wait a minute."

Dwight's puzzled exclamation gave her an excuse to look at him and away from Cosmo. "What?"

"What's with you two?" Dwight waggled his forefinger between them. "Last night when Ben came to get Jason—"

Julie felt a rush of relief. "Jason's out of jail?"

Dwight nodded. "On bail. Anyway, Ben asked if I'd seen you, Julie, said something about you not comin' home from work, and it was almost ten o'clock by then. So where the hell was you?"

"Why, I was..." She looked desperately at Cosmo, seeking help.

He looked over her head, focused on some middle distance. There'd be no help from that quarter.

Dwight added suddenly, "And wearin' the same clothes you had on yesterday, except now they look like you slept in 'em. Julie Cameron, what have you been up to?"

"None of your business!" She took a couple of duck steps, then rose into a crouch behind the patrol car. "Okay, I'm going! Are you both satisfied?"

Cheeks fiery, she bent over and ran behind the cop cars toward the line of trees. She didn't blame Dwight, not at all. She blamed Cosmo. Just because they'd slept together didn't mean he owned her.

Apparently it didn't even mean he *wanted* to own her.

ONCE SHE'D GONE, Max gave in and uttered every four-letter word he knew, some of the more descriptive ones twice.

Dwight waited until he'd finished before announcing, "That was some plain and fancy cussin', but damned if I know what set you off."

Max jerked his head toward the café. "That's my fault," he said grimly.

"How you figure?"

"I've been playing around with these guys, treating them like harmless hayseeds. Talk about piss-poor judgment." He clenched his hands into fists. "If anybody gets hurt..."

"Nobody's gonna get hurt," Dwight said. He clapped the other man on the shoulder. "Hell, I'm glad to have you here. I need all the brain power I can scare up." He looked a little uncomfortable. "But first I think I gotta tell you..."

Max's antennae went up, his full attention on Dwight.

Whose mouth curved down in displeasure. "The LAPD's lookin' for you. You been cleared, boy. They want you back ASAP. Hell, they're fixin' to pin a medal on you. There's already been a story to that effect in the Los Angeles papers, so I understand."

JULIE WORKED HER WAY through the trees and around toward the back of the café without any specific destination in mind. She simply wanted to get the lay of the land and see what was going on.

Not much back here. A police car was parked at the curb, an officer crouched behind it watching the Spur's back door. He didn't see her and she started to wave, then decided against it. Maybe, just maybe...

What were the chances that Beau or Johnny had thought to lock the back door?

Slim and none, she decided, since they weren't really pros at this lawbreaking business. They were nothing more than a couple of hell-raisers who'd gone a bit too far. At the moment they were probably as scared as their so-called hostages.

If she could talk to them, she'd bet dollars to doughnuts she could convince them to give up peacefully. What a relief that would be to old Ethan.

If wishes were horses... She gasped with sudden excitement. She really could; she *knew* she could! All she needed was a few minutes alone with them.

But a deputy stood between her and the back door, a deputy who was now turning in response to a shrill whistle from behind the real-estate building. She couldn't hear what was being said, but she read the pantomime easily enough: someone had brought the officer coffee.

Someone who didn't want to cross that open street to deliver it. The lawman gestured impatiently, but the other man just shook his head, held out the thermos and refused to budge from the shelter of the building.

At first it didn't look as if the deputy would budge, either. Julie sent a telepathic message: *Please, please, please. Go get your damned coffee!*

At last he did. When he started moving, so did she, slipping like a shadow through the trees to the point closest to the building. Then, drawing a deep breath, she crouched and ran for the door.

Her fingers touched the knob and she twisted, expecting at any instant to hear a shout announce her discovery. But no shout came, no sounds of feet running to intercept her. Instead, the door banged open and she fell inside, kicking it quickly closed behind her.

For a moment she lay on the linoleum in the hallway, trying to catch her breath. Pushing up to her elbows, she congratulated herself on a job well—

"Well, well, well," a gravelly voice intoned. "Look what we got here. If it's not little Julie Cameron, the sweetheart of Cupid High."

She didn't have to look any further to know she'd got her wish. The muddy boots moving into her field of vision belonged to one Johnny King: rustler, back shooter and hostage taker.

Once her gaze reached his scowling face, she wondered if maybe she should have been a little more careful what she wished for.

CHAPTER FOURTEEN

JOHNNY GRABBED Julie by the scruff of the neck and dragged her down the hallway into the restaurant proper. Off-balance and struggling against his harsh grip, she finally managed to throw off his hand and stumble away.

"Damn you, Johnny King!" She straightened, rubbing her bruised neck beneath her hair. "Where do you get off manhandling me that way?" Without waiting for an answer, she looked around and gasped at what she saw.

Beau Turner held a shotgun on Nancy Wyatt, Avis Vaughn and a half-dozen others, who huddled around tables next to the huge glass windows in front. Although the blinds were drawn, Dwight and the other lawmen doubtless knew that the hostages were being used as human shields—at least Julie hoped they knew. From where Beau stood in a corner between two windows, he could peek out front from time to time without being seen.

Nancy, who'd positioned herself between the gunmen and her customers, looked exceedingly unhappy. "What are you doing here, Julie?" she wailed.

Johnny waved his pistol at the woman, but she didn't flinch. "Shut up and let me ask the questions," he blustered. "Julie, what the hell are you doin' bustin' in through the back door that way? You could've got shot!"

"Don't be so melodramatic." Julie looked at him with scorn. "You're no killer, Johnny King."

"Ha!" Johnny glared triumphantly at the huddled masses. "Ain't I been tellin' you? I'm no outlaw. I'm just a victim of circumstances. It's society that's all screwed up, not me."

Julie laughed; she couldn't help herself, even if it earned her a baleful glance from those fiery eyes. "That's not what I said," she corrected him. "You're no killer, but you *are* an outlaw, not to mention dumb as a post for thinking you could get away with a stunt like this. The jig's up, Johnny. Everybody knows you and Beau and Scott Hale are responsible for the rustling that's been going on around here. Why don't you just—"

Beau swung around, the muzzle of his shotgun wandering. Hostages ducked. "Everybody knows? Johnny, you said nobody would ever pin that on—"

"Shut up, you damn fool. She's guessin'. Nobody knows shit from apple butter."

"Johnny," Julie said gently, "we found your horse trailer. We found your hideout. We have a corroborating witness."

Beau looked confused. "A corob—a what?"

Johnny took a threatening step toward Julie, his eyes mean little slits. "She means your grandpa. If that old fool's been talkin'—"

"Calm down." Julie held up her hands in a gesture meant to placate. She'd known Johnny a long time and she'd seen him lose his temper before, but never had she seen him in such a rage. It gave her an idea. "I'm on your side," she announced.

"The hell you are."

"I am. Have I ever lied to you?"

He curled his lip. "I don't know. Did you mean it when you called me dumb?"

"With all my heart," she flung back. "Sometimes you *are* dumb, but maybe...maybe this time you're right. Maybe it's not entirely your fault."

"Yeah, well, that's what I said."

Johnny began to walk back and forth between Julie and the other captives, who watched him with the wary respect they'd accord a rattlesnake. Julie knew them all: in addition to Avis and Nancy, there were a couple of teenage girls who worked part-time as waitresses, two local merchants and a couple of housewives. She just hoped they kept their cool and stayed out of this.

Johnny stopped suddenly. "I hate this town!" he announced with feeling. "They've treated me like trash my whole life, all of 'em." He waved his pistol at the little group, and when they recoiled, he laughed. "Buncha damn cowards, ever last one." Again his narrowed-eyed gaze zeroed in on Julie. "'Cept you."

"That's because I know you, Johnny," she said, seeking to soothe him. "I understand you."

"Like hell. Nobody knows what I been through."

Which was just what she'd been waiting to hear. "You're right, and your story should be told. Tell *me* and I'll tell the world."

"Huh?" He blinked, looking confused.

"That's why I'm here—to see you get a fair deal," she rushed on earnestly. "I want to tell your side of the story, yours and Beau's. I can make you famous. You'll be, I don't know, the Robin Hoods of the new West."

Beau's expression brightened. "Hey, I like that."

"You dumb..." Johnny swung on his partner. "We never give anything away!"

"You think Robin Hood did?" Julie inserted quickly. "It was all public relations, trust me. And I'll do the same for you, just as soon as..." She flicked a meaningful glance at the hostages.

"No!" Johnny shook his head violently. "No way! I need my hostages. We're fixin' to trade 'em for a helicopter and a million dollars."

"To hell with the boss," Beau chimed in, nodding agreement.

"Screw the boss. We don't need him anymore. From here on out, *I'm* the boss."

It was all Julie could do to keep from making some caustic comment about the viability of Johnny's plan, but this was no time for smart remarks. If he'd just release the hostages... "Let them go and keep me," she urged.

Johnny stared at her. "That's just what I'd expect from a Cameron."

"Bravery?" she guessed.

"No. The gall to think one of you is worth eight of them."

Then she did laugh. "That's good, Johnny. But seriously, one hostage is as good as a bunch. It'll be a whole lot easier to keep an eye on just me, especially when you know I'm here because I want to be. I mean, you're smart enough to realize that with so many people, all they'd have to do is jump up and rush you and it'd be all over."

"Yeah, for them!" He glared at his hostages as if she'd planted new suspicions in his mind.

Julie saw an advantage and leapt for it. "How many could you get before they overran the two of you? Sure, you've got the drop on everyone now, but what happens when you get tired, or... or Beau has to go to the bathroom and you're here alone, or..."

And she talked on, soothingly and calmly. If she could just convince him she was on his side...

MAX AND DWIGHT watched Jason Cameron dash toward them in a crouch, slipping behind the police cars. The tall cowboy hunkered down beside them, breathing hard.

"How's the finger?" Max asked.

Jason grinned. "Son of a bitch hurts like hell."

"Good. Anybody who's that bad a shot deserves to have his trigger finger broken." Max turned away to peer over the hood of the vehicle. It'd been a good fifteen minutes since he'd detected any movement inside the café, and the inactivity was making him antsy.

Jason nudged Max's shoulder. "Hey, you wouldn't happen to know where Julie is?"

Max shrugged. "She was here a few minutes ago. You know where she went, Dwight?"

"Thataway." Dwight jerked a thumb toward the trees. "We told her this was no place for a woman."

Jason laughed. "She loves that kind of talk. Uh...either of you know where she was last night? She didn't come home, and Grandma's fit to be tied."

Dwight glanced at Max but said nothing.

Max kept his gaze glued to the front door of the café. "We . . . kinda got caught in the snowstorm."

"We? As in, you and Julie?"

"Yes, we as in— Jeez!" Max strained forward. "Somebody's coming out of the Spur. Let's hope none of your men gets trigger-happy, Dwight."

Nobody did, which was fortunate, because after a few tentative steps, the hostages surged forward in a bunch. Once they'd been corralled at a safe distance, Dwight called for calm—and an explanation.

Nancy Wyatt provided it. A normally composed woman, she had tears in her eyes when she said, "Julie got us out. We owe it all to her."

"Julie!" Max, who'd been standing to one side with Jason while keeping his ears open and his mouth shut, jerked as if he'd been slugged.

Nancy nodded. "She slipped in the back way, told Johnny she was on his side and never stopped talking. She promised to make him as famous as Robin Hood or Jesse James, said she'd tell his side of the story in the *Chronicles* and make him a national hero."

"So why," Max asked evenly, "isn't she with you?"

Nancy's gaze darted toward the café. "Because she convinced those two boys they only need one hostage, that the rest of us were so much deadwood. We're to tell you their demands."

"Demands!" Jason choked on the word.

Dwight resumed control. "Which are?"

"A helicopter and a million dollars. There was some talk about whether or not they also want Scott Hale, but they finally decided . . ."

As she talked, Max turned away blindly. Coming face-to-face with a tall pine, he pressed his forehead against the pebbly bark and tried to keep himself from going ballistic. In this he was only partially successful, banging his fists against the trunk so violently he could feel the skin on his knuckles rip.

The pain felt good, but not as good as it'd feel to take those two jerks and—

"You're takin' this awful personal."

Jason's voice, taut and accusing. Slowly Max straightened. "So would you," he snarled, "if the woman you love was being held hostage by Billy the Kid.''

Jason's mouth dropped open and he stared. Max felt as if his own mouth was probably hanging open, too, but he wasn't about to take anything back.

It was true. He loved Julie Cameron: pushy and competitive, conceited and brash Julie Cameron. He threw back his head and let out a howl of anguish. He'd get her out of this or die trying.

Jason stared. "You're shittin' me, right?"

"Hell, no. Now all I've got to do is save the woman's life so I can tell *her*." Yeah, that and a helluva lot of other stuff.

With a new sense of urgency, Max scooted back behind Dwight's car and peered over. A window blind quivered, then a corner lifted, and he saw the man toward whom all his fury was directed. Johnny King was waving a handgun around, all the while beating his chops at someone unseen.

With a clear shot presented on a silver platter, Max reached for the pistol he didn't have. His hand closed on thin air, and a shocking realization ran through him.

Julie was in there somewhere; thank God he wasn't armed, because no power on earth could have kept him from shooting that son of a bitch for daring to threaten her. He sucked in a deep breath, knowing this was one showdown he'd have to handle with wit, instead of weapons—and not entirely sure he was up to it.

"—SO WAS THAT FIRST HORSE theft all Scott's idea?" Julie looked expectantly at Johnny, pen poised over her notebook while she tried her best to look cool.

She didn't feel at all cool. Johnny was acting and talking so irrationally he was making her nervous; maybe it hadn't been very smart of her to come in here like this. But the die was cast; at least she'd have a lot to tell the marshal when she got out of this, not to mention the readers of the *Cupid Chronicles*.

She'd just have to brazen it out and hope for the best.

Which was what she was doing, sitting on the counter with her feet on a stool and dutifully writing down every word Johnny said. The horse thief himself slumped on a nearby stool, eating Betsy's pumpkin pie out of the pan with a tablespoon. Beau had found a jar of peanut butter and was devouring it off a knife with great gusto. Neither of them had looked out the front window in at least five minutes. Apparently they were so taken with the charm of their own story they were getting sloppy.

She hoped so.

Johnny swallowed the last of the pie and cleared his throat ostentatiously. "Nah, rustling hosses was *my* idea. Scott's idea was to stay away from Cupid, which was pretty damn dumb. I mean, wouldn't that make it kinda obvious that we live here?" He threw out his chest. "All the good stuff was mine—takin' the Arrow pony and snatchin' Gwendolyn. Beau didn't want to do it, either, but I had me a score to settle with Gene

Varner and that Mackenzie SOB and the Camerons.''
His grin was wolfish. "Present company excluded,
'course."

Beau hunched his shoulders. "I always kinda liked
old Gwendolyn," he muttered. "She—"

The door opened and Cosmo Mackenzie walked inside. "Excuse me," he said, closing the door behind
him, "but I've got a message from the marshal."

Johnny came up off his stool, dropping his spoon
and grabbing his pistol off the counter. Bringing it to
bear on Cosmo, he tightened his finger on the trigger.
"What the hell do you think you're doin', walkin' in
like you own the place?"

"Hey, I'm sorry!" Arms held high, Cosmo shrugged
helplessly. "I'm just an innocent bystander. If you
don't want to know what Marshal Deakins has to
say..." He lowered one arm cautiously to fumble behind him for the doorknob.

Johnny gave a nasty little laugh. "Give it up," he
suggested. "Innocent bystander my ass!" He exchanged a knowing glance with Beau, who just kept
nodding no matter what his henchman said. "Everybody knows you're this big L.A. fuzz, but you ain't
lookin' any too big at the moment. We caught you flat-
footed."

Julie almost fell off the counter. Completely confused, she looked from Cosmo to Johnny and back
again. "What in the world are you talking about,
Johnny? Cosmo isn't—"

"The hell he isn't." Johnny gave her a pitying glance. "He's a two-bit phony who got in trouble back in California for shootin' some poor innocent suspect. We figure he just come here to bust the rustlers and make us locals look bad."

"No." She shook her head; what a ridiculous story. "No!"

Johnny was relentless. "Hell, it's old news, Julie. Scott told us. The old boy who fenced the horses we took had a newspaper clipping about it, and Scott checked it out."

She frowned, recalling all that Johnny had said in the past half hour and how much of it had been wishful thinking. "I'd know if it was true," she decided. "Cosmo would've told me himself, especially after we—"

She bit her lip, remembering how close they'd been. Could he really be so deceitful as to make love to her under false pretenses? Surely not, and yet...

It would explain a great deal. It would break her heart, but it would explain a great deal. At last she raised her eyes and looked directly at Cosmo for answers.

SHE LOOKED AT HIM with those big shocked eyes, and at that moment Max wished he *did* have a gun, because he'd rather shoot himself than have Julie find out this way. How could he explain himself under these circumstances?

Dammit, he'd messed around with these amateurs long enough. Feigning innocence, he took a wandering step toward the man with the gun, then another. He spread his arms wide, hands palm up. "Where'd you get an idea like that, Johnny?" Max inquired mildly. "I'm just a simple insurance salesman from California."

He saw the triumphant relief flood Julie's face and felt even worse.

"See?" she cried, turning on Johnny. "I told you so." She took a swing at him with her notebook, which glanced off his shoulder. "If he was a trained lawman, would he just walk in here like some nerd and let you get the drop on him? He'd have a plan." She hit Johnny again, and he yelped, reaching to rub his shoulder with his gun hand. "He wouldn't just—"

Max sprang, grabbing for Johnny's gun. The two men grappled for control of the weapon.

"—let you—"

Julie stopped talking. From the corner of his eye, Max realized she was staring at the titanic struggle with horror on her face. He also saw Beau brace himself to jump the counter. Max tried to shout a warning to her, but Johnny had one hand around his throat, cutting off his air and his words. Little son of a bitch was a handful when he wasn't falling down drunk.

Fortunately the warning wasn't necessary. As if she'd read his mind, Julie picked up the big glass container of pennies next to the cash register, the one collecting money for charity. Without hesitation, she brought it down on Beau's head with all her might. It hit his skull with a great *thonk,* and Beau went down like the *Titanic.*

"—hold us all hostage." Julie stood up on the bar stool and screamed. *"Cosmo, what are you doing?"*

What he was doing was beating the living daylights out of Johnny King, who was on the floor and rolled up in a ball with his arms curled over his head. If Marshal Deakins hadn't come roaring through the doorway with pistol drawn, Max really might have killed the little punk.

Dwight pulled Max off the whimpering outlaw. "Good work," Dwight panted. "You big-city cops have plenty of nerve, I'll give you that." He pumped Max's hand with enthusiasm.

Max groaned and let his chin sag onto his chest for just an instant, thinking how that would sound to Julie. He turned, his pleading gaze meeting her anguished one. Everything else faded away until it was just the two of them.

"I can explain," he said, the desperate and defensive note he heard in his voice a shock.

"Don't even try." Her voice cracked, threatening to break. She finished on a little sob, "We're through. Goodbye, Cos—whoever you are."

Max shuddered beneath the impact of the last bullet, the one he couldn't possibly dodge.

ANGER WAS Julie's only defense, and she pulled it tight around her. Everyone had been in on what could only be described as a bad joke at her expense. *Everyone*—her boss, her family, even her grandmother. She blamed them all, but most of all she blamed Maxwell Cosmo Mackenzie.

Naturally she refused to see him or speak to him. In fact, the only person she *would* see was Marshal Deakins, to whom she gladly gave the notes she'd taken from Johnny's rambling dissertation.

But when he tried to defend Cosmo's deceit, she wouldn't listen. Instead, she went home and locked herself in her bedroom, where she brooded, wept and brooded some more. That she, Julie Cameron, should make such a fool of herself took a little getting used to.

In the meantime she refused to go to work or accept telephone calls or visitors. She told herself she needed time to mourn the death of something that had been . . . beautiful.

Still, she finally had to face facts. She'd been seduced and abandoned, brought low by a man who'd raised deceit to a new level.

She decided to hate him until the day she died.

But she wasn't dead yet. On the third day, she walked downstairs with her head held high, just daring anyone to say a word crosswise to her. They didn't; indeed, her family greeted her return with loving and sympathetic relief.

They also filled her in on what had happened during her hiatus.

With the exception of Julie's broken heart, everything appeared to be turning out splendidly. All three horse thieves were in jail, and the Outlaw Grandpa had been completely exonerated. Perhaps most wonderful of all, Gwendolyn had been located at a packing plant in Texas mere minutes ahead of the grim reaper.

That got through to Julie. "That's wonderful!" she cried. "How...?"

From their guilty expressions, she knew. Cosmo had rescued the old gray mare, so Julie didn't want to hear any details; her love for Cosmo must remain as dead as her dreams. "Don't say it," she warned all and sundry. "I don't even want to hear that man's *name*. In fact, come to think of it, I don't even know what his name really *is*."

They'd looked unhappy to hear this but hadn't pressed the issue until later. It was Jason, leaving the next day to resume his interrupted rodeo career, who'd apparently been elected to defend the indefensible.

"Look," he began uneasily, "I know you won't want to hear this—"

"Then don't say it," she suggested sharply.

"I've got to." He squared his shoulders. "I think you ought to know that when Max found out—"

"Who the hell is Max?"

Jason looked surprised. "Max Mackenzie, who else?"

"Oh," she said with acid in her tone, "you mean *Cosmo*."

"Yeah, I guess so. Anyway, Mackenzie almost came unglued when Nancy Wyatt told him you were inside that café with those two idiots. For a second there, I thought he was going to do something really stupid.''

"Like he didn't? You call it smart for him to go waltzing in there without so much as a . . . a gun or anything? He could've been killed!''

Jason grinned. "I knew you cared.''

"Cared? *Cared!* I wish Johnny had shot him! I wish—''

"No, you don't.''

"Don't tell me what I wish! Cosmo, or Max or whoever he is, is the most obnoxious, lying, two-faced—''

"Shut up and listen to me.''

Only her twin brother could get away with grabbing her by the shoulders and giving her a good shake.

He softened it with a smile. "Before the man walked into the jaws of almost certain death—''

"Oh, puh-leeze.''

" '—he said he loved you. And Jewel, he meant it.''

Julie's lips parted on a soft gasp. Cosmo had never told her he loved her, not even when they were in a position that practically demanded it. She swallowed hard, suddenly vulnerable again, and her gaze sought her brother's for confirmation.

Jason nodded. "It's true. He went in after you because he couldn't stand to leave you in their hands another minute. If anybody got shot, he wanted it to be him, not you. Can't you find it in your heart to give him another chance?''

"AND WHAT DID SHE SAY when you said that?" Max asked, daring to hope.

Jason shook his head regretfully. "She said she wouldn't give you another chance even if you ate worms. She said she wouldn't give you another chance if you took out an ad in the *Cupid Chronicles* and begged her. She said—"

"I get the picture," Max cut in, thoroughly deflated.

"She said until you'd suffered the same kind of public humiliation she'd been put through, she had nothing to say to you, period."

"She did, did she." A thought occurred to Max, a long shot so desperate he had to swallow hard to keep from groaning.

JULIE FINALLY WORKED UP enough courage to go into Cupid on Thursday. With a list of errands as long as her arm, she made a point of avoiding the *Chronicles* office. Her first stop was the dry cleaners to retrieve a silk blouse for Betsy.

The silly girl behind the counter started giggling the minute she saw Julie and never stopped. At the drugstore to pick up Grandma's vitamin pills, Julie's reception was the same.

The cashier at the grocery story greeted Julie and then collapsed into helpless laughter; the manager had to come out to check the order. Julie was well and truly irritated by the time she pulled into the parking lot of the Rusty Spur. Betsy was working today, and at least she, Julie knew, had the sensitivity not to laugh.

Deep in her own dark thoughts, Julie stepped into the café—and all the customers burst into spontaneous applause. Confused, she blinked and glanced around, wondering if she'd walked into a Chamber of Commerce luncheon or something.

Betsy hurried around the counter with a big smile on her face. Throwing her arms around her sister-in-law, she gave a startled Julie a big hug.

"Julie, I'm so glad you made it! We all are."

"Thanks, but why?" Julie glanced around at all the smiling faces.

"Lots of reasons." Betsy's grin became even broader and more mischievous. "First of all, we love you."

"Well, gosh, that's great. I love all of you guys, too. Will that and fifty cents get me a cup of coffee?"

"No sarcasm, if you please." Betsy steered Julie toward a seat at the counter. "Second of all, we're very grateful to you for helping bring that whole hostage thing to a successful conclusion."

"Hear, hear!" Everyone clapped and cheered.

"Thank you, thank you." Julie dipped her head in acknowledgment. "You're too kind. Is there a third of all?"

"As a matter of fact," Betsy said, "there is!" Reaching into her apron pocket, she produced a newspaper and whipped it open to display the top half of the front page.

Julie didn't want to look at it; she was mad at Gene Varner for his part in her humiliation, so naturally she was mad at the *Chronicles,* too. But the banner headline screaming across the top was too big to ignore: MAXWELL COSMO MACKENZIE LOVES JULIE LAVERNE CAMERON. Her stomach clenched and she almost fell off the stool. "What is this?" she cried. "Has the man nothing better to do than humiliate me?"

"Humiliate you!" Nancy Wyatt leaned on the cash register, her grin as wide as Betsy's. "We should all have handsome macho cops so crazy about us they'll bare their souls in pitiful public displays of devotion like this. The boy has put the most abject apology you ever heard right there on the front page for friend and foe alike to read."

A new voice sang out, "Marry him and put him out of his misery, Julie—him and half the single men in Cupid!"

She looked around and saw Charlie Gilroy, the bartender from the Hideout. "For your information," she said with dignity, "he hasn't asked me. He's just... messing with my mind." *And one or two other things.*

Heads bobbed eagerly. "Yes, he *has* asked you, the only way you'd let him," Betsy interpreted. "Right there." And she pointed to a box on the front page.

A box with a sidebar story and a headline that read: BUT WILL SHE MARRY HIM?

MAX FOUND JULIE sitting at the counter in the Rusty Spur Café, laughing so hard tears streaked her cheeks. When she saw him, she tried—and failed—to get hold of herself.

And then something wonderful happened and she was in his arms. He hung on to her with all his might, determined to keep her there forever.

"Let's get out of here," he whispered in her ear. "We've got to talk."

"Not a chance," she countered, pushing him away. "You made a fool of me in public. Now if—and I mean that, *if*—we're going to work this out, it might as well be in public, too."

"Fine." He drew a deep breath. "When you threw yourself at me at the line shack and insisted we make love—"

She shrieked and lunged to clap a hand over his mouth, her cheeks the red of American Beauty roses. "Privacy," she gasped through the delighted laughter and catcalls of their audience. "My God, have you no sense of decorum?"

Coming from Julie Cameron, that was rich.

THEY DUKED IT OUT behind the Rusty Spur, going nose to nose and toes to toes.

"You deceived me! How could you?"

"I deceived everyone, or at least I tried to. Damn, don't you get it? I came here to do a job for my uncle, a job I was more than qualified to do. How was I to know—"

"—that some stupid local girl would fall for your line of malarkey? When I think of how miserable I was when I realized I was falling for a nerd..."

"How do you think I liked pretending to *be* a nerd? I didn't give a damn what anybody else thought of me, so long as they didn't get between me and what I'd come here to do. But to have you believe—"

"You made love to me! You made love to me and never told me—"

"You made the first move, if you recall."

"What's that supposed to mean? That you *wouldn't* have? If I hadn't—"

"I didn't say that."

"You didn't say a helluva lot of anything."

"How could I? You hit me like a thunderbolt. I wanted to tell you who I really was the next morning, but Ethan showed up and it was too late."

"But I told you that I loved you and—"

"—scared the hell out of me. I didn't return the favor at the time because...dammit, because I didn't know."

"Oh, but you know now, I take it."

"Yes, God help me, I do. When I learned you were in danger..."

"I wasn't in danger. I was—"

"—being held hostage by two outlaws with guns? You don't call that danger?"

"Danger is...loving someone who doesn't love you back. It's baring your soul—"

He touched his fingers to her lips to stop the flow of words. "I know. That's what I just did, in the most public forum I could find. Hell, I put it in the *Cupid Chronicles!*" He shuddered, then continued bravely, "And I'd do it again if it would convince you to give me another chance."

"Then do it now," she whispered. "Do it now. Privately."

And he did.

EPILOGUE

IT TOOK a little over six months for Maxwell Mackenzie and Julie Cameron to get together on a permanent basis, but it was worth the wait. The bride had never looked lovelier, and if the bridegroom wasn't a nervous wreck, he sure gave a good imitation.

Poor Max confided to his best man and soon-to-be brother-in-law, Jason Cameron, that after all Julie had put him through to win her following what he liked to think of as his "little deception," the actual wedding should have been a piece of cake.

It wasn't. The road to this church in the Colorado mountains had been a long and rocky one.

When Max had gone back to California to resume his previous life, Julie had gone with him—but only on a trial basis, she'd warned. No permanent commitment.

They'd found a new apartment after she took one look at the dump he called home. Then with typical Julie confidence, she'd found a job. It wasn't the *L.A. Times* but still a respectable tabloid daily, she'd insisted, although Max considered that an oxymoron.

He'd thought she loved her job, and so he'd thrust aside his own misgivings about his return to the force and pretended everything was all right. But then Dwight Deakins called to say he was actually going to retire after talking about it for years, and if Max was interested in coming back to Colorado...

Max was, but it took him another month to find just the right time to broach the subject with Julie. He loved her so damned much that he didn't know what he'd do if she hated the idea of going back to Cupid.

To his joy, she didn't. Instead, she'd burst into tears and confessed that she was so homesick for the mountains she could hardly stand it. How soon could they leave?

Just as soon as she set a wedding date, he'd countered, seeing his chance and grabbing it. And that was how it happened.

Now, on the day he was to marry the woman he loved, Maxwell Cosmo Mackenzie, the new marshal of Cupid, Colorado, was a happy—if slightly overwhelmed—man.

JULIE WORE the gown of her dreams, the beautiful Edwardian reproduction Betsy had specially made for her years ago for a wedding that never took place—to everyone's relief, including Julie's.

The Cameron clan was out in full force for the occasion. Matron of honor was Maggie; bridesmaids were Blair Britton, Maggie's beautiful teenage stepdaughter—and Betsy. Ushers were Ben, and Chase Britton—Maggie's husband.

Lisa Marie turned her flower girl into a star-making turn, tripping lightly down the aisle in yellow organdy, strewing rose petals with joyous abandon. Joey, almost ten and above such shenanigans, refused to do more than sit in the front pew with Grandma and entertain his young half sister, Catherine. Defying tradition, Max's mother had joined the Camerons on their side of the aisle, where she sat beaming approval of her son's choice of wife. At her side, Gene Varner looked equally pleased.

Throughout the beautiful ceremony, Betsy fought back tears. Even though Julie had made tough-guy Max jump through hoops before she forgave him, Betsy had never believed the final outcome was in doubt.

Everything else had turned out equally well.

Johnny and Scott had been tried and convicted and were serving time for rustling. A much-subdued Beau, always the follower, had been put on probation and was a guest at the wedding, along with his grandpa Ethan and most of Cupid.

Jason had been cleared in the shooting of Scott Hale, since he'd been aiming in the opposite direction. But the experience had taught the young cowboy a hard lesson. Although still traveling the rodeo circuit, he'd settled down considerably. Then there were Chase and Maggie, who looked almost as happy as the bride and groom.

Awash in sentiment, Betsy got teary-eyed thinking about the day she'd first driven into these mountains—also on the first day of May, she realized with a start. She'd arrived five years ago today in a snowstorm, a stranger with a small child. At the time she'd never dreamed there could be as much love and happiness in the world as now surrounded her.

"I now pronounce you husband and wife. Max, you may kiss the bride."

At the words concluding the beautiful ceremony, the bride and groom turned into each other's arms for a kiss that spoke of their love and commitment. Then, amidst applause, they hurried down the aisle, their faces wreathed in smiles. The double doors of the church swung wide and they stopped short in the entry, turning to each other in wonder and amazement.

It was snowing!

With a gasp of pleasure, friends and family burst into spontaneous applause.

HOLDING HANDS, Max and Julie dashed out into the big fat lacy flakes of a spring snowstorm. Looking like a bride and groom in a crystal snowball, they moved into each other's arms to exchange a lingering kiss.

Maggie, watching them, snuggled back against her husband's solid chest, welcoming the comfort of his arms around her waist—her thickening waist, for she was four months pregnant. Chase had been as ecstatic as she, wanting to shout their news from the rooftops. She'd insisted they wait until after the wedding, though. She didn't want to steal even a tiny part of the spotlight from the bridal couple.

Chase leaned down to kiss her ear. "Are you all right, sweetheart?"

"Always." She could barely force that single word from her lips her throat was so clogged with emotion. All she could hope was that Julie and Max would find the same kind of happiness she and Chase had, the same kind Betsy and Ben had.

MAX LOOKED UP into a sea of smiles—from his mother and Uncle Gene, Ben and Betsy, Maggie and Chase, Jason and Grandma Cameron, Ethan and Beau Turner, Dwight and everyone else. Standing there in his tuxedo before the little church, holding his gorgeous new wife in his arms while snow practically blinded them, Max realized that his previous cynicism had been replaced by a bone-deep contentment.

He'd found everything a man could ask for right here in Cupid, Colorado. And he'd cherish her for the rest of his life.

Weddings by DeWilde

Since the turn of the century the elegant and fashionable DeWilde stores have helped brides around the world turn the fantasy of their "Special Day" into reality. But now the store and three generations of family are torn apart by the divorce of Grace and Jeffrey DeWilde. As family members face new challenges and loves— and a long-secret mystery—the lives of Grace and Jeffrey intermingle with store employees, friends and relatives in this fast-paced, glamorous, internationally set series. For weddings and romance, glamour and fun-filled entertainment, enter the world of DeWilde . . .

Twelve remarkable books, coming to you once a month, beginning in April 1996

Weddings by DeWilde begins with
Shattered Vows
by Jasmine Cresswell

Here's a preview!

"SPEND THE NIGHT with me, Lianne."

No softening lies, no beguiling promises, just the curt offer of a night of sex. She closed her eyes, shutting out temptation. She had never expected to feel this sort of relentless drive for sexual fulfillment, so she had no mechanisms in place for coping with it. "No." The one-word denial was all she could manage to articulate.

His grip on her arms tightened as if he might refuse to accept her answer. Shockingly, she wished for a split second that he would ignore her rejection and simply bundle her into the car and drive her straight to his flat, refusing to take no for an answer. All the pleasures of mindless sex, with none of the responsibility. For a couple of seconds he neither moved nor spoke. Then he released her, turning abruptly to open the door on the passenger side of his Jaguar. "I'll drive you home," he said, his voice hard and flat. "Get in."

The traffic was heavy, and the rain started again as an annoying drizzle that distorted depth perception made driving difficult, but Lianne didn't fool herself that the silence inside the car was caused by the driving conditions. The air around them crackled and sparked with their thwarted desire. Her body was still on fire. Why didn't Gabe say something? she thought, feeling aggrieved.

Perhaps because he was finding it as difficult as she was to think of something appropriate to say. He was thirty years old, long past the stage of needing to bed a woman just so he could record another sexual conquest in his little black book. He'd spent five months dating Julia, which suggested he was a man who valued friendship as an element in his relationships with women. Since he didn't seem to like her very much, he was probably as embarrassed as she was by the stupid, inexplicable intensity of their physical response to each other.

"Maybe we should just set aside a weekend to have wild, uninterrupted sex," she said, thinking aloud. "Maybe that way we'd get whatever it is we feel for each other out of our systems and be able to move on with the rest of our lives."

His mouth quirked into a rueful smile. "Isn't that supposed to be my line?"

"Why? Because you're the man? Are you sexist enough to believe that women don't have sexual urges? I'm just as aware of what's going on between us as you are, Gabe. Am I supposed to pretend I haven't noticed that we practically ignite whenever we touch? And that we have nothing much in common except mutual lust— and a good friend we betrayed?"

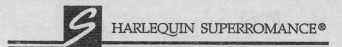

HARLEQUIN SUPERROMANCE®

WOMEN WHO Dare

If you enjoyed THE SECRET YEARS by Margot Dalton,
you'll love the chance to revisit some of the residents
of Wolf Hill, Alberta, in her newest Superromance novel

The Hiding Place

Laurel Atchison—or Laurie Atkins, as she's now calling
herself—doesn't dare tell her new neighbors who she really
is or why she's come to Wolf Hill. Fortunately, the trusting folk
of this small town don't ask too many questions. But there's
another newcomer, Jonas O'Neal, who has none of
the local respect for privacy....

Watch for *The Hiding Place* by Margot Dalton.

Available in May 1996
wherever Harlequin Superromance books are sold.

WWD96-4

HARLEQUIN SUPERROMANCE®

The Baby Contract
by Lynn Erickson

Bettie Gay Bryson is pregnant and alone.

Late one night, she finds herself sitting in a police station in
Tucson, Arizona, because her boyfriend—*ex*-boyfriend—
robbed a highway convenience store. He escaped, leaving
her to face the law.

Now the County Attorney's office—in the person of handsome
investigator Greg Tyrrell—is offering her a deal. No
prosecution, plus her living expenses paid—if she'll go
undercover to help him trap the head of a baby-selling ring.
She and Greg will be working closely together....

B.G. agrees. What other choice does she have? And this
decision marks not only the beginning of her new life but the
beginning of love.

> An exciting and moving new novel by Lynn Erickson,
> author of *Aspen*, described by *Publishers Weekly*
> as "suspenseful and tumultuous...a sharply
> plotted page turner, abetted by loads of colorful
> secondary characters."

The Baby Contract is available in May, wherever Harlequin
books are sold.

HARLEQUIN®

Don't miss these Harlequin favorites by some of our most distinguished authors!
And now, you can receive a discount by ordering two or more titles!

HT #25645	THREE GROOMS AND A WIFE	
	by JoAnn Ross	$3.25 U.S./$3.75 CAN. ☐
HT #25648	JESSIE'S LAWMAN	
	by Kristine Rolofson	$3.25 U.S.//$3.75 CAN. ☐
HP #11725	THE WRONG KIND OF WIFE	
	by Roberta Leigh	$3.25 U.S./$3.75 CAN. ☐
HP #11755	TIGER EYES by Robyn Donald	$3.25 U.S./$3.75 CAN. ☐
HR #03362	THE BABY BUSINESS by Rebecca Winters	$2.99 U.S./$3.50 CAN. ☐
HR #03375	THE BABY CAPER by Emma Goldrick	$2.99 U.S./$3.50 CAN. ☐
HS #70638	THE SECRET YEARS by Margot Dalton	$3.75 U.S./$4.25 CAN. ☐
HS #70655	PEACEKEEPER by Marisa Carroll	$3.75 U.S./$4.25 CAN. ☐
HI #22280	MIDNIGHT RIDER by Laura Pender	$2.99 U.S./$3.50 CAN. ☐
HI #22235	BEAUTY VS THE BEAST by M.J. Rogers	$3.50 U.S./$3.99 CAN. ☐
HAR #16531	TEDDY BEAR HEIR by Elda Minger	$3.50 U.S./$3.99 CAN. ☐
HAR #16596	COUNTERFEIT HUSBAND	
	by Linda Randall Wisdom	$3.50 U.S./$3.99 CAN. ☐
HH #28795	PIECES OF SKY by Marianne Willman	$3.99 U.S./$4.50 CAN. ☐
HH #28855	SWEET SURRENDER by Julie Tetel	$4.50 U.S./$4.99 CAN. ☐

(limited quantities available on certain titles)

	AMOUNT	$
DEDUCT:	10% DISCOUNT FOR 2+ BOOKS	$
ADD:	POSTAGE & HANDLING	$
	($1.00 for one book, 50¢ for each additional)	
	APPLICABLE TAXES**	$_____
	TOTAL PAYABLE	$_____
	(check or money order—please do not send cash)	

To order, complete this form and send it, along with a check or money order for the total above, payable to Harlequin Books, to: **In the U.S.:** 3010 Walden Avenue, P.O. Box 9047, Buffalo, NY 14269-9047; **In Canada:** P.O. Box 613, Fort Erie, Ontario, L2A 5X3.

Name: _____

Address: _____ City: _____

State/Prov.: _____ Zip/Postal Code: _____

**New York residents remit applicable sales taxes.
Canadian residents remit applicable GST and provincial taxes.

HBACK-AJ3

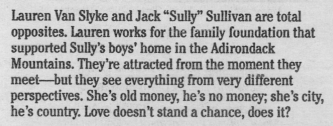

UNLOCK THE DOOR TO GREAT ROMANCE AT BRIDE'S BAY RESORT

Join Harlequin's new across-the-lines series, set in an exclusive hotel on an island off the coast of South Carolina.

Seven of your favorite authors will bring you exciting stories about fascinating heroes and heroines discovering love at Bride's Bay Resort.

Look for these fabulous stories coming to a store near you beginning in January 1996.

Harlequin American Romance #613 in January
Matchmaking Baby by Cathy Gillen Thacker

Harlequin Presents #1794 in February
Indiscretions by Robyn Donald

Harlequin Intrigue #362 in March
Love and Lies by Dawn Stewardson

Harlequin Romance #3404 in April
Make Believe Engagement by Day Leclaire

Harlequin Temptation #588 in May
Stranger in the Night by Roseanne Williams

Harlequin Superromance #695 in June
Married to a Stranger by Connie Bennett

Harlequin Historicals #324 in July
Dulcie's Gift by Ruth Langan

Visit Bride's Bay Resort each month wherever Harlequin books are sold.

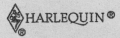

BBAYG